Praise for the novels of
Viola Estrella

"Estrella's quirky and endearing characters ensure an enjoyable reading experience that should satisfy paranormal romance fans."

—Carol from Bitten By Books

"This was a fast paced story that keeps the readers attention from start to finish. Viola Estrella writes a wonderful tale of true love."

—Gabrielle from Got Romance Reviews

"Kudos to Viola Estrella for one Spicy Hot Romance read."

—Larkspur from Long and Short of It

"... a witty, funny, sexy piece of fiction. It is so well written that you will lose yourself in the pages."

—Brit from Bitten By Books

"Viola Estrella combines suspense and action with a bit of humor and the paranormal to make for one intense read."

—Romance Junkies

"This is pure creativity and imagination with the purpose of entertaining."

—The Romance Studio

Viola Estrella

Books by Viola Estrella

Paranormal Romance

BEWITCHING YOU - Bewitching Women: Book
One - Sofia and Gray's story

FINDING FATE - A Bewitching Women short story

HAUNTING YOU - Bewitching Women: Book Two
- Rachel and August's story

Coming Soon!

Bewitching Women: Book Three - Becca's story

Urban Fantasy

ANGEL VINDICATED - Abby Angel: Book One

Coming soon!

ANGEL UNLUCKY - Abby Angel: Book Two

Viola Estrella

Haunting You

You

Viola Estrella

HAUNTING YOU

By Viola Estrella
Copyright 2014 Viola Estrella

All Rights Reserved

ISBN-10: 0-9856198-4-8
ISBN-13: 978-0-9856198-4-8

More information about Viola Estrella can be found at:
www.ViolaEstrella.com

Cover art by Estrella Cover Art: www.estrellacoverart.com

Copy Editor: Helen Hardt: www.HelenHardt.com

Proofreader: JoAnn Collins at Twin Tweaks Editing

DEDICATION

To those who believe and those who've loved, lost, and
continue to love.

To my father-in-law, Richard aka "Tata", for giving all of
your heart to your family. You've inspired us all to do the
same. You're forever in our memories.

ACKNOWLEDGEMENTS

There are so many people to thank.
My family always comes first. Thanks to my husband,
Mark, my sons, my daughter-in-law, and my new adorable
baby granddaughter for always supporting me, making me
laugh, and bringing so much joy to my life.

Thanks to my critique partner, Patrice, for reading and
rereading and rerereading the many revisions of this story
and helping me whip it into shape.

Thanks to my beta readers, Holly and Libby, for reading
the unedited version and giving me your valuable
opinions.

Thanks to my copy editor, Helen, for your priceless
feedback with the story and the blurb.

Thanks to Margie Lawson for your genius suggestions for
the first page. Your workshops inspire me.

And always, always, thanks to my readers for purchasing,
reading, and supporting my books!

Chapter One

Rachel Spencer was not going to have another panic attack. *Not. Not. Not.*

She peeked over her flashcards at the most recent figment of her imagination. This one—a woman with warm blue eyes, defined laugh lines, and a determined set to her rose-painted lips—wasn't as scary as some of the other transparent trespassers who had been plaguing her lately. No, this one Rachel could imagine bumping into at the grocery store, the library, or the hair salon. Only they weren't at any of those safe places.

They were in Rachel's bedroom. Alone.

Rachel sat at the head of her bed, pretending to study for her next attempt at the bar exam. The unwelcome visitor perched at the other end with straight posture and daintily clasped hands.

The others hadn't been as calm. Lucid.

Rachel had done her best to get rid all the rest, ignoring their outbursts until they finally grew frustrated and went away. But this one's persistence deserved a first-place ribbon. She'd been hanging around Rachel's

1

apartment for *weeks*. Talking, moping, pacing, staring, and sighing.

Today's tactic was a different one.

"I'm not going to hurt you," the woman said in a soothing motherly voice. "All I need is a small favor."

They all needed favors.

Rachel crushed her pillow to her chest as a familiar pain expanded from her rib cage to her abdomen.

Not another panic attack. *No. No. No.*

"Really, don't be afraid of me." The intruder smoothed the comforter with her ghostly hand.

Strange. None of the others seemed to have the ability to touch or move objects. This one was different. She *felt* different. Stronger. Vibrant. More real.

"I'm sorry." Curiosity won over logic, and Rachel met the woman's shadowed eyes. "I can't help you."

A broad smile spread on her visitor's face, revealing a deep dimple on each hollowed cheek. "I just knew you could see me."

"Well...yes," Rachel admitted, which was probably a mistake. She pulled a harsh breath into compressed lungs. The bottle of sedatives the doctor had prescribed sat in her nightstand, useless. They didn't help anyway, not if she wanted to stay alert and awake. And she did.

"But," she continued, easing out the breath, "before you ask me for anything, I want you to know you're wasting your time. Really, I can't help you."

The woman's eyes brightened. "I figured you couldn't ignore me forever. Though I was about to give up."

Fabulous.

"My name's Ella. I probably mentioned that a few times." She leaned forward and offered her hand to shake.

"Nice to meet you, Ella. Um..." Rachel didn't want to seem rude, but she also didn't want to touch what was not real and further her ride to insanity in the process. She stood and guiltily ignored Ella's outstretched hand. The flashcards fell to the bed, but she kept the pillow pressed to her center as she paced across the rug.

"Sorry. It's just that I'm trying to cure myself of these hallucinations." She faced Ella. "No offense."

Ella dropped her hand, but her smile remained warm. Rachel wondered what it would take for this phantom interloper to lose its temper. Like some of the others had.

She strode to her old battery-operated boom box— her MP3 player had gone kaput months ago—and clicked off the background music. Men at Work's "Who Can it Be Now?" faded to a stop.

Her life hadn't always been this way. She hadn't always seen these people. People? Maybe at some point they'd been flesh and bone. Now they were three-dimensional manifestations. Like a hologram. Holograms that could speak, whine, scream, or throw tantrums. Or smile patiently like the woman in front of her.

Rachel plopped back down, jouncing the bed. Yet her visitor didn't bounce with it.

Who was she kidding? She knew exactly what they were. Ghosts—spirits trapped in this earthly realm. She knew this because two years ago she'd said goodbye to the love of her life twice. The first time at his funeral after he'd died a senseless death. The second goodbye had been after he'd returned to her in his afterlife.

Hayes Phillips. She sighed at the memory. She hadn't seen him since he'd crossed over to somewhere beyond this dimension. Beyond her vision. Beyond her touch.

Instead, she'd been bombarded with other spirits who, for some reason, thought she could help them with their unfinished earthly business. She had a good guess how they'd found her. A hospital was just across the street. Out her balcony window, she could see them flitting around. If she accidentally made eye contact with one or gave any indication she could see them, she suddenly had a new uninvited roommate.

3

Rachel didn't want any part of that. Pretending they weren't real was much easier. Because what would it mean if they were? Familiar tingles fluttered along the base of her neck, and she shivered. She didn't want to be a medium or a psychic or whatever those people called themselves. She was just Rachel Spencer, a loyal daughter/sister/friend, destined to one day pass the bar exam and join her father's law practice. Her path was so simple yet way too complicated.

Ella laughed softly, breaking Rachel's thoughts. "Don't fret so much, sweetie. You're going to give yourself a migraine."

Or another anxiety attack. The pain in her chest remained manageable this time, thankfully. If she could just keep it under control when everything around her was out of her control.

She caught a glimpse of herself in the oval mirror above her vanity and quickly smoothed the worry crinkles on her forehead. Her mother always warned her she'd get premature wrinkles from some of the faces she made. God forbid nature took its course.

"You're quite the thinker."

"What?" Rachel forced herself to loosen her grip on the pillow before she ripped it open.

"I said you're quite the thinker. My oldest son, Nicholas, is the same way. He'll sit for hours and do nothing but think. He's a smart boy, but I fear he worries too much. Like you." She winked. "It's hard for me to not be able to talk to my sons. There's so much I want to say to them. I left them so abruptly." Her dimples disappeared as her cheeks hollowed, shadowed. "They need my guidance. Honestly, my brother is in over his head. I fear for their well-being."

Rachel remembered Ella had mentioned her sons during one of the prattling episodes Rachel had tried to ignore. Something about her brother being incompetent and a bad role model for her sons. Definitely not life-threatening for the children and not something that wouldn't work itself out in the long run.

Besides, someone else's life was none of her business. With interning for her father's practice, re-studying for the exam, and trying to lead a normal, sane life, she had enough on her plate to worry about.

Ella produced yet another warm smile as she nodded toward the flashcards. "You're studying to pass the bar?"

"Again." Rachel spat out the word before she could restrain herself. She still felt the sting of shame for failing, and her parents had never seemed so disappointed.

"You know, I was an attorney before I…well, when I was at my prime. I was a very good attorney, actually."

"Really?" Rachel's intrigue got the best of her. "What specialty?"

"Family law. Mostly custody hearings and divorce settlements. Everyone was always trying to get away from each other and hold on tight at the same time. The cases were depressing on occasion, but when I could save a child from harm's way, it made up for all the other stuff. Know what I mean?" She leaned forward, pinning Rachel with a mischievous gaze. Her navy blue eyes sparkled against the sun streaming through the sheer curtains. "Children are helpless in this world without adults to guide them. They need us."

The strain in Rachel's chest fizzled. Amused, she bit back a grin. She may not have passed the bar, but she sure the heck knew when someone was trying to manipulate her. "I know where you're taking this, Ella. How bad could your brother be? He's not abusing them, is he?"

Please say no. Ignoring the mostly selfish requests from the others had been easy, but if a child was truly in danger, Rachel wouldn't be able to look the other way.

Ella rolled her eyes—the first time Rachel had seen her act less than proper. "No, Auggie would never physically hurt Nicholas and Zachary. He barely disciplines them at all. That's part of the problem."

Thank God. "Auggie? Is that your brother's name?" Why did she ask? This was all becoming way too personal.

"August, actually." Ella inched a little closer, her expression frozen in place. "August Kline. My son's are Nicholas and Zachary Kline. I took back my maiden name after their father left when the boys were little. And my parents have passed, so August is all they have."

"At least they have someone."

"You don't understand. I love August, but he doesn't have a clue about raising children."

"I'm sorry."

"Stop apologizing and just help me. Please. I beg you to at least visit the house and see them."

Oh, geez. Rachel wished the woman would stop staring with those big, pathetic eyes. "I honestly don't see how I could help."

Ella's face fell, transforming to a sadness Rachel knew all too well. Of mourning and grief. Of desperation and the need to fight to hold onto a loved one.

She'd gone through all those emotions when Hayes had left her for good. Pulling herself together and moving on with a normal life had been difficult. Well, as normal as she could be with her daily visitors.

With a sigh, Ella swiped at a pearl-drop tear trailing down her cheek. Rachel got the impression crying wasn't something this woman had done often in her life, and her resolve softened.

"Think about it this way," Ella said, determination setting back in. "One way to conquer anxiety is to face a problem head-on. You help me and I go away. Problem solved. Anxiety gone."

"What do you know about my anxiety?" Rachel's gaze veered to the nightstand that held the sedatives her doc had prescribed, and the pressure in her chest built again.

6

"I know a lot about you. I've watched you. You like listening to eighties music." Ella pointed to the numerous sticky notes Rachel had littering her bureau mirror. "And you like making lists."

To-do lists, some completed, some not. It was time to organize her organizational tactics. Only the idea deflated the air out of her achy lungs.

"Check me off your list, Rachel, and I'll be gone. You'll have done something wonderfully generous in the process. You seem like a giving person. Am I wrong?"

Oh, yeah. Rachel was being taken on a guilt trip, and she was following right along. But maybe Ella had a point. Maybe this was the solution she needed. She could attempt to help this spirit, quickly and efficiently, of course, and then they could both move on. Besides, what would it hurt to visit the children's home, to verify they were indeed all right? She'd help ease Ella's soul so she could cross over and erase her own guilt. Checkmark. Done.

Then she could get back to studying.

Her visitor tilted her head, her charming smile low wattage as she waited.

"I'll do it." The words slipped before Rachel could talk herself out of the decision.

"Yes?" The wattage amped up.

Thinking with her heart rather than her head had gotten Rachel into a mess or two in the past. This time she'd think with both. "I guess it wouldn't hurt me to make a brief visit, if it will help you move on, that is."

~ * ~

August Kline cursed under his breath and kicked the washing machine a second time. The loud clunking sound sped up its rhythm and then whirred to a deafening stop.

"No. No, no, no. Don't break down on me now, you son of a bitch." He lifted the lid and looked inside.

His clothes were drenched in sudsy water, nowhere close to being clean or ready to transfer into the dryer. Oh, hell. A dryer that had suddenly and unexpectedly sparked and almost caused an electrical fire. How could he have forgotten? He was officially losing his mind.

"Shit-damn." He slammed the lid shut and tried to think of what else he could wear that wouldn't make him resemble a transient. Everything he owned was either dirty or in the damned washing machine. At the moment, all he had on were boxer briefs and his old NYU T-shirt. The mustard stain below the "U" might do well in a I-see-Jesus's-face-in-this-food contest, but it was entirely inappropriate for the office.

Guess that's what you get for waiting until the last minute to wash your clothes, dumbass.

He should've predicted the machine would break down, considering everything else in the house was on the fritz. The dishwasher, the television, the microwave. Thankfully the ancient refrigerator was still working, though it seriously needed to be defrosted.

Probably needed to call an electrician before the house burned down. The house was so old. No doubt faulty wiring hid within the walls. Either that, or the spring storms they'd had produced multiple surges.

August kicked the washing machine one more time just for the hell of it and strode into the kitchen.

Still no boys. Double damn. They were going to miss the bus, and he'd have to drive them again. He grabbed two pots sitting on the stove and banged them together. "Nicholas! Zachary! Get up and out of bed or you're walking."

That should get them going. He dropped the pots into the already crowded sink, turned up Prince's "Let's Go Crazy" on the boom box, and poured himself a cup of strong coffee.

These boys were fourteen and sixteen years old, and they acted like they needed constant supervision. How had Ella done this by herself? August had been their guardian for less than a year, and he was already exhausted.

Ella.

God, he missed her, strong personality and all. Even if the majority of their last conversations had been desperate pleas for him to drop his band and return to his medical practice.

His gut still hollowed when he thought of her.

She'd died disappointed in him. Which felt like hell. His peers had called his sudden career change a classic burnout. He'd been running on exhaust fumes and coffee, and he'd needed a break. Besides, it had only been one more checkmark in his big sister's ever-growing list of *How Auggie Fucks Up His Life.* If it wasn't his career choice, it was his place of residence, taste in clothes, or choice of women. Or more like lack of choosing one woman and settling down.

The decision to leave his practice and his patients had been hard. But the decision to transfer his energy to music had been the easiest thing he'd ever done.

He'd been drawn to it his entire life, just like his mother—thanks to his mother—and he ended up joining an eighties tribute band with a woman and two guys he'd known in college. They'd wanted him back then, liking his bottomless mental music library and how he could play any instrument they put in front of him, but he had to decline at the time.

After the *medical meltdown,* he'd given up fighting the urge to play and contacted them. They'd gladly welcomed him. The gigs hadn't paid much, but he'd had the time of his life. For an entire year.

Until Ella died.

Now, for Zach and Nick, it was time to grow up. He would play doctor just like Ella had always wanted him to, at least for the next few years until the boys went off to college.

Frantic footsteps on the floor above him told him the

boys were awake. They'd probably rolled over, saw what time it was, and decided to get their butts in gear. Finally.

Ah, the teenage years. School, girls, and friends were all they had to think about and not necessarily in that order.

August chuckled quietly, took another gulp of his coffee, and sat down at the kitchen table in front of his laptop that was surrounded by another two coffee cups he'd failed to take to the sink.

He'd clean up later. Right now it was time to break out the credit card and buy some stuff.

He pulled up a department store website and scanned the page. He could live without a dishwasher and a television, but there was no way he would walk around town wearing dirty clothes.

Women didn't dig guys who smelled, and he wasn't willing to give up sex altogether, although he hadn't had much luck the past year. Not in this town, that was for damn sure. Curlville, Indiana, where single women were a rare species. *Attractive* single women were nonexistent.

Which reminded him...

He glanced out the window. Dana Finnegan—aka Dana the Desperate Divorcee—was busy with her morning routine of watering her lawn, making sure her little white T-shirt accidentally got wet in just the right places.

It was a sad day when the artificially enhanced bleached blond who lived across the street started to look tempting. August had a mild distaste for synthetic women.

As if her man radar were on full alert, she smiled his way and waved her fingers. "Hi, August," she mouthed with those overly plump, pink-painted lips.

Damn. Who was he to be picky?

"Down boy," he warned his wayward groin and turned back to the computer screen.

Back to business. Clean clothes. That's what he

needed. Not sex. Sex could wait.

Priorities, August. Think priorities.

First on his list were a washing machine and dryer, a dishwasher for when he had enough time to clean up this pigpen…and maybe a new refrigerator that had enough room in it for some actual food. That would be good.

A stainless steel fridge with a water and ice dispenser caught his eye, but the price made him cringe. Money had never been an issue until he realized he had two food-sucking cyclones to sustain morning, noon, and night.

He'd thought about commuting to the next largest city like Ella had, but August didn't have the patience to drive long distances. And he had zero desire to drive over *that* bridge every day.

The older bottomless pit, Nicholas, shuffled into the kitchen. His shaggy light brown hair and dark brown eyes reminded August of the kid's father. The same guy who'd tried to be August's father for a short portion of his life—Grant Golding. Ella had changed her last name, as well as Nick and Zach's, back to Kline after Grant disappeared. August had given him hell back when he was in high school, and he couldn't help but wonder if that had been the reason Grant had ended up leaving Ella.

Nah. Grant was just a deadbeat loser with a tactless temper. Plain and simple. And Ella had always been too good for him.

Nicholas, frowning as usual and dressed all in black, walked with his gaze glued to the linoleum, grabbed a granola bar from the pantry, and headed out the door without saying a word.

"Morning to you, too, Nick," August called out after him. "Stay out of trouble at school. I know how you like to chatter—"

A slamming door ended August's fun.

Lord, that boy had issues. The most Nick spoke was to himself, mumbling under his breath. Unintelligible words. Probably cursing August. Certain members of the community had worried Nick's shyness was a result of his mother's death, but August remembered Nick had always been quiet. It was just how he was.

August respected that. He had no clue how to relate to the kid, but it wasn't like his nephew was supposed to be his best buddy. Nope, August was there to make sure these kids had a roof over their heads and food in their bellies.

He could handle that. No problem.

He just hoped he wasn't screwing these kids up more than a normal parent would. Plus the therapist he sent the boys to for monthly grief counseling hadn't expressed any real concern.

No worries, right? *Right.*

"Zach is here. Nothing to fear." The younger one sprinted into the kitchen. His dark brown hair was spiked, stiffened by hair gel. His too-large blue eyes glinted with mischief.

The quintessential Kline. Ella had always said Zach was a carbon copy of August and also bore a strong resemblance to August's old man. The boy had charm, charisma, and a killer smile even with a mouthful of metal braces. How could August argue with that?

"What's up, little man? You better get out to the bus stop. I wasn't kidding about making you walk."

Zach shrugged and dipped his hand into a bag of potato chips that had been sitting on the counter all night. "I got it covered." He stuffed a handful of crumbs into his mouth.

August grabbed the chips and handed Zach a granola bar. "How so? The school's four miles away."

"Dana said she'd be happy to drive me whenever I miss the bus." His changing voice squeaked at the word happy, and August stifled a grin.

"No way, little man." August shook his head,

12

wondering just who would have to pay for Dana's generosity. "No taking favors from Ms. Finnegan. Or anyone else for that matter. Get your ass out there."

As if on cue, August heard the squealing of bus brakes and the whoosh of its opening doors. He shot his thumb toward the window.

Zach put up his hands. "Chill, dude. I'm going. I'm going."

~ * ~

Rachel slid her Volvo into park and glanced around the parking lot filled with a mixture of cars and Amish horse-and-buggies. If she'd known Ella's family lived so far away, she wouldn't have given in so easily. But now she was here, two hours away from Indianapolis, sitting in front of a shopping plaza in the town of Curlville, Indiana.

Ella had insisted that Rachel go to her brother's place of business instead of his home because the children had undoubtedly left for school already. Rachel hadn't argued, wanting to get this over with. One little peek at the brother would hopefully ensure the man was a capable guardian.

"He's right in there." Ella pointed to a sign on a glass door that read "Robert P. Williams, MD." She sat in the passenger seat, looking just as tangible as any flesh-and-blood person would in her burgundy sweater-set and white capris.

Rachel made sure no one was watching and then shifted in her seat to meet Ella's gaze. "He works in a doctor's office?"

"He is the doctor." Ella strummed her fingers on her thigh. "Dr. Williams died of a heart attack about a year ago and Auggie took over his practice. It's so like my brother to wait to change the name on the door. He's the worst procrastinator."

"Your brother's a *physician*?"

"Now he is." Ella rolled her eyes. "He took an entire year to follow some ridiculous pipe dream of being in an

13

eighties tribute band. Now he has no other choice than to act like a responsible adult."

"The man can't be all that awful if he's holding a stable job." Geez, what was she doing here? Even if the guy was a musician, there was no reason to believe the children were in harm's way.

"Stable? Auggie doesn't know the meaning of the word. You should see my house."

"Nooo. Don't need to do that."

"Auggie moved in there with the boys," Ella continued. "He's let everything go to heck. The appliances are broken. There are dirty dishes everywhere. Opened food containers. The laundry hampers are overflowing. My garden…" She clasped a hand to her heart. "My garden is ruined. He let all my hard work wither up and die."

The lights on the dashboard flickered and the radio spurted to life and then died just as quickly. Perfect. This had happened before when she'd angered the others, the ones she'd ignored. Strong emotions seemed to trigger the phenomenon.

"All those hours of pruning and pulling weeds and mulching and—"

"Okay. I get it." Rachel stopped her before the woman did irreparable damage to her car. "You're worried. I understand."

She wondered if the woman was this neurotic in her living days as she was in her afterlife. The ghosts Rachel had encountered had all been obsessed over something they'd left behind, and this didn't seem to be different. At least Ella's temper wasn't nearly as bad.

Ella cleared her throat. "I'm sorry. It's just so upsetting."

"It's fine," Rachel said, looking toward the office.

Through the glass door, a woman with black rim glasses sat behind a desk. She was laughing and talking on the phone while typing on her computer keyboard. From this distance, she appeared to be in her fifties or sixties.

"That's his nursing assistant, Loretta. She loves to gossip, so she's going to love you. Just wait until she sees there's a—God forbid—*stranger* in town." Ella eyed her. "And a gorgeous redhead to bat."

Gossip? Rachel hadn't planned on approaching anyone, much less giving them something to gossip about. An aching pressure compressed in her chest. She drew in a calming breath to relieve it. "What exactly do you want me to do here?"

"Well... He does take walk-ins." Ella's sly grin did nothing to alleviate the ache, which cranked up to a burning softball-sized knot.

"You want me to pretend to be a patient?"

"It's the best way for you to meet and chat with him."

"Chat? I'm not comfortable with that idea at all. I wouldn't have the slightest idea what to say or do." This whole day had been way out of Rachel's comfort zone. She could only imagine what her mother would say if she were here.

You need to think things through before you act, Rachel. This isn't appropriate behavior for a young woman.

Ella bit her lip and gave Rachel the once over. "You're a pretty girl."

"Thank you." Her stomach turned. "I think."

"August is a sucker for pretty girls."

"A sucker for... No. No way." She pressed the brake to the floor, as if that could stop what was happening. "I'm sorry, but I am not going to flirt with a complete stranger for you." The pressure in her chest swelled. Her heart beat angrily against her ribs.

Ella laughed. "No, not flirt. Just show a little leg. August's easy. I'm positive that'll get you invited back to the house or at least on a date."

"A date?" What was she thinking coming here? Her life wasn't even her own anymore. Not with these ghosts invading her privacy and driving her nuts.

She couldn't ignore the facts, no matter how absurd they were. Rachel Spencer saw dead people. She *communicated* with them. She was crazy. Certifiable, for crying out loud. She shouldn't have agreed to this. She should've have ignored Ella until she went away. Like the rest of them did eventually.

Perspiration beaded on her upper lip. "I need therapy. I need help."

"That's the spirit, but I'm afraid August isn't that kind of doctor."

Rachel pressed her trembling fingers to her forehead, feeling lightheaded and out of sorts. Her chest compressed. Punching in the brake a couple more times, she grabbed for breaths of air her lungs didn't have room for.

God, was she dying?

No, it was just another panic attack, right?

Just breathe, Rache. Inhale. Exhale. Inhale. Exhale.

"A panic attack, huh?" Ella leaned toward Rachel. "That'll work. Let me help you out with that."

"No," Rachel managed to say. Her chest hurt so badly she thought she might pass out. Or croak right there in the middle of Nowhere, Indiana.

A knock on her window startled her, and she veered her attention upward. Up, and then up some more to see a man staring down at her. Crisp navy-blue eyes, the same shade as Ella's, narrowed at Rachel as he bent down to her level.

"Are you okay?" was the last thing Rachel heard before blacking out.

Chapter Two

Rachel breathed in the familiar scent and nuzzled her nose into bare skin, taut warmth with a thumping heartbeat. A man's neck. She indulged in another sniff of the aroma—a hint of spicy-musk aftershave. Masculine and inviting.

The scent reminded her of someone.

Hayes.

She kept her eyes shut, loving the feeling of being in his arms again. It wasn't often she was able to dream of him, and she wanted to savor his presence. Real or not, any time with Hayes was precious.

The urge to press her lips to his skin and kiss him was a natural instinct. "I miss you," she whispered and brought her hand to his jaw.

"She's coming to." A deep *unfamiliar* voice came out of Hayes's body. "Let's get her in to the exam room. Is it ready?"

Exam room? Her dream was fading, taking on a life of its own. "Hayes? Don't leave me yet."

"Of course it's ready." A husky woman's voice ground out. "But, Dr. Kline, we don't even know if the girl has insurance."

"Loretta, priorities, please. Move that pillow out of the way."

Dr. Kline? Okay. Enough. This wasn't Hayes, and it certainly wasn't a dream. Rachel dared to open one eye and saw the man's profile. Strong jaw line, olive skin, dark brown hair with side burns that needed a trim. She kept him in view as he lowered her onto a padded table. He had nice lips. Lips that spread into an effortless grin as he glanced down at her. A grin that said, "you're going to be just fine."

Who was he?

Damn, she needed to shake this fuzzy feeling. She sat up, letting her gaze settle on his eyes—a dark navy blue with specks of warm gold, welcoming and calming. His lips moved, saying something. Words she couldn't quite absorb.

"What?" Rachel tore her attention from him and glanced around the room.

A medical license hung in a simple black frame on the wall just to the right. Light aqua green walls. To the side was an oak counter with a sink and several drawers. Matching cabinets hovered above the counter.

Typical doctor's office.

A doctor's office... Oh, no. It was all coming back to her now. Ella and her *procrastinating, screw-up* physician brother. That ghost had done this to her. Ella had somehow gotten her way, and now Rachel was sitting in his office. Wonderful. So much for being nice to her hallucinations.

"You passed out in your car." The so-called screw-up leaned forward and flashed a light into her eyes. "You seemed to be hyperventilating just before that. I noticed you from my window. How are you feeling now?"

"Good. I'm good. I, uh, I guess I had a panic attack. I've never fainted before, though." She was going to kill Ella…er…*never mind*.

"It's very rare to lose consciousness from an anxiety attack." He clicked the light off and dropped it into an open drawer behind him. "If you don't mind, I'd like to look you over." Before Rachel could answer, he grabbed her wrist and pressed two fingers to find her pulse.

The abrupt touch of his warm hands shot her heartbeat up. She drew in a breath to calm herself and tried not to notice his fingers had a rough callused texture, unusual for a doctor.

Curiosity piqued and she assessed the rest of him. A faded NYU T-shirt stretched against his broad chest. The muscles underneath were firm and well-defined—every one of them from his shoulders…down to his abdomen. Athletic build. She glanced up, thankful to see he concentrated on his wristwatch, timing her pulse, so she dared to continue her observation. He wore faded jeans that looked soft to the touch and hugged his hips and legs. She smiled when she saw what he wore on his feet. Tattered white running shoes with shoelaces tucked into the sides.

"Laundry day." He chuckled. "I don't usually dress like a college student. Not here, anyway."

"Oh." Rachel's cheeks grew warm. She hadn't meant for him to notice her gawking.

His soothing smile didn't fade as he grabbed a stethoscope from the open drawer. "So, are you seeking help for these attacks?"

Help? With the ghost-induced panic disorder? She didn't like to admit she had this problem, not even to herself. Though after the last attack, she'd forced herself to make an appointment with her regular doctor. Hence the bottle of sedatives sitting in a drawer at home.

It had only happened twice before. The first time when she'd initially encountered an unwelcome ghost. The second time after one of them had visited her while she was taking her bar exam. On the second day of the exam, he'd been relentless, threatening her life if she didn't leave and help him find his body. He'd yelled in her ear until her chest squeezed and her breathing strained. She'd barely made it back to her apartment before she broke down and cried, realizing she'd left too early. She hadn't finished, and she'd failed the exam.

But she couldn't seek further help. What would she tell a therapist? That her panic attacks were caused by ghosts? Yeah, right. Her psychological medical history would forever be tarnished. Worse, her parents would find out.

Rachel shook her head. "It's not a problem. I have it under control."

"Okay. I don't make it a habit to argue with patients." He reached around her and pressed the stethoscope to her back. "Take a deep breath for me."

She did as he said, using the opportunity to check him out further. So this was Ella's brother? Rachel didn't see anything wrong with him at all. He looked fine. Handsome. Laid back. Easy going. Like the type of person who didn't care what anyone thought. How could that be a bad thing? She wished she could be the same way.

"Okay, let's get your blood pressure."

"Listen, I really didn't mean to put you out. I'm sure you have more important things to do." She slid off the exam table to the floor, ignoring the urge to take one last sniff of his intoxicating scent. This man reminded her of Hayes in more ways than she cared to admit.

Time to get away from him. She didn't need the reminder of a love that could've been but never would be.

"Really sorry to bother you." She headed toward the door.

"And now you're leaving. So soon?"

His lighthearted tone made her want to stay and small-talk—discover more about Dr. Screw-up.

Obviously she'd gone too long without a date.

She turned the doorknob and slipped out of the

room. "Sincerely, I am so sorry. I really have to go," she said over her shoulder as she dashed to the front door. "I'm late for…you know. Thank you!"

"Wait a minute. Hey, I don't even know your name."

"Paperwork," the woman behind the desk shouted. "You haven't filled out your paperwork."

Rachel pretended she hadn't heard and hurried out to the parking lot. She had a few choice words for Ella, if the apparition ever showed up again. This whole experience had been beyond mortifying.

~ * ~

August scratched his head as he watched the mystery woman leave the parking lot. He'd followed her out, but after seeing the look of panic on her beautiful face he'd let her go without an argument. He hadn't wanted to trigger another anxiety attack. Well, that and she scared the hell out of him.

The feel of her soft lips on his neck when he'd carried her into his office had done crazy things to his body—things he hadn't felt in a long time. The way her analyzing cocoa-brown eyes had looked him over had left him uncharacteristically nervous. And how her long strawberry blond hair had actually smelled like strawberries had him wanting to explore the rest of her body. Women like her didn't exist outside his fantasies. Women like her could convince a man like him do just about anything. Including letting her leave his office before he was finished examining her. One look at those soft, smooth pink-glossed lips and he'd lost all common sense.

He heaved a sigh and considered finding the nearest wall to bang his head against. Loretta was going to throttle him for not making his anonymous patient fill out her paperwork. There were too many reasons to count why he should've gotten the woman's medical history and personal information.

His duty as a physician was to diagnose and act accordingly. He hadn't done his job. He hadn't even found out her name. She wasn't from around here. What if she had another attack while driving? Where had she come from? Where was she going? And who the hell was Hayes?

"Damn." He kicked a loose stone on the sidewalk. "Should've kept her here, dumbass."

Loretta pushed open the glass door and raised a condescending eyebrow. "Are you coming back inside anytime soon, Einstein?"

August shrugged. "That depends. Are you planning to verbally assault me?"

The middle-aged woman planted a hand on her robust hip and huffed out a breath. "If it would do any good, I would, Dr. Kline."

Oh, Lord, here we go again. When it came to nagging, Loretta was worse than Ella had been. A distressing thought.

"You're lucky I stuck around here to help you out after Dr. Williams passed away. God bless his soul. He knew how to be a doctor. He was so good in fact, he actually got paid once in a while. What do you think about that?"

"I—"

"Don't argue with your elders, child. Didn't Ella teach you better than that?"

August bit his tongue, mainly because an audience was forming outside of Dolly's Hair Salon two doors down. Then there were the reclusive Amish people gathering outside of Albert's Food Market. They quietly pretended not to listen in like they did so often.

If August gave a damn what anyone in this town thought, he would've apologized for the spectacle Loretta was making. But he didn't care, so he just ducked his head and walked back into his office.

"I don't want to hear anymore about it," he called over his shoulder before taking a seat at his desk on the opposite side of the room. He wasn't sure how Dr.

Williams had kept his sanity, having to work in the same room as Loretta for nearly thirty years. If August had the extra cash, he'd purchase the empty space next door, blow out the walls, and make a private office.

"Oh, really." Loretta waved to the ladies in front of the hair salon and closed the door. "You don't want to hear about how that woman left her handbag behind?"

August's ears perked up. "Her what?"

Loretta held up a purple leather purse. "This la-dee-da thing right here. If Miss Rachel Spencer can afford one of these designer bags, she can surely afford to pay for your services. I just did an internet search on how much one of these here cost and—"

"Rachel Spencer?" August took the purse from her and looked it over. He knew nothing about designer anything, but the accessory in his hands wasn't something he'd seen any of the women of Curlville carrying around. New York? Definitely. Not here. He fought the urge to dig through it like his nosy assistant undoubtedly had. "How did you get this, Loretta? I didn't bring it in with her."

"I took it from her car while you two were in the examination room. Couldn't leave it out there to be stolen, could I?"

"Right." August shook his head at her boldness. "Curlville's crime rate has blossomed since the Amish took over. We should all be worried." He narrowed his eyes. "Why didn't you take the keys out of the ignition?"

"Now you're being silly." Loretta shrugged and veered her gaze back to the computer screen.

August tried to act angry but a grin stretched wide.

Mystery Woman had a name. Rachel Spencer. And if she cared anything about this purse or the contents inside, he was sure to see her again.

~ * ~

Rachel's heart was still thudding as she drove down Curlville's Main Street, trying to find the access road to the highway. Whatever Ella had done to her to make her pass out had put her in a vulnerable position. An uncomfortably embarrassing position. That poor doctor probably thought she was deranged. And his diagnosis wouldn't have been far off.

Her thoughts were interrupted as a stray dog jumped into the middle of the two-lane road. She stomped on the brake, barely missing the cute matted-haired mutt. He stared up at her through the windshield, barked once, and ran off into the cornfield bordering the side of the road.

"Sweet mother of…" Rachel clenched the steering wheel and took in a calming breath, thankful no one had been behind her. She would've caused an accident for sure.

You're fine. Everything's fine.

She glanced around to see if anyone had noticed her near-homicide experience, but all she saw was a gas station about a hundred yards away.

Good. A bright side. She was running low on gas…which seemed odd because she remembered filling up yesterday. Besides this trip, she hadn't traveled anywhere, and her little car got excellent gas mileage.

Oh, well. With the way her luck was going, she'd better not take any chances driving back to Indianapolis without refilling. She pulled into the one-pump station and cut the engine. The small building in front of her had white-ish paint flaking off its siding, and its only window was cracked and too dirty to see through.

No one came out to greet her, and the pump didn't have a slot for credit cards, so she reached in the car for her… Oh. Wait. Where was her purse? She checked under her seat and the passenger seat as well. Nothing. Damn. Where could it be? She never left home without it, so—

"Oh, no."

Dr. Kline or Loretta must have grabbed it from her car when she'd passed out.

"Lovely. Could this day get any worse?"

Her cell phone sang from the change tray in her

console. At least she had her phone. Another bright side. She picked it up and saw that her mother was calling. Yep, the day could get much worse.

"Hi, Mom." She answered, knowing how relentless her mom could be. No point in trying to avoid the phone call.

"Rachel, where are you? I'm in your apartment, and you're not here."

"I'm, um, visiting a friend. Why are you at my place?" Rachel didn't bother asking how she'd gotten in. Her parents had agreed to pay her rent, but the price Rachel paid was her privacy. Her mother, Dora, had her own key and had an unsavory habit of making surprise visits.

"Do I need a reason to see my daughter? Besides, Rebecca told me you were having trouble concentrating on studying. You need to pass the exam, dear. July is right around the corner, and you've already wasted enough time by taking a semester off to plan a wedding that didn't happen. Then of course there's always the possibility of you failing again. What are you going to do then?"

Mental note: Never talk to Becca again.

"Mom, I'm fine. I'm studying, and I promise I'll pass. I was just having a bad day when I talked to Becca. It's not a big deal."

"It's a big deal to me and your father, young lady. How can you treat this as if it's not important when your father and I have spent so much time and money putting you through school? Do you know how much it hurts me to hear that you're not grateful?"

Rachel rolled her eyes shut as the familiar words bounced around her mind. "I am grateful," she said sincerely, guiltily—like a mantra. "I owe you and Dad everything. I promise I'll pass the next time. I still have almost two months to prepare, and I've been studying every day."

"How can I trust you, Rachel? How do I know you won't fail again?"

Rachel wrapped her arm around her belly. She had no idea if she'd be able to pass the second time. The way her life was going she couldn't predict what would happen in the next sixty seconds. But she couldn't tell her mother that. "I give you my word, Mom."

"Well, I guess that'll have to do." Her mother's signature martyr's sigh gusted through the receiver. "Your father is deeply worried about you. You know how much this means to him."

"Mom, I've been interning for the firm whenever he needs me, learning as much as possible." Though what she'd learned hadn't been exactly inspiring. The firm seemed to attract some shady—insanely wealthy—clientele. Money spoke, and Spencer & Donovan, LLC tended to listen. Becoming a criminal defense attorney seemed less and less appealing. But...

"He wants you to succeed, like he has."

"I understand." Even though her father would never admit his feelings to Rachel, ever, he must be embarrassed by her failure. He'd always been a man of few words, fewer emotions, so when he'd asked her to consider following in his footsteps, she'd easily agreed. She could still remember the brief grin that had appeared on his face.

"I worry about you, sweetheart. If you could only find a man to take care of you, like your father has taken care of us."

Then there was her mother's wish. Two paths had been set out in front of her, and she'd chosen the one where she'd least likely end up like her mother. Spoiled and bored out of her mind.

Another exaggerated sigh. "In any case, I don't suggest you come home for dinner tonight. Your father is having a colleague over, and he doesn't want your *setback* to be brought up."

"Of course. I understand." She'd agree to just about anything to cut the call short.

She said goodbye, trying not to sound too hasty, and dropped the phone back onto the console.

"Isn't she a delight?" Ella's otherworldly body materialized in the passenger seat.

Rachel did the usual glance around to see if anyone was watching before speaking. "I don't appreciate you listening in on my phone calls. And where have you been? You left me with him. Do you know how embarrassing that was? Don't ever mess with my body like that again."

"Sorry." Ella threw her hands up in surrender. "I promise I'll be good from here on out. And I left because I needed to rest."

"You sleep?"

"Descend into blackness is more like it. My energy only lasts for so long before I fade. Very annoying." She scrunched her nose. "So how did it go? Do you see what I mean about August? He's a complete mess."

Rachel's anger renewed. There wasn't anything wrong with August Kline, other than he'd had a pushy control freak for a sister. "Your brother is fine." He was better than fine; he was gorgeous. Her stomach tumbled at the possibility of seeing him again to retrieve her purse. Perfect. A silly crush was the last thing she needed. Her focus needed to be on studying.

She could always forget about the purse and order a new drivers license and bank card. Everything else in there was replaceable, as well. In the meantime, she had a credit card at home her parents had given her for emergencies. A lost purse would constitute an emergency, right?

But she'd still have to find a way to fill her gas tank...

"Did you notice what he was wearing?" Ella said. "You can only imagine what my home looks like. It's falling apart, and he's done nothing to keep it together. The man is a walking domestic disaster. Do you have any idea what my boys are eating? How they're living? You have to help them."

Rachel barked out a nervous laugh. If only a pinch

could end this nightmare. Ella wasn't just a control freak, she was obsessive, much like all the other ghost invaders. How was Rachel going to get rid of her now?

"I have an idea." Ella's eyes widened. "We can make a deal. You help me, and I'll help you."

"Oh, boy." Rachel tapped her fingers on the steering wheel and shot another glance at the deserted gas station...

Only to see it wasn't there anymore.

"Where—?" Baffled and slightly freaked, she leapt from the car and took in her surroundings. New surroundings. All that encircled her were rolling hills of tall grass with a house way off in the distance. She'd driven off the road into a field, apparently. How had she mistaken this for a gas station?

"I couldn't let you leave." Ella stood beside her now. Her hair whipped around in a breeze that didn't exist. In this dimension, anyway. "I need your help, Rachel."

Boy, she really was nuts. "How did you do this? Where's the gas station? I know it was here." She was sure of it.

A hint of guilt fluttered across the ghost's face. "I had to play a little trick on you. To keep you here. I'm desperate. I'll do anything."

"A little trick? You mean on my mind?"

Ella shrugged. "Your perception, I suppose. The dog, the empty gas gauge, the gas station. You see what others can't. You see what I see and what I imagine to see."

"Wait. Back up. You imagined it, and I saw it?" That wasn't possible. Was it?

Funny, Rache. Rational reasoning had been thrown out the window months ago.

"I had to try. I hope you'll forgive me."

"So I'm not out of gas?" Another thought occurred. "Wait, did you also steal my purse?"

"No and no. You're at three-quarters of a tank.

Good gas mileage on that one." She gestured to Rachel's two-door hatchback. "And I believe the purse-snatching was Loretta's doing. August has it with him now." She grinned coyly. "At my home."

"Nooo, Ella." She pressed her hand to her throbbing temple. "You can't control me like this. I have my own life, my own troubles."

"I'll help you with them, I promise."

Rachel shook her head. She'd never cared for the purse anyway. It had been an extravagant gift from her mom, who'd been more than happy to toss her old department store handbag. She'd get a new one…and simply break down and use the emergency credit card, making it a priority to replace the essentials. Yes. That was it. She'd go back home, continue to study, continue to ignore her rising insanity, and everything would work itself out. It had to.

She returned to her car, snapped her seatbelt on—because that's what normal people did—and turned the key.

The engine sputtered and died.

She tried again.

No luck.

"Just hear me out." Ella sat beside her again, her hair lying flat now in its too-perfect style.

Rachel tried the engine again. Still nothing.

"You have to take the bar exam, and I can guarantee you'll pass the next time. I've taken it before, and I did rather well. What I can do for you is simply stand over your shoulder and tell you how to answer."

"I didn't fail because I didn't know the answers," Rachel snapped. She'd had it with being thought of as a failure. She would have passed that damned exam if it hadn't been for the hostile ghost. "I failed because a spirit screamed in my ear, trying to manipulate me just as you are now. I'm tired of it, Ella. All I want is to be left alone."

"No need to get testy. I'm only trying to do right by

my boys. I didn't mean to upset you."

"So you'll leave me alone?"

"Well. I don't know."

"For the love of..." Rachel grumbled as she flung the car door open, preparing to walk home if she had to. But Ella grabbed at her hand. The cold ethereal contact passed through Rachel's flesh, and she shivered.

"Wait," Ella said. "I've got the answer. I'll protect you from the other spirits. I'll keep them at bay for as long as it takes to get my house in order and for you to pass your exam."

"You can keep them away?" Rachel settled back into her seat.

"You bet." Ella smiled wide. "Is it a deal?"

The offer was incredibly tempting. To be rid of the annoying and sometimes frightening visits would free her to study more…and just be normal for once in two years. Normal and back in control of her destiny.

Yes, she'd do just about anything.

"What would I have to do?" She closed the car door and braced herself.

"Simple really. I need someone to whip my home back into shape, someone to make sure my boys are eating their vegetables, taking their vitamins, doing their homework. Until August gets a handle on things, he needs guidance. And, well, he needs a housekeeper."

"Oh." Rachel stretched at her blouse's collar. Why was she suddenly so hot? "I don't know, Ella. I have zero experience running a household."

"You've never cleaned a house? Cooked a meal?"

"Yes, I've done those things, just not for an entire family. That's a lot of work. A lot of time." Not to mention she'd have to convince August to let her into his home.

"Then you'll have to decide what's worse. Obnoxious spirits or cleaning toilets? What do you say?"

Chapter Three

"There it is." Ella pointed at a two-story home with grey vinyl siding and black shutters flanking each of the windows. A quaint home in an even quainter neighborhood. Seemed harmless.

Rachel pulled up to the curb and took a closer look. A large porch with white railings stretched across the front of the house, and on it was a lopsided porch swing that needed some TLC. The front yard consisted of overgrown grass with scattered dandelions and a couple of large oak trees needing trimming. And, of course, the infamous wilted garden sat in between the house and the detached one-car garage.

"Do you see what I mean?" Ella waved a gesture at the house.

"There's nothing that can't be fixed, I'm sure." Rachel shut off the engine. The car was working fine now, which wasn't surprising after having agreed to Ella's deal. To know this particular ghost had so much power was alarming, and Rachel wondered what would've happened if things hadn't gone Ella's way.

She'd weighed her options: go home and try to ignore the spirit visits, which seemed to be increasingly worse

31

every day. Or deal with Ella, who was a little pushy, but not nearly as scary as most.

She'd chosen Ella and her scheme to help her family.

The offer had been too hard to refuse—an assurance that she would pass the bar exam and a guarantee she wouldn't disappoint her parents again. She couldn't allow herself to fail. Caring so much about her parents' approval was silly. She was a grown woman with needs and wants of her own, but the yearning to please them had never ceased. Just once, she wanted to hear them say how proud they were of her. *One time.*

If she accomplished that, she could accomplish anything.

Besides, being a housekeeper for this family couldn't be all that difficult. Rachel figured she could clean while they were gone during the day and leave before they returned. All in exchange for some sanity. Well worth it, she thought.

She just had to convince Dr. Hotstuff that she wasn't a lunatic.

Easy-smeasy. Right?

Probably not so much.

"It's a pretty home." Rachel gulped down her anxiety. She could do this. No problem.

Ella sighed and wrung her hands. "It used to be."

Poor woman. Rachel considered patting her on the shoulder to comfort her but thought better of it. Could a ghost feel a touch? They could certainly feel emotions. As they stared at the home where Ella had raised her sons, tears slid down her pale, hollow cheeks. It broke Rachel's heart.

"Thank you so much for doing this." Ella swiped away the watery line that trickled to her chin. "August and the boys are inside. I'll be back soon."

"Wait. You're leaving? What if he says no? What if he doesn't want help?" What if he thinks I'm a nutcase and throws me out of his house?

Ella's lips curled up into lopsided grin. "Oh, he won't have a choice," she said, and disappeared.

~ * ~

"I'm hungry." Zach stuck his head in the fridge for the tenth time since he'd come home from school, making August grit his teeth in irritation.

When wasn't the kid hungry?

"I'll order pizza after I get back from the Laundromat." August threw the last pair of wet jeans from the washer into the plastic laundry basket nearest him. There were five baskets at his feet overflowing with dirty clothes. Usually, he made Zach and Nicholas wash their own clothes, but since their new washer and dryer wouldn't be delivered for another six to eight weeks, he decided to get it all done in one trip.

"We have pizza like every other night." Zach slammed the fridge door shut. "No way am I having it again."

August counted to ten in his head and reminded himself that his nephew was a hormone-ridden, girl-crazy, and essentially brain-warped teen until at least the age of twenty. He remembered those years, therefore he'd give the kid a break. This time.

"What?" Zach knotted his eyebrows together. "Why are you looking at me like that?"

"You do see that I'm slaving over your laundry, do you not? If you don't want pizza, make your own dinner. Got it?" August stacked two baskets on top of each other, picked them up, and walked into the living room, proud of the fact that he hadn't raised his voice. Much.

These boys had to learn a little respect, especially Zach, who was maybe a little too similar to August when he was that age. A boundless spirit with an attitude. Nicholas, on the other hand, stayed in his room for the most part.

August didn't know what was worse—being annoyed or being ignored. At least having the lively Zach to banter with occasionally made this whole situation a little less lonely.

"You know Dana said we could use her washer and dryer." The boy skipped after him and laughed. "She said she wouldn't mind getting her hands on your tighty whities. Gross, right? I can sorta see why you avoid her. She's kinda weird."

"You're catching on," August said over his shoulder, and then stopped short when the doorbell rang. Oh, no, no, no. He dropped the baskets and headed to the door. "I swear, boy, if you said anything to that woman—"

Before he could finish his threat, Zach retreated into the kitchen, laughing the whole way.

"Coward," August yelled and opened the door. "Hi, Dana—" He clamped his mouth shut when he saw who stood on the other side.

She offered him a partial smile and timidly pushed a coppery-blond lock behind her ear. "Rachel. My name is Rachel Spencer. I believe I left my purse at your office?" She bit into her bottom lip. Plump, delicious-looking lip.

"Uh…" Lord, his brain was here a moment ago. He cleared his throat to waste some time while he gathered his cool. Looking like an ass in front of this woman was not an option. "Yes. Yes, you did. I brought it home with me, actually. Didn't want to leave it at the office."

"Great. I hope you don't mind me stopping by your house. Your office was closed, and someone directed me here." Her gaze drifted behind him then met his again. "Can I come in? You know, to get it?"

"Absolutely." He swung the door open and realized too late the house was a disaster.

Tennis shoes, dirty socks, backpacks, and various sporting equipment littered the living room floor. A dumping ground that never seemed to be cleared. The kitchen, dining room, and upstairs were worse. He didn't even want to think about the bathrooms. God only knew what was growing between the cracked tiles. He just hoped like hell she didn't have to go.

Keeping her in the living room was his best bet. "Have a seat." He tossed Nicholas's backpack from the sofa to the floor and shoved away a few stray comic books, as well as the last two Sunday newspapers and the TV remote.

"Sorry about the mess. I'm raising my two teenage nephews. Alone. Definitely alone. No woman whatsoever in my life." He cringed at his idiotic choice of words, unable to recall the last time a woman had made him this jumpy.

Nope, he'd always been the one to make them nervous. Over the years, he'd learned just what look or touch made them shiver. A simple sweep of his fingers over the inside of the woman's wrist. A brush of his knuckles down her cheek. A searing gaze from across the crowded club that told her she was the most gorgeous woman he'd ever seen.

Which, of course, hadn't been true.

But this woman—Rachel—he wasn't so sure he'd ever seen a woman as stunning. Either that or he hadn't had sex in so long he was starting to lower his expectations.

Nah.

She sat on the sofa, her long legs and shapely ass bending against stretchy dark-washed jeans. His gaze lingered to her slim waist. Then up to the hint of creamy ivory skin peeking out from her snug V-neck. Higher then to her elegantly lean neck that begged to be licked and kissed. Shiny coppery hair that cascaded down mid-back, which he imagined scraping against his chest as she sat on top of him and rode—

"That's very noble of you."

Her words yanked him out of his fantasy.

"I'm sorry?" *Snap out of it, August.*

"Taking care of your nephews"—she licked her bottom lip—"without any help is honorable. Unselfish."

"Oh. Right. They're good kids for the most part." He rubbed his hand across his chest. "Do you want something to drink? Water? Soda? Beer, wine?" He had one nice bottle he was saving for a special occasion, but what the hell? A beautiful woman in his home was a special occasion.

"Water would be great, but I don't want to put you out. Were you about to leave?" She glanced at the laundry baskets.

"That can wait." Everything could wait. "I'll get your water. Don't move." He walked backward, talking to her as he made his way to the kitchen. "Really. I'm holding your purse hostage so don't even think about disappearing on me again."

She smiled and a blush tinted her cheeks. August took that as a good sign and pushed open the swinging door into the kitchen. The sound and sight of a dozen eggs dropping from Zach's hands to the tile squashed his mood.

"Shit!" Zach swooshed up his hands in surrender. "They slipped, dude. It's not my fault. I swear."

"Clean it up," August whispered through his teeth. "And watch your mouth, kid. I have company in the other room."

"Dana?"

"No. What're you doing with the eggs anyway?"

Zach rolled his eyes and grabbed the paper towels off the counter. "I'm making my own dinner. Remember?"

"Making more work for me is more like it."

"Is everything okay in here?"

Rachel's voice sent a shiver of dread down August's spine.

He turned slowly while blowing out a breath. If she scared easily, she'd surely be running out of here stat. What sane woman would be interested in a man with two teenage hurricanes and a disaster area for a house? Damn. He was never going to catch a break.

36

"Oh," she said from the doorway. She smiled at Zach, whose mouth dropped open, revealing every bracket on every tooth. "Do you need some help cleaning that up?"

"No, thanks," August said, almost covering Zach's enthusiastic "Yes."

Before he could stop her, Rachel took the paper towels from Zach. "Get me the garbage can, and we'll have this cleaned up in no time."

"You don't have to do that." August shot his nephew a threatening glare, but it seemed the boy was under her trance. Easily so. "Zach can clean this up. Why don't we go back in the living room?"

"I don't mind helping, Dr. Kline." She dropped to her knees beside the mess. "I believe I owe you."

"Please call me August. And no, you don't owe me a thing. I promise." August would've protested further, but the sight of Zach picking up eggshells without whining surprised him. The pair exchanged introductions while they worked together. Since when did the boy follow directions without complaining?

"I'll get the mop." Zach bound toward the broom closet. His nephew knew where the mop was located? Wait, he knew what a mop was?

Rachel swiped up the rest of the splatter and threw the paper towels into the garbage can. "In any case, thanks for helping me today." She dusted off her knees. "I've been under a ton of stress lately, and I think I just let it build up too long. Know what I mean?"

August nodded. He wanted to reach out and touch her somehow. Give her a little comfort. But he didn't. Hell, she really was the most beautiful woman he'd ever seen. And the most terrifying. A woman like this couldn't be just a one-night stand. A woman like this needed to be savored. Thoroughly.

"Will you stay for dinner?" He heard himself ask before his thoughts had time to settle.

"Great idea," Zach said, slopping the soaking wet mop on to the floor. "You don't want pizza, do you? Because I'm so tired of that crap."

"Zach," August warned, but bit his mouth shut when he felt Rachel's hand on his arm.

She looked up at him with pretty golden brown eyes and those sweet pouty lips. "I'd be happy to put something together. I love to cook."

August shifted on his feet, suddenly uncomfortable because the woman's voice was spurring a hard-on. Her voice! Soft and honeyed. Like her face. And her body.

"I can't let you do that," he said. "I'm sure I can whip something up."

Zach grabbed his throat and pretended to gag. "Please...no more...mac and...cheese."

For God's sake, the boy was going to muck everything up.

Count to ten, August.

At least Zach's antics made Rachel laugh. The sound of it filled the room with a sweetness August hadn't felt in a long time. Not since Ella had been alive.

She grasped his forearm with both hands and knocked him over the head with a sexy grin designed just for him, causing his knees to almost give. Yep, she was terrifying all right.

"Don't deny it," she said. "You guys need some help, and I have plenty of time on my hands. Why don't you get that laundry done while I make dinner? It'll be ready by the time you get back."

This woman was too good to be true. August brought her hand up to his lips for a kiss. "You're an angel sent from above, aren't you?"

Her smile faded ever so slightly. "Something like that."

~ * ~

The thudding of the rubber ball on the hardwood floor was driving Nicholas nuts. How many times could a ghost play jacks before getting bored?

Bounce. Scoop. Catch. Bounce. Scoop. Catch.

Ach! Her celestial voice vibrated in his head. *Why can't I ever get to tensies, Nicholas?*

He shrugged, pretending he didn't care. But he knew why. Her hands were too small. Just like the rest of her body. For a girl who lived to be sixteen, she sure was short.

In a cute and petite sort of way, he guessed.

Nicholas thinks I'm cute. Nicholas thinks I'm cute. Joanna sang and dumped the jacks on the floor again.

"And a pest." He stood from his bed and lightly thumped her on her head with his classroom copy of *Animal Farm*.

"Ouch." She giggled and pushed her white bonnet back, scratching the area right behind her hairline. A few loose blond strands fell forward.

Nicholas wondered what her hair looked like down, out of that stupid Amish cap. How would it look free of its tightly braided constraints, flowing over her shoulders? He wondered how she'd pull off normal-girl clothes, like shorts and a T-shirt, instead of that ankle-length dull grey wool dress.

She'd probably be pretty hot. She didn't need any makeup with the way her long lashes framed her big blue eyes and the way her cheeks blushed by themselves. But he couldn't help but imagine her spreading on some of that glossy lip stuff, the kind that smelled like tropical fruit. He'd like to kiss lips like that.

"Your mind is sinful," she said aloud, and threw the rubber ball at his chest.

Yeah, well, get out of it then.

No. It's…interesting. Besides, you're the only one who can hear me. Her pink lips twisted to a frown. *After what happened.*

Right. The big secret. He didn't bother asking her again how she'd died, not after the last time, when she'd lost her temper and broke his hard drive. Or the time before that, when the downstairs TV started smoking and almost caught on fire. The girl had major anger management issues. Every time she got mad, something blew up or fried.

She especially hated it when he went to school and left her alone.

No surprise everything was breaking around the house. He *had* to go to school. He didn't mind giving up the dances or the baseball games—okay, he sort of missed the baseball team—but there was no way he'd drop out just to stay home with a ghost. It was bad enough he knew she existed.

He didn't want to see ghosts. Like that time he looked out his window a few months ago and saw his mom floating through the garden. Yeah, that'd been weird. And sad. He shook that memory from his head, not wanting to go there.

Everyone thought he was a freak to begin with. What would they say if they knew he saw dead people?

"I'm not dead." Joanna shoved her blond hairs back into her bonnet and glared at him.

Whatever. He wasn't even going to provoke an argument. Not when his new cell phone was in her vicinity.

A knock on his door made her gasp.

"Nick?" Uncle Auggie called through the door. "Time for dinner."

Joanna scurried into his closet and curled her legs up against her chest. *Make him go away!*

Nicholas rolled his eyes. *Chicken. It's just my uncle. I'll be back in a little bit.*

"Nick?" August called again and pounded harder against the door.

"Coming." Nicholas glanced at Joanna's pursed lips, flushed cheeks, and angry scrunched up eyes. "Just need to grab my cell phone."

Chapter Four

Rachel helped August clear off the table, careful not to bump into him as they crossed paths in the kitchen. She'd never thought she was a great cook, not having had much practice. Living alone, she mostly survived on the essentials, so she'd been surprised when August and his nephews went back for a second and third helping of her chicken and dumplings—a recipe she'd learned from her childhood housekeeper. Therese would be delighted her recipe had given these boys so much satisfaction. Rachel felt a tingle of delight as well. She'd accomplished something good here. A small deed but well worth the time and effort.

And one checkmark on the mental list to helping Ella crossover and getting Ella to help her pass the bar ghost-free.

"Thanks, Rachel. That was so much better than pizza," Zach said over his shoulder as he darted from the room and away from any cleaning responsibility.

Rachel held her tongue, not wanting to insert herself into this household more than was necessary.

"Thank you, Ms. Spencer." Nicholas nodded politely. "Dinner was delicious."

41

"Call me Rachel."

She smiled at him, and he blushed.

"I...I have homework, so..." He let his words fade as he followed his brother out the door, also leaving without offering to help with cleanup.

Despite their lack of responsibility, they were both adorable. Heartbreakers in the making. Just like their uncle. Rachel had stolen glimpses of him throughout dinner. The man even ate sexily. Pleasing him had warmed places that had no right to be heated. She took one last peek at him as he cleared a space on the cluttered counter to stack more dirty dishes.

He gave her a small grin and a shrug. "Sorry about the mess. The dishwasher's broken and things have piled up on me."

"I'd be glad to help you clean up." This was what Ella wanted, after all.

Where was that woman anyway? Rachel had felt a presence in the house all evening. Was she hiding? Saving up her energy, or whatever it was she did to stay in this realm?

August crossed his arms and leaned against the kitchen counter. "That's sweet of you, but I think you've more than earned back the rights to your purse. That meal was delicious."

More warmth flooded her, reaching areas that hadn't been *inspired* in a while. Sad how a simple compliment from this man could turn her on. She whooshed out a breath and reminded herself to concentrate on the reason she was here in the first place.

"I still owe you for the doctor's bill," she said. "I shouldn't have left without paying. That was rude of me, and I'd like to make it up to you." She maneuvered around him and began filling up the sink with sudsy warm water.

"No, Rachel." He reached around her and shut off the faucet, pressing the weight of his body against her side in the process. "I appreciate the thought, but the last thing

I want you to do right now is wash my dishes."

"I don't mind at all. I'd like to help." The words squeaked out of her mouth. Blah. She'd always been timid around men, but this man gave her shyness a category all its own.

He backed away but not before gripping her wrist. "Come on. Let's get some fresh air. The weatherman assured me we have at least a few more days of unseasonably warm weather."

"Oh." She looked around for a reason to resist. "My hands are wet. See?" She gestured toward their connection. His perpetual smile broadened even larger. How was it possible for someone to seem happy all the time?

"Here."

He tore off a paper towel from its holder and dried her hands, reminding her of the rough texture of his fingers. What did the doctor do to get callused hands?

"Good?"

Really good. Too good. She nodded, avoiding eye contact, wanting to shrink away from his undivided attention.

"Excellent. Let's get out of this house." He led her through the cluttered living room and out the front door, past the creaky screen door, and onto the porch, where he finally released her hand.

He jabbed his thumb toward the porch swing. "I've been meaning to fix this. Shouldn't take long. We can sit and talk. Get to know each other better. You don't have to be anywhere, do you?" He didn't wait for her answer. Instead, he began to work on the chain link holding up the swing.

Rachel fought the urge to retreat. One small conversation wasn't going to kill her…or ignite another panic attack. She didn't think so, anyway. Those episodes were unpredictable. So far they'd only been provoked by ghosts, and not one apparition had made an appearance tonight. Well, besides the presence that still lingered, only

43

slightly different. This one was larger than the one inside. It took up more space and wasn't hiding from anyone.

Must be Ella. She'd promised to keep other spirits away, and so far she was sticking to her part of the bargain. But what was with the presence inside the house? If that hadn't been Ella, it must be something—someone—else. She hoped she hadn't brought a spirit with her. This family didn't need some ghost wreaking havoc on their home. They had enough to deal with as it was.

She moved closer to where August stood. "I'm free to stay for a little while. I need to talk to you about something anyway."

"Oh, yeah?" He finished unlinking and linking the chain to make the swing level and then sat and patted the seat next to him. "Zach and his buddies were messing with this a few days ago. Seems safe enough now. Have a seat."

"Sure." She sat on the far end of the swing. Her mind sped as she tried to think of a way to convince August to allow her into his house on a daily basis.

He shimmied to face her and rested his arm on the back of the swing, taking up all the space his long athletic body needed. Confident. Casual. He pinned his vibrant blue gaze on her. "Did you need to talk about what brought you to Curlville this afternoon?"

"What brought me here?" Now she was just stalling for time. She clasped her hands together. Ella's giggling nearby confirmed they indeed had an audience. Darn her.

"Yeah, I couldn't help but check out the address on your driver's license. Curlville isn't exactly in your proximity. You live in Indianapolis, right?"

She nodded and delayed a little longer by watching a young family ride by on bicycles. From what she'd seen, Curlville was an adorable little town. A shopping plaza and of couple of churches outlined several streets of quaint two-story homes. Miles of farmland and scattered white Amish homes surrounded the town.

Not much to do here for entertainment other than

hang out with the family or curl up with a good book. She liked the idea of that, but she wondered if this lifestyle bored a man like August. A man Ella had said used to play in a rock band in New York City. What a change of scenery.

"Rachel?" He brushed her shoulder with his fingertips and leaned closer. "Did I lose you? I didn't mean to put you on the spot."

"You didn't. Not at all. You asked a simple question." She paused, thinking this through. She could either lie, wrapping herself in a web of deceit, or she could spill the truth and hope he believed her. Not probable. "I don't know how to explain what brought me here without sounding crazier than you already think I am."

His smile faded but quickly returned. "Crazy? I don't think you're crazy, honey. You puzzle me, but I kind of like puzzles. Keeps me on my toes."

A puzzle. He had no idea. She gulped down the knot in her throat. "I—"

"Who's Hayes?" The question slipped out as if it had been on the brim of his lips.

"Where did you hear that name?" Rachel thought back to the contents of her purse but couldn't think of a single thing that would lead August to ask about her former love.

He leaned in more—a few inches and their mouths would be touching. She wasn't comfortable being this close to anybody, much less a man who could easily haunt her fantasies. She held her breath and forced herself not to back away. He had her full attention.

"You called his name when I carried you into my office."

"I did?"

"And then you kissed my neck." His gaze dropped to her mouth.

"I did not." Had she? She couldn't remember. She'd been in such a fog.

"Trust me. My skin is still blazing from the scorch of your lips." He rubbed his neck, just under his jaw.

"Scorch of my lips? Are you joking?" She couldn't tell with the way he was always smiling.

"Was that too corny?" He chuckled, deep and whispery. Sexy. Masculine. Just like his voice and just about everything else about him.

Rachel crossed her legs, ignoring the warm fluttering in her belly. She shrugged and waited for him to say something else. Anything.

"Who is he? A boyfriend? Or someone you're running away from?"

Anything but that. Talking about Hayes with a man she was attracted to felt wrong—like she was cheating on his memory. But Hayes wasn't here, and that wasn't any fault of her own.

She cleared her throat. "We never quite made it to the boyfriend-girlfriend stage. He died before we'd had a chance to commit to a relationship."

"Ah." The smile disappeared. "I'm sorry. Was he special to you?"

"Yes." She blinked her stinging eyes as old emotions hit full-force. Just when she'd thought she was getting over him. Damn. "He was the love of my life."

"The love of your life," August repeated. "Meaning there's only one love per lifetime? That's pretty extreme, binding yourself to one person no matter what. Especially since he, you know…" He let his sentence fade.

"You don't understand. If he'd lived, I'm sure we would have married and been together forever. I felt that strongly for him."

"Interesting." August picked something from her shirt—a stray hair—and let it fall to the ground.

His proximity and scrutiny made her incredibly nervous. And excited at the same time. If it weren't for Ella, she'd leave.

She spread her hands and lifted a shaky shoulder.

"So?"

"So tell me more about this guy. What made him the one and only?"

Memories poured into her thoughts. Hayes's face. His laugh. He'd been the most exciting thing to ever happen to her. He'd been larger than life, too large, in fact, for her to hold on to.

"He was," she started slowly, "carefree. Charismatic. I loved the way he inspired me to feel as if nothing else mattered in the world other than that moment in time. Because he felt the same way. The next breath of air hadn't been important to him as long as this breath was the sweetest."

She met August's gaze directly and unexpectedly inhaled his scent, the same scent that reminded her so much of the man in her memories. "That was how he'd lived, and that's how he died. He'd gone parachuting with friends. No one checked to make sure his equipment worked properly, and—"

"Stupid," August said so softly, Rachel barely heard the word. Barely.

"He wasn't stupid."

"No? Sounds like he was either an adrenaline junkie or just a plain old junkie. Which was it? 'Cause no breath is sweet enough to be my last, that's for sure. I've seen enough death in my life to know that much."

"Hayes never touched drugs," she said, louder than she'd intended, but she didn't care. She wouldn't allow this stranger to smear Hayes's memory. "The accident wasn't his fault, not entirely. He didn't mean to die." God, she didn't think so anyway. A stubborn tear broke free. She swiped it away.

The wooden swing creaked against the movement of August's lengthy body as he sat back...away from her. "I'm sorry. Didn't mean to upset you. It's just that I've lost so many important people through no fault of their own and to hear about someone treating life like a sport really sets me off."

Ella. He'd lost his sister and apparently other family members, since he was alone raising Nicholas and Zach. Rachel didn't like that August thought poorly of Hayes, but she understood his frustration. She could relate to the anger, the grief.

There they had a connection. She studied August's profile as he stared ahead, seeming to want to hide emotions of his own past. She didn't like being the reason his perpetual smile disappeared. His frown seemed unnatural.

She inched closer to his side of the swing and pressed her hand to the soft cotton expanding across his chest.

"I'm sorry about Ella."

No. Right as the words left her lips, she realized her mistake.

His gazed snapped to hers, and he grabbed hold of her hand, squeezing just a little too hard. "How do you know my sister?"

Rachel wiggled free and stood. "I can explain."

"You better." He sat forward on the edge of the swing.

A twinge of anxiety hit her. The man seemed to suck the wits straight out of her head, especially when he touched her. She needed to pace. Her mind worked better when she moved. And she really needed to think this through.

"Tell him you worked with me." Ella appeared in front of her, forcing Rachel to stop mid-pace.

"I can't lie." Or at least she wasn't comfortable lying to August.

"Okay," he said, watching her as if he were searching for a diagnosis. "Good to know. So is Ella the reason you came to Curlville today?"

Rachel swiveled and faced him, happy to answer that particular question, at least. She looked directly at him and said the next words, "Yes. She was—is—the reason I'm here."

Ella touched Rachel's back, sending a thick chill up her spine. "Tell him we were good friends and you were worried about the boys."

"No."

"No what?" August stood and softly gripped her upper arms. "Are you feeling okay?"

Rachel leaned in, toward the tempting heat radiating from his body, but she still couldn't escape the cold. Was she okay? She wasn't so sure. How could she tell this man she saw his dead sister? Someone he'd said goodbye to over a year ago. Tell him all this when she didn't fully believe it herself.

"You can't," Ella's whisper felt a thousand miles away, though her icy presence surrounded Rachel, enveloping her body, coursing through her veins. "Please don't. He won't believe you. And if he does, it'll only upset him."

She'd read Rachel's mind. Not good when her thoughts often deceived her. Great. Too much to think about now. She shook her head and decided to focus on the issue at hand.

"I'm fine," Rachel said, finally meeting August's concerned gaze. "I'm just..." She waved her hand, trying to summon her next words. "She was a friend of mine. A mentor, really, since I'm studying to be a lawyer. We had lunch on several occasions." The lies seemed to flow now. "She'd told me about you and her sons, and after she died, I couldn't stop thinking about them and wondering how they were."

August's frown lifted just so, easing Rachel's guilt just a bit. "You were worried about people you've never met?"

"Yes. Ella always spoke so highly of her sons. I felt like I knew them." That wasn't such an awful lie, was it?

"And you were aware I was a single mom," Ella urged her on.

"And she also told me you were the only family she

and the boys had left, so I figured you'd be alone in raising them."

He slid his warm palms down her arms until his hands found hers and intertwined. "Kind of you to come all the way out here for us."

Oh, wow, she was going to burn on brimstone for this. Her true reasons were far less benevolent.

Ella coughed. "Keep going before you lose him."

Rachel sighed, hoping her lies wouldn't hurt anyone in the long run. "I want to help you, August. Ella did so much for me." Or was about to if all went as planned. "I never had the chance to thank her for all her advice and encouraging words."

His hands tightened around hers. "Help me how?"

An icy jab shoved Rachel forward, making her fall against August's chest. He caught her before she collapsed on to the porch. Her cheeks blazed, and she quickly stepped away, pulling from the warmth of his body.

"I'm so sorry. I must've lost my footing."

"No problem." He reached out again but seemed to think better of it. "Listen, I'm glad Ella made an impression on you, but please don't worry about Nick and Zach." He gestured toward the front door. "We might not be the most organized bunch. We make messes, and things might seem a little chaotic at times, as you probably noticed. But we manage. They're going to be okay. I'll make sure of it."

"I know," she said, without hesitation. "I don't doubt that for one second. I think those boys are lucky to have you." This part was not a lie, and it felt good to tell him. "I don't know you that well, but you seem like you're a wonderful father figure for them."

He shrugged one shoulder and stuck his hands in his pockets, taking an all-too-familiar stance. Hayes's stance. "Thanks. I'm trying."

Rachel couldn't help but smile. He was adorable and sweet and gorgeous and— She cut the list short and straightened out her expression. This wasn't the time to gush over a man. August might remind her of Hayes in a lot of ways, and that was confusing.

But they were two different men.

"Rachel, what's on your mind?"

She eased out a breath. "Starting tomorrow I'd like to come over and help you get organized."

"Organized?"

"Yes. You said it yourself—you're not the most organized. I can help with that."

"You mean like clean up?" He muffled some words as he rubbed his hand over his mouth and then straightened, meeting her gaze full-on. "Rachel, that's very generous of you, but I can't accept."

Don't give him a choice. Ella's voice whispered through the warm breeze.

"I won't take no for an answer," Rachel said, with a rush of determination. "I'll see you tomorrow." She turned and headed down the porch steps before he could say anything else, hoping like hell this worked.

"Wait just a second. Let's talk about this."

"No need," she yelled over her shoulder. "Truly, I insist. I'll be by your office to pick up the house key. See you then!"

"Rachel," he called after her. "Hold on."

She ignored him and dropped into her car seat.

There. She'd taken the first step. Checkmark.

She didn't care about anything except getting back home to study in silence, with Ella standing guard against any other spirits. Just imagine. A quiet evening to herself with absolutely no supernatural activity to make her think she'd lost her mind.

This deal was going to work out wonderfully.

Though, one last glance at the man standing on the porch steps sent a stream of concern through her. A big wide grin curved his lips as he waved, obviously coming to terms with their conversation. He leaned against the porch frame—broad shoulders and a lengthy athletic body—and watched intently as she started the engine. The man looked so sexy, every erogenous zone in her body lit up.

Seriously?

She was in trouble. If only Ella could guard her from him.

Chapter Five

Nicholas stuffed his feet into his high-tops and slung his backpack over his shoulder. He was running late this morning and didn't want to miss the bus, knowing how much Uncle August hated to drive him. Listening to his uncle grumble was the worst. Not as bad as how his mom used to nag, but it still sucked. At least his mom had always had good reasons. August just seemed to like to cuss under his breath. A lot.

He took one last glance at Joanna, who was pouting in his closet again with her knees pulled up to her chin. August had told him about a possible visit from that woman—Rachel—later today, so Nicholas had warned Joanna not to freak out. Of course, she'd had a temper tantrum, frying every electronic device within a ten-foot radius.

So much for his new cell phone. Not that he ever got any phone calls. Who wanted to hang out with a loser with no social life? And now he would have to hear it from August about how he and Zach never took care of their things.

"Stay in here today, Jo," he whispered, giving her a look he hoped might make her take him seriously. Yeah, right. "Rachel won't bother you. My room's clean, so she should stay out. Got it?"

August had made him pick up all his stuff the night before, which didn't really make any sense to Nicholas. If the lady wanted to clean up after them, why should they care what the house looked like? Dumb. But at least now she'd have no reason to go near his room.

Joanna rolled her eyes.

Good enough. He was late. "See ya," he said, and ran downstairs and out the front door just as the bus pulled up.

~ * ~

August said goodbye to his ten o'clock patient. Barb Smyth—a pregnant patient who was struggling through her third trimester with her fifth child and too stubborn to travel to the next town over to see an OBGYN—squeezed past him with a toddler and a four-year-old in tow.

"You have my emergency number, Mrs. Smyth," he said. "If contractions set in, call, no matter the time. You've been through this before. I trust your judgment."

"Yes, Dr. Kline. I'll do that."

"I know you don't have a problem staying active, like we talked about, but remember, it's not a sin to take a nap once in a while." He hated seeing the woman so swollen and just plain exhausted.

On cue, the toddler grabbed her skirt and begged to be picked up. Barb sighed and ran her fingers through the boy's dark curls. "Thanks, Dr. Kline. I'll keep that in mind."

He didn't believe her for a second, but how could he argue? Especially when the baby inside of her was doing just fine. The pregnancy was about as textbook as they came, which was a relief since obstetrics had not been his specialty. "See you in two weeks, Barb."

She nodded, gave him a weak grin, and continued to her car...bypassing Rachel in the process.

Rachel—in leg-hugging jeans, a soft pink top, a cute

ponytail, and tennis shoes—waved to the kids as she walked past them, heading in his direction. So she actually wanted to go through with this?

Fantastic. No, more like embarrassing. And wrong. So wrong.

A beautiful woman had popped into his life like a granted wish and all she wanted to do was clean his house.

He stepped outside, letting the glass door close behind him, and smiled at Rachel because, well, he found it hard not to when in her presence. Rosy-glossed kissable lips, light coppery hair, delicate features, and seductive eyes framed by thick lashes compelled him to be happy. Hell, to be ecstatic. The woman magnetized him. He was a goddamned moth and she was the brightest lamppost on the block. Only question was when would he get zapped?

"Hi." She stuffed her hands in her pockets and rocked on her feet. Cute and sexy. Lethal combo.

"You came back." *Obviously, dumbass.*

"I hope you don't mind. Helping you and the boys would mean a lot to me."

When she put it that way, it seemed kind of rude to object. But… "I really don't think this is a good idea."

"I want to. Besides, I owe Ella for all her mentoring. She helped me so much. And this is how I'd like to repay her."

"I don't know." Why couldn't he just say "no"? Where were his balls? They were there a moment ago.

"I insist, August. So…" She lifted her hand, palm up. "Hand over the house key. You're not going to win this argument. I'm a soon-to-be lawyer. I don't back down easily."

"I can see that." He dug into his pocket and pulled out his set of keys. "I'm going to pay you for whatever you do." Truth be told, he should have hired a housekeeper before it had come to this. If he had, maybe Rachel would be more interested in his bed than his dirty dishes.

"No, you're not." She grabbed the key from his hand

just as he unlatched it. "I won't accept anything but extreme gratitude."

"Extreme gratitude could come in many forms." He instinctively reached out to touch her, brushing two fingers down the inside of her forearm.

Her cheeks flushed pink as she inched ever so slightly away from him. She averted her gaze to the parking lot. "Um, I'll get started. Should I bring the key back to you before I leave?"

So she was shy all of a sudden? Too bad. He could have some fun debating with Ms. Soon-To-Be-Lawyer. But shyness was good too. The word "challenge" sprang to mind.

He leaned against the concrete plaza wall and inclined toward her, catching a whiff of strawberry. He hadn't gained women's interest in the past by being inhibited. And he wasn't going to start now.

"You could spend the night," he said.

Yep, that got her attention.

She jerked her head back, warm chocolate eyes wide and alert. "Pardon?"

August kept his cool, something he'd learn to excel at over the years in NYC, where the women he'd run into weren't quite as innocent as this one. He hitched up one side of his grin and lowered his eyelids somewhat—a look several of his ex-girlfriends had told him was sexy.

Yeah, he was desperate.

"I mean, if you're planning on coming back tomorrow, there's no point in driving four hours round trip." He winked. "With gas prices and all."

Every inch of her body seemed to tense, including her clutched fists at her sides. "My car's pretty efficient," she mumbled, glancing at his lips before settling on his eyes.

"Safety then. It's a long drive." As subtle as possible, he reached out again but this time to see if her hair was as silky soft as it appeared. Her skin certainly was. He ran his fingers across her smooth cheek, sweeping a thick lock of unbelievably soft reddish-blond hair away from her face and behind her ear.

She tilted her head toward his touch, and he hoped to God the two ladies who had just walked out of Dolly's Hair Salon wouldn't scare her away from the kiss he was about to give her.

He cupped her cheek and moved in closer.

She pulled her bottom lip in to bite and then released it, making him want to taste her even more.

"Thanks for the offer, but I'll pass."

Before he could make his move or argue it was the best idea he'd had in years, she took three sharp steps away from him, leaving his hand caressing nothing but air.

"I'll return the key in a few hours." She turned on the heel of her tennis shoe and race-walked to her car.

Ah, hell. "All right," he called after her, trying to sound as if he hadn't just tried to make a move on her in the middle of a shopping plaza. And failed miserably. "See you soon."

"Hey, Don Juan." Loretta heaved the door open, grabbing his attention. "You collect payment from Ms. La-dee-da, or is she planning on paying you the old-fashioned way?"

August spun around and pointed a finger at her. "You know I could fire you, right? You realize I'm *your* employer and not the other way around?"

She rolled her eyes. "Hon, you would be lost without me."

Shit, she was probably right. He blew out a breath. "Don't insult Rachel, got it? She was a friend of Ella's. And she's going to be helping me out around the house as a favor."

"A friend of Ella's?" Loretta scrunched her black-dyed eyebrows together. "I don't recall Ella ever mentioning her, and she told me everything."

August shrugged. "Maybe there was more to Ella

than you know."

"Hmmph. I doubt it. I know everything about everyone in this town, and if Ms. Spencer is planning on sticking around Curlville for a while, I just might have to check her out."

~ * ~

Rachel parked her car in the driveway and walked up the porch steps, trying to ignore the woman staring through a window across the street. The neighbor yanked her curtains open and made no attempt to hide the fact that she was watching Rachel's every move.

She was attractive, with long blond hair, a fitted T-shirt that accentuated large breasts, and a golden tan Rachel only achieved once in her life—the summer after her freshmen year in high school when she volunteered to be a lifeguard at the local public swimming pool.

Heck, she'd spent most of her high school existence volunteering for something as a way to build up her resume for college. That along with homework and various extra-curricular activities had been exhausting. Too exhausting to have a decent social life.

Funny how times hadn't changed much.

August's door opened with a gentle nudge. It hadn't been locked. Huh. Small-town mentality.

Did everyone leave his door unlocked? Even single women? Rachel shot the neighbor woman one last glance.

A woman like her probably had a great social life. The blond narrowed her eyes to bludgeoning slits before she jammed the curtains shut.

Huh. Was she August's girlfriend? An ex, maybe?

The thought of August having been with a woman who looked like a swimsuit model wasn't surprising. Annoying, maybe, but not surprising. The way August talked, acted, and responded to Rachel showed her he was probably used to getting women to fall for him. Fall right into his bed, that is.

He was smooth, all right. The way he'd cocked his

grin and given her those practiced bedroom eyes. The way he'd been brave enough—confident enough—to touch her. And the way he'd spoken in that deep, rumbling voice, trying to say just the right things to keep her guessing. Yes, very smooth.

There had been a time when she liked that type of guy, a time when she would have found him thrilling. Tempting.

Who was she kidding? August was tempting, in a one-night stand sort of way. It wouldn't be hard to talk herself into thinking this could be a short fling. Sex. Orgasms. Running her fingers through his thick head of hair as he molded those powerful lips to hers.

She shivered and pushed the door open. The idea of sleeping with August made her anxious—and turned her on at the same time. Her cheeks burned like they had when he'd suggested she spend the night.

Yes, he was too tempting. Too bold. Altogether too much.

She set the plastic bag of cleaning supplies on the floor and gave the living room a once over. How strange. The room wasn't that bad. Well, not as bad as it had been the evening before. The clutter had disappeared. The tossed clothing, shoes, and socks she'd seen scattered all over the floor were out of sight. The baseball bats, gloves, and various-sized sports balls were gone. Nothing was left but dust and crumbs on the hardwood and a few stains on the beige and brown rug that sat in front of the couch.

August must've had a late night.

This should make Ella happy, wherever she was. She'd visited for a couple hours the night before so Rachel could get some studying done. Not one ghost had appeared. It had been so peaceful. So normal. And then this morning bright and early, Ella had awoken her before the alarm clock. She'd been excited that Rachel was actually going to go through with this.

The entire situation was a win-win.

Rachel lifted the bag of cleaning supplies and started toward the kitchen, wanting to get the worst of it over with. There was no way the trio could have cleaned up all of the mess. But before she reached the doorway, an odd thudding sound distracted her. She turned toward the wooden staircase as the noise grew louder.

Thud. Roll. Thud. Roll. A quarter-sized ball bounced down the stairs one step at a time.

The hairs on Rachel's arm stood on end. She'd thought no one was here. The red ball plunked to the floor and continued to roll on the hardwood until it tapped the tip of her sneaker.

Maybe one of the boys had stayed home from school.

"Hello?" she called out as she picked up the ball and studied it. Just a small rubber ball one might play jacks with. "Hello?" She looked to the top of the stairs.

No answer.

She remembered the eerie feeling she'd gotten the night before. The sensation was hard to describe, but she imagined it was like tension after a heated argument—the negative energy that clings to the air, making it hard to take in full breaths. A thick energy that shouldn't exist, not in this house, not now.

She could only assume the phenomenon was a spirit. She'd sensed them many times before. But for some reason, this one wasn't showing itself.

"I know you're here." She dared only to whisper and waited for a cold chill to hit her as had happened with so many other ghosts. But she felt nothing. Maybe this one was harmless. Possibly a child, considering it had rolled a ball down the stairs. All of the spirits who had visited her before had been adults. Angry and confused. With the exception of Ella, of course.

"Okay," she said a little louder, "I'm going to clean now. I won't bother you if you don't bother me."

A door slammed somewhere on the second floor and Rachel took that as a positive sign. The spirit didn't want to be disturbed and neither did she. She just hoped she hadn't brought this one with her. Ella would have told her about the phantom visitor, otherwise. Right?

Rachel blew out a breath and walked into the kitchen, where every dish had been cleared off the counters and placed into the sink. The opened bags of chips and boxes of crackers and cereal had been closed and put away or thrown away. This room had also gotten some attention and wasn't nearly as bad as it had been.

How late had August stayed up to do this? It must've taken him hours. Still, these results wouldn't make Ella happy. And who knew how bad the upstairs looked?

She picked the dishes out of the sink and stacked them on the counter. August had mentioned the dishwasher was broken, and this seemed to be the biggest task in the room. She filled one side of the sink with hot soapy water. If she washed these dishes, wiped down the table and counters, swept and mopped the floor, and vacuumed the rug, she could call it a day. Checkmark—done.

Oh, yes, and she still needed to find her purse. She shrugged, deciding to look for it later. No point in provoking the ghost.

She began scrubbing sauce off a plate when her cell phone rang in her pocket. Her mother or her sister, Rachel guessed. The few friends she had didn't bother to call anymore. They'd gotten tired of being rejected—of Rachel's many excuses not to go out in public unless she absolutely had to. Studying and interning at her father's practice was about all she'd dared to do with the possibility of agitated ghosts following her around.

She pulled the phone from her pocket. The caller ID said it was indeed her mother. Wonderful. The usual knot tightened in her belly.

Just get it over with, Rache.

"Hello?"

"Rachel, thank God you answered."

"I always answer." *And you always act surprised.* "What's up, Mom?"

"I need a favor, darling."

A favor. Not again. The last time her mother had asked for a favor, Rachel had ended up on a date with Frederick St. Thomas, a son of one of her mother's wine club friends. The date wouldn't have been horrible if Fred hadn't been twenty-plus years her senior and still living with his parents. Her mother had thought they'd make a nice couple since they were both "timid but promising." Promising as in Frederick was to inherit his daddy's Fortune 500 Company within the next two to ten years. The best part of the date had been when it ended. Rachel had driven him home—Freddie didn't have a driver's license—and waved goodbye as he jogged up to his house to meet his waiting mother.

So not going to happen again.

"I, uh… What sort of favor? This doesn't have anything to do with Fred, does it?" Rachel held her breath.

"Fred? Oh, you mean the St. Thomas boy?"

"Mom, he wasn't a boy. He had hair growing out of his ears instead of his head, he was so old."

"Now, Rachel, there's nothing wrong with dating a mature man. He had potential, unlike those starving artists you used to date before you met Grayson. It's a shame you two couldn't work it out. He was such a lovely man."

"Yes, a shame, alright." Why bother arguing or explaining why the engagement had ended? Grayson had been Hayes's twin brother and Rachel's fiancé, at one time. After Hayes had died, both she and Grayson felt the need to cling to what was safe, so they'd gotten engaged, even though they weren't in love. Her heart had always been with Hayes, and so the engagement was doomed from the start. And now Grayson lived across the country and was very much in love with someone else. It was for the best. Grayson deserved a woman who could give him her entire heart. He had that with Sofia.

"What favor do you need, Mom?" She braced for the worst.

"Your sister is coming back home this weekend, and your father and I thought it would be nice to have a dinner party for her on Friday evening."

"Oh." Her younger sister, Becca, was a pain at times but not awful enough for her mother to use up one of her favors… Unless there was more to it. "And?"

"Well, you know how much Rebecca looks up to you."

"She does?" Rachel left the sink full of dishes and sat down at the table. This conversation was getting too interesting not to give her full attention.

"Of course, Rachel. Don't play naïve." She sighed into the phone. "You know Rebecca has always had a difficult time concentrating. She's the free spirit of the family. But she's also very impressionable."

That was a nice way to put it. Then again, her mother had a knack for making excuses for her younger sister. Just six months ago, Becca had dropped out of college to run away to Cancun with one of her professors. Considering she had a history of running away to exotic locations with strange men, Rachel figured Becca had tired of the professor and was back to refuel. If only Becca could find what she was truly looking for.

"Go on." Rachel bit her fingernail and waited for more.

"Well, since you are such a huge influence on your sister, I'd like for you to bring a respectable date to the party. If she sees you with someone who is living his life like a successful man should, maybe she'll follow in your footsteps. You two were always the best at inspiring one another."

"Ah." Hence, the favor.

"And my good friend Dorothy has a nephew I think you'll adore."

Rachel dropped her head to the table and listened as

her mother described the forty-two year old gynecologist with a good pedigree and just the slightest of a lisp.

"What about August?" Ella's voice whispered from not far away.

Rachel jerked her head up to see her sitting at the other side of the table. Startled, she asked, "August?"

"August?" her mother said. "No, darling. It's May. I was thinking this Friday evening."

"Sorry. Hold on a minute, Mom." Rachel lifted her phone from her ear. "What about August?"

"He's somewhat respectable when he cleans up." Ella smiled and shrugged. "You could ask him to go with you to this little soiree. I'm sure he'd say yes."

"You're kidding. I can't ask him to do that." Her mother would eat him alive, after a thorough dissection of character and background. Worse, she'd find out that Rachel was cleaning his house. God forbid Dora Spencer's daughter stoop to manual labor.

"You're right," Ella said. "Go with Dorothy's nephew. He sounds like a winner. Marry him and you'll have free pap smears for life."

"When you put it that way." Rachel pressed her palm to her clammy forehead.

Ella shook her head. "Auggie may not be the ideal parental figure, but he can be charming. Your mother will swoon."

"She's not the swooning type." She also wasn't the type to back down until she got her way. Shoot. "You really think he'd say yes?"

"I've never known my brother to turn down a date with a woman." Ella smirked.

"Oh." Hmm... That confirmed Rachel's theory about August being a ladies' man, to put the term nicely. He'd hit on her in a parking lot, hadn't he? He'd asked her to spend the night—under the guise of safety and saving gas—and she barely knew him.

In any case, an evening with August had to be better

than any man of her mother's choosing. "Mom?" Rachel put the phone back up to her ear. "I might bring my own date, actually."

Chapter Six

"Before you disappear again, I need to ask you something." Rachel finished wiping down the counters and reached out to pat Ella's hand, but then remembered there was nothing there to touch. It was easy to forget her new friend wasn't a living, breathing person. She was nice to talk to and friendly.

As long as Rachel agreed to go along with the housecleaning plan.

Ella bunched her eyebrows together and floated a circle around the kitchen, the toes of her black pumps inches off the ground. "I don't know. Can you work and talk at the same time?" She pointed to a speckling of crumbs on the tile floor just under the oven. "I've been waiting a long time for someone to clean that up. August misses it every time he sweeps, and it drives me mad."

Rachel bit back a laugh. She'd always thought *her mother* was uptight and fussy. The immaculate museum of a house Rachel and her sister grew up in proved that. But any woman who came back from the dead to ensure her house stayed tidy took *control freak* to an impressive level.

Neurotic ghosts.

"Sure, no problem." Might as well check off that task.

Rachel grabbed the broom and swept the crumbs. The day was far from over. She still had to return the key to August. Then step way out of her comfort zone and beg him to go to dinner at her parents' house. Her mother had agreed not to invite the slurring gynecologist, thankfully, after Rachel had revealed August was a physician. She just hoped her mother wouldn't grill him about his income. Rachel had a feeling he didn't earn much in this little town. What he did make probably went to taking care of his nephews.

The thought warmed her heart. He might be a playboy, but he seemed like a good guy.

Ella hovered in front of Rachel, breaking her thoughts. "What did you need to ask me?"

"Oh, yes." How could she forget? "There's a spirit in this house. Did you know that?"

"A spirit?" Ella silently dropped to the floor.

"This one's hiding. I guess it doesn't want to be seen."

Ella frowned and gave her attention to another crumb mess. "I'm sure it's your imagination. I wouldn't worry about it. Just stick to cleaning and everything will be just fine."

Her imagination? Rachel couldn't be sure and didn't want to take any chances. "I'm not worried as long as it keeps to itself. But if another irate ghost starts bothering the guys or me, you'll have to step in and get rid of it. You can do that, right?"

"Yes. If there's a harmful spirit, I'll protect my family." She pointed to a minuscule pile of dust on the floor. "Could you get that mess, as well?"

~ * ~

Happy to get off work early and—what the hell?—excited to see Rachel again, August bound through the front door and stopped short when he heard the woman's voice coming from the kitchen. Who was she talking to? The boys were still at school.

67

He listened closer and questioned for the first time if it had been a good idea to hand over his house key to a stranger. A lickable, sexy, beautiful stranger but a stranger, nonetheless.

Damn. This wouldn't be the first time a woman had blindsided him with beauty. The female lead singer in his old band hadn't been made lead singer solely for her vocal abilities. No, Kiera had many other qualities. Some, he found, weren't as appealing as her breasts and ass. Not when she'd shared them with the bassist. And the drummer. She'd been sleeping with everyone in the band as far as he knew, which had made moving from New York to Curlville a lot easier. Women like that ran rampant in his old scene. He'd learned to expect it and not ask for more.

But from what he'd observed so far, Rachel was nothing like his ex-fling. Or any other woman he'd come across, for that matter.

From the other side of the kitchen door, August listened to her sweet murmuring voice. He couldn't make out what she was saying, nor did he hear anyone answer. Weird.

"Rachel?" he called out, to give her a little warning. She did suffer from anxiety, after all. No need to startle her.

A pause. "Yes?"

He pushed open the door to see her standing wide-eyed with a wet mop in hand. A few coppery strands of hair had broken loose from her ponytail, and the front of her shirt was damp in certain spots. He swept his gaze over the room, now immaculate and smelling like pine. She was alone.

"You okay? I heard you talking."

She set the mop into a pail and wrapped her arms around her waist. "I, um, was just talking to myself. I do that sometimes when I clean."

"Really?" He smiled because he just couldn't help

himself. She was odd in an adorable sort of way. Some people hummed or sang when they cleaned; she had a one-sided conversation. Who was he to judge?

She nodded, unsmiling. "Do you want me to leave?"

"What? No. Are you kidding?" He stepped toward her. "Dang, look at this kitchen. It hasn't been this clean since Ella lived here, and even then I'm not so sure." The pine scent reminded him of the cleaner Ella used to stockpile, and he wondered if Rachel had found it in the house somewhere.

She jerked her head to the side and then, after a moment, rolled her eyes and said, "Whatever."

August chuckled at her unusual response. "You don't believe me?"

"I believe you. It's just that…never mind." She grinned and shook her head. "Thanks, August. But unfortunately I've spent all day in here and haven't gotten to any other rooms."

"Believe me, this is more than I could've ever hoped for. I really appreciate your help." He took another step toward her.

She stepped back.

He inched closer.

She bumped back against the fridge.

"You all right?" He cocked his head.

"Of course."

She didn't look all right. She looked nervous. What was up with that? Maybe she hadn't unwound in a while.

"Is there any way I can make it up to you?" Any way at all. Something physical, he hoped. Or maybe just something to help her relax around him. One step at a time.

"No." She pulled her rosy bottom lip in with her teeth, and her cheeks flushed just as rosy. So fucking beautiful. And she was right here in his house. Alone—he glanced up at the clock—for at least another hour. Oh, the possibilities.

"Actually," she said, her voice shaky, "there might be something you could help me with."

"Name it." He raked his fingers across her cheek to push back a lock of her fiery hair. Her skin was soft and warm, her lips moist, plump, and bare of any makeup. He wondered if she'd object if he tried to kiss her.

Slow down.

She shifted on her feet and gestured nervously with her hand. "You see, my mother is having a dinner party on Friday."

"A dinner party?" Not what he expected, but he continued to listen.

"Yes, and she has this terrible habit of setting me up with men who aren't exactly appealing."

"That is terrible." He widened his smile, liking where this was going. "Do I appeal to you?"

"You?" She blushed and looked away. "Well. Yes."

August decided to give her a break. "Would you prefer for me to take you to this party, so you don't have to deal with some chump?" He backed away and stuffed his hands in his pocket to give her some space. Her nervousness might have dissuaded him if she hadn't just admitted she found him attractive—in a way. One point for August.

"Would you?"

"Absolutely." Was she joking? A woman this beautiful had her pick of men. But maybe her timid demeanor scared them off. He could see how that could be mistaken for disinterest.

She relaxed her shoulders and let out a breath. "Thank you."

"I'd be happy to be your date." He emphasized the last word so there was no doubt it would be a date, not a favor. Call him selfish or desperate, he didn't care. It'd been a long time since he'd been with a woman. A night out with Rachel was just what he needed. And he wouldn't complain if the night stretched into the morning.

"Sure, a date." She dropped her gaze for a moment before meeting his eyes again. "To warn you, my mother is sort of, um, finicky."

"Finicky?"

"You know, she's particular about certain things. I guess you could say she's hard to please."

Ah-ha. That explained a lot about Miss Rachel Spencer.

"No need to worry. Moms love me." Who was he kidding? He'd always avoided them at all costs, but that little fact wouldn't do anything to ease Rachel's nerves. "Should I wear a suit?"

She smiled, and he felt the linoleum melt underneath him. "Just something nice. I'm sorry, I don't mean to make her seem so harsh. She's lovely to most people." She reached out and planted her hand on his chest. "I'm sure she'll be pleasant."

About that, he didn't give a damn. But if her mom liked him, maybe Rachel would too. He didn't want to screw anything up before it started. And her hand on his chest reminded him just how much he wanted to start something. Anything. "Something nice. You got it."

"Great." Her smile broadened, and she tugged on his shirt playfully. "Hey, do you think I've earned my purse back yet?"

"Definitely. Follow me. It's in my bedroom."

~ * ~

Rachel followed five steps behind, her gaze plastered on his tight jean-clad ass as he walked down the basement stairs. All common sense had fled her mind after he'd said the word "bedroom" and gave her that come-hither grin. Lord, she was in trouble. And she had exactly two days to gain control of her libido before the dinner party Friday night. A date? She hadn't thought of it that way, not until the word left his gorgeous lips. Now she had no choice but to go through with it. She only hoped he wouldn't expect a kiss…or more.

Oh, heck. The way she looked right now with her hair and clothes a mess, he probably wanted nothing more than to pay her back for cleaning his house. She readjusted her ponytail, tucked a few loose strands behind her ear, and hoped she didn't smell like oven cleaner. At least Ella wasn't around to distract her anymore. How embarrassing that he'd caught her talking to herself. He was sweet not to make fun of her. Or throw her out of his house.

He opened the door at the bottom of the stairs and turned the knob. To his bedroom. Oh, geez. What was she doing following him there of all places?

Get a hold of yourself, Rache. Just grab the purse and get out.

He glanced back and smiled. "Don't worry. It's more of a studio than a bedroom."

"Studio?"

He pushed the door open and flicked on the light. "Come in. I'll show you."

Curious more than anything, Rachel walked by him into the large basement room with wood-paneled walls, low ceilings, and yellow shag carpeting. She would have called it depressing if not for what filled the room—every musical instrument she could imagine. A baby grand piano stood in the center, taking up much of the space. Along one of the walls hung an array of acoustic, electric, and bass guitars, probably ten in all. Below them sat several different sizes of amplifiers. Fascinated, she looked to the other side of the room. Hanging from that wall was a violin, a cello, a saxophone, and a trumpet.

She would've mistaken it for a music store if August's queen-sized bed hadn't blared at her from the far corner of the room. An electronic keyboard sat on top of the navy down comforter, with pieces of white paper scattered around it.

"You're a musician." It was easy to sound surprised, although Ella had told her about his year with his band. "Can you play all these instruments?"

"I can, actually. Though some of these are just

keepsakes." He looked as though he wanted to tell her more but held back. He was somewhat modest, at least.

"That's impressive, August. How did you learn?"

"My mom's doing. She used to call me a musical savant because I was a fast learner. A prodigy, she'd claimed to everyone she met." He chuckled. "Typical mom. She'd been so excited to see what I could do next she started collecting instruments from garage sales and secondhand stores. Before I knew it, we had a room full. I kept them all these years. Well, Ella kept them for me. In here." He frowned but quickly recovered.

"What's your favorite?" Rachel found herself leaning toward him, magnetized. She'd dated a musician in the past, finding him sexy. Yet it hadn't lasted more than a few dates.

"The piano's my passion. It's what I learned first, but like everything else in my life"—he paused and winked—"I can't help but dabble with all the other possibilities."

She wanted to ask him what he meant by that but was distracted when he grabbed her hand and led her to the piano bench.

"I took a year hiatus from medicine to play in a band. Before coming out here to take care of Nick and Zach." He sat down and drew her to sit beside him. "Do you like eighties music? We mainly played that era and some early nineties. Our gigs were night clubs to weddings and anything in between."

"I listen to eighties and nineties all the time. But I love most music." She held back from mentioning the musician she'd dated. The short relationship with the indie musician had never bloomed. Just a couple of dates and then he stopped calling, probably because she hadn't wanted to take it to a physical level. It had always been difficult to let a man in that close. Making love was like giving her heart away. She'd confirmed that painful scenario with Hayes.

"I thought you would," August said, easily luring her

from her thoughts as he stroked the keys in front of him. Bruce Spingsteen's "Dancing in the Dark" permeated the room. "Do you play?"

She shook her head, mesmerized by the liquid movement of his long fingers. They worked together yet individually, slow here and fast there, pressing and tapping the keys just so. The sight was almost as beautiful as the seductive sound he created—deliberate and poignant with a hint of hope. What talent. She could only dream of having the ability to create music or art or anything that required thinking outside the box she'd been living in all her life. And to witness someone else dance around the outside of that damning restraint was exciting. And refreshing.

"I've always wanted to learn," she admitted aloud.

"I can teach you." His voice was a rumble close to her ear, sending shivers down her body and settling a blanket of warmth between her thighs.

"Thank you, but..." She dared to meet his attentive blue gaze, which was a mistake. The music halted and silence thickened the air. "Don't stop. It's lovely."

"But what?" He brought his hand up to cradle her jaw. The light touch electrified—her face flamed hot to match the rest of her body.

"I don't know." What had they been talking about? She couldn't focus with him so close, his eyes so heavy, his lips so tempting.

Before she had time to question whether she should leave, he tilted his head and met her halfway for a kiss—a kiss she hadn't known she wanted so badly until that moment.

She kissed him back, and yes, their lips curved together like they were built from the same mold. Of course. She knew he'd be a good kisser. Too good. And delicious, she realized as his cinnamon tongue slipped into her mouth and found hers. Was it cinnamon? Not quite, but there was a spicy flavor to him along with something else she couldn't identify. He tasted smooth and potent. So robust she could barely think to do anything but savor him.

Oh wonderful. August Kline was addictive.

He maneuvered his legs and straddled the bench. Just as quickly, he gripped her waist and gathered her close so she was tight against his athletic chest. Light-headed, she clutched his broad, solid shoulders and held on while their mouths discovered each other. Lips colliding and tongues consuming. A kiss for lovers.

Lovers?

No. She wouldn't go that far. A kiss was innocent, and she was happy to discern August was nothing like Hayes in this department. Two different animals, yet she couldn't deny August's mouth was just as skilled. Or was her memory of Hayes dwindling?

Damn it. She didn't want to forget, but August was making it hard for her to think of anything but this moment.

If she could just stop thinking altogether...

His strong arms wrapped around her in an insistent embrace that crushed her breasts to his chest. She sighed as his hands slid up and down her back, massaging and holding her close. How had an innocent kiss transcended into pure lust?

He broke away but trailed kisses to her ear, burning her skin. "I want you, Rachel," he whispered and tugged at her lobe with his hot mouth.

"Can't," she managed to say when her body was begging to differ. "I'm sorry. I can't." She pressed her hands to his shoulders, and he released her but kept a grip on her hips.

"That's okay. I'm fine with that." He didn't sound fine with the way his husky voice rasped. "It's too soon. I'm pushing it."

Rachel almost changed her mind when he brought her hand up and kissed her palm. She still felt his lips on hers and his taste lingered on her tongue.

It would always be too soon, she reminded herself. Too much. And August was a dangerous man. Or was it her love-starved body? In any case, she let her hands slide from his shoulders, past his solid chest to his ribbed stomach and then back up again. Oh, wow. What had come over her?

He drew in a deep breath and pierced her with a covetous gaze. "I like it when you touch me."

She crossed her legs to stop them from trembling. If she didn't leave now, she'd undoubtedly make a huge mistake.

A day after meeting him!

Get it together, Rache.

She wasn't in August's life for any other reason than to help his sister's spirit cross over—after Ella aided her in passing the bar exam. Having a sexual relationship with him would only complicate things. Especially if he discovered her little gift. She hoped he never found out why she was really in his home.

Would he think she was deranged if she blabbed the truth? That she was cutting a deal with his deceased sister? Would he believe her? Or would he hate her? One thing was certain—he'd never look at her like he was at that moment, with adoration and longing. She shivered at the current feeling, at how he studied her with his blue eyes, wanting her.

"What's on your mind, Rachel?" Those gorgeous lips eased up to a full grin. "I don't think I've ever asked a woman that question. They usually have no problem giving me an earful. But you're not like other women, are you?"

If he only knew. "I guess I'm not." She forced her hands from his body and clasped them in her lap. "I was just thinking I should go before I do something I'll regret. I barely know you." Though it felt she'd known him much longer. Odd.

He brushed his fingers down her arm, renewing the

blaze. "I don't want you to regret anything you do with me. Just realize that I don't plan to quit trying."

She averted her gaze from his determined stare. "I'm guessing you tend to get what you want." She thought about the woman across the street and how she'd glared.

"No, not always." He edged her chin up so she couldn't avoid his eyes. "But I get the feeling you're worth all the effort it's going to take to get you naked and in my bed."

Chapter Seven

That couldn't have scared her away any faster. August listened to Rachel's frantic footsteps as she sped up the basement stairs, through the living room, and out the front door.

Shit.

He scrubbed his hand over his mouth where her sweet flavor still lingered. Her lips were just as supple and delicious as he'd imagined. So good, he'd wanted to suck on her tongue and nibble on those pouty lips. Hell, he'd considered doing a lot more than that, but he'd restrained himself. Until he couldn't anymore.

She'd kissed him back almost as hungrily, pressing her unbelievably soft breasts into his chest.

Next time he'd have to keep his mouth shut. And there would be a next time. Now that he'd sampled a kiss, there was no doubt they had chemistry.

The phone rang on his bedside table, and August jumped to get it. He cleared his throat, just in case it was Rachel changing her mind. Then he remembered he hadn't had a chance to give her his number. Fantastic.

"Hello?"

Silence.

"If this is one of Zach's little buddies again, I'm gonna—"

"August?" A man's voice. Familiar.

"Who's this?" Curious, August checked the caller ID. It was a blocked number.

"Is this August Kline? Ella's younger brother?"

The voice brought back a rush of memories. The pompous tone gave him away. Grant Golding. Ella's ex, and Zach and Nicholas's biological father, who'd left them all high and dry over twelve years ago.

August sat up. He'd had a speech prepared for this very day but had long since forgotten it, thinking it was wasted space in his memory. "What do you want, Grant?"

The man dared to chuckle. "You remember me?"

"I wish I could forget. What the hell do you want?"

"Easy now. I just heard about Ella."

It'd been a year and the dipshit was just now getting a clue? August didn't believe it. This was Grant-speak for *I want something.*

"And?" August kept his tone firm, his fists clenched. "What does it mean to you?" This wasn't a possibility he'd let himself ponder—the question of Grant coming back into the picture. He'd been gone so long without any contact. The courts hadn't been able to track him down after Ella passed. And August hadn't tried to find him.

Grant didn't deserve to be in Zach and Nick's life, biological father or not.

"How are the boys doing?"

The boys? Did he even remember their names? Well, August wasn't going to remind him. "They're great." He gritted his teeth.

"I heard you were made their guardian."

"What's it to you?" August stood and paced, attempting to calm his rage. How could a father disappear for twelve years and then have the nerve to call up out of the blue just to say hi? Fuck him.

"Just relax, August. You always had such a hot

temper."

"You don't get to call my house after deserting my nephews and my sister and expect a warm greeting. If you think I have a temper, just try me. I've been dreaming about kicking your ass for years. And I'm not a puny teenager anymore. You will feel pain."

August took in a deep breath. If he didn't get a grip, Grant might think there was a reason to worry about Zach and Nick. Truth was, August hadn't been accused of having a temper since the last time he'd blown up at this idiot. There'd always been something about the guy that grated August's nerves.

"I'd like to see them." Grant's words sat like a heavy brick in August's chest.

"That's not a good idea." No way in hell.

"They're my sons. I don't need your permission."

"Actually, yes, you do. I'm their legal guardian. The courts appointed the boys to me. I'm more of a father to them than you ever were." The words left his tongue so easily just before pride clogged his throat. Zach and Nick were his. Smart mouths and all, they belonged to him. They were his family. And he protected his family.

"I'll look into that. Until then, you better take good care of them."

"Fu—" Before August could spit out his next words, the line went dead.

August slammed the phone down and dropped his head into his hands. This wasn't good. The last thing Zach and Nick needed was to have their deadbeat dad back in their lives. Would they even remember him? Zach had been a toddler and Nick a preschooler when Grant had left.

The dirtbag wouldn't stay for long, August was sure. No, Grant wouldn't last a month with his track record. And he'd no doubt leave two broken hearts in the process. The only question was why he wanted to come back in the first place.

One thing was certain—August wouldn't give his nephews up without a fight.

~ * ~

Dana Finnegan peeked through the curtains to see the cute redhead Loretta had warned her about run out of August's house, jump into her car, and drive away. Finally. The little twit had spent most of the day there "helping" August. According to Loretta, Rachel Spencer had been Ella's friend at one time. Dana found that hard to believe. Ella had never been one to hold back on the details of her day-to-day life, and she hadn't once mentioned anyone named Rachel.

What did the woman want? August's attention? Good luck with that. He had to be gay or on some celibacy mission from God. He looked sometimes, but he'd never asked Dana out or made a move on her no matter how many clues she'd dropped. She hadn't felt this frustrated since her ex's thingie stopped working. That no-good son-of-a-bitch hadn't satisfied her for the last fifteen years of their marriage, and there was only so much a woman could take.

Now that she was free, she could do whatever and whomever she damn well pleased. Only problem was she was obsessed with the one guy who wouldn't give it up.

"Baby." Grant's voice grabbed her attention. She turned to watch him walk from her bedroom, his phone in his hand.

She'd almost forgotten he was here. What kind of hostess was she? She let the curtain drop and turned to face her guest. He was just as handsome as he'd been twelve years ago. The crow's feet and laugh lines didn't take much away from his warm brown eyes, olive skin, and cut masculine features.

Dana had always thought he could be a movie star. He certainly had the looks and some of the charm.

Now he was here, in her home. He'd shown up early this morning without warning, but she hadn't dared protest. She'd always had a hard time denying Grant anything he wanted.

He set his phone on the coffee table and tapped the couch cushion next to where he sat. "Come sit with me."

"Sure." She gave him the smile that had won her the esteemed title "Miss Curlville" three years running and walked over. "Did you talk to August?" She patted his leg as she sat. "You getting the boys back?"

It puzzled her that Grant would want them now, after all this time, but who was she to judge? Besides, a hot single man like August probably wanted to return to his bachelor life anyway. He could go back to New York and rejoin that band of his. Maybe she could take a trip and visit him to watch him play.

And then not leave.

Then he could see how serious she was and how much she desired him.

Grant sighed and put his arm around her. He smelled of cigar smoke and whiskey. Already. "I'm afraid it's not going to be that easy, sweetheart. August is just as stubborn as ever. I'd have to go through the courts, but I'm sure any sane judge will give me my rights back as their father." He lightly ran his fingers down her arm. "Now that Ella's gone, they need me."

Dana shivered from his touch. It had been a long time since a man had valued her body. And she remembered too well how much Grant had appreciated hers. When he'd moved in across the street with his family, it had taken him no time to show his interest. Dana had been flattered, especially since her husband at the time was so neglectful. She was somewhat ashamed of their little affair—every morning after Ella left for work and sometimes on the weekends. But it hadn't been her fault. Her ex-husband hadn't loved her properly, and she would've rather died than go without human contact.

Ella hadn't found out, thankfully. She never would've forgiven Dana. And the affair had only lasted a few months before Grant decided to take off. Out of the blue, it seemed, he'd said he'd needed to spread his wings. Small town life was suffocating him and it had been a huge mistake to move to Curlville.

Dana had thought maybe his sudden departure had something to do with that pretty little Amish girl who used to come around all the time to help Ella with housecleaning and babysitting. She'd disappeared around the same time.

He'd always had an eye for her, strange as it seemed. She'd been so young and, well, Amish. With dark long dresses, her hair always up in a bonnet, and not a touch of makeup, she wasn't a beauty queen, like Dana. But the girl had potential, and Grant had probably noticed.

He'd always had a way with words. Dana wondered if maybe, just maybe, he'd convinced that pretty little thing to run away with him.

She looked through the corner of her eye at the handsome man sitting beside her. Nah. Her imagination was running wild again. Her mind liked to do that sometimes.

"I'll tell you what," Grant said. "As soon as I get the boys back, maybe we can all move out of this shit-hole town. What do you say about that?"

"Are you asking me to marry you?" Dana wasn't sure she liked that idea. Grant was handsome and all, but he wasn't as young as he used to be. Definitely not as tempting as the doctor across the street.

Grant winked. "We'll see, sweetie. For now, I'd like to maintain a low profile and keep my ears and eyes out across the street. If you don't mind me staying here for a bit, that is?"

"Oh. Well." She shrugged, not sure what to think. "I suppose that's all right."

"And you can keep quiet about me being in town? I don't want to cause a stir."

"Keep quiet? Sure. I can do that."

Chapter Eight

Rachel patted the perspiration from her forehead and swept a scrutinizing gaze across the living room. Not a single dust mite. Nothing more to be done. The rug in the living room was vacuumed, the hardwood floors were mopped and shined, the windows were spotless, and everything else had been dusted, fluffed, spruced, and arranged just so. There wasn't one more thing she could think to do. Checkmark, checkmark, checkmark.

Too bad she didn't have the final say. This list seemed endless.

"Anything else?" she asked over her shoulder.

Ella shook her head. "This is fine for now. Let's head upstairs."

"Upstairs?" Rachel glanced at her watch. August had arrived home around this time yesterday, and she didn't want to see him again so soon. Not until she had her hormones under control. The kiss they shared had flipped a switch on inside of her somewhere and she couldn't figure out how to turn it off. Now all she could visualize and think about was August and those three words he'd whispered into her ear.

I want you.

Lord help her, she wanted him too. She couldn't deny the instant and overpowering chemistry between them, but she'd always been able to resist men. No matter how much she was attracted to them. What was so different about August?

The answer boiled down to one thing. He made her forget about Hayes—the one man who'd succeeded in blasting through her guard.

Which was not a good thing. She'd promised herself Hayes would always live on in her memory, and anything or anyone threatening that memory was nothing but trouble.

"I'm not starting on the upstairs today, Ella. Sorry. I have to go."

Ella rolled her eyes. "Are you afraid there's a ghost upstairs, or are you afraid my brother might find the key to your chastity belt? Stop being such a prude. You obviously want to sleep with him."

"Excuse me?"

"You forget I can see your thoughts, although I try not to since they're so depressing most the time." She set her ghostly hand on her hip. "It might do you some good to get laid, sweetie."

See my thoughts? How mortifying. "I didn't know for sure that you could. Oh, geez. Please don't do it anymore."

"Relax." Ella gave her a sympathetic grin. "It doesn't matter what I think. All you should care about is what makes you happy, and I think getting that Hayes character out of your system is just what the doctor ordered." She broke out into a giggle. "Get it? August is a doctor."

"Very funny."

Ella's laughter halted when the doorbell rang. "Wonderful. It's Dana."

"Dana? Who's Dana?"

"The neighbor woman. I'm leaving, but don't let her

get to you."

"Why? What is she going to—"

Before Rachel could finish, Ella faded away.

"Fabulous." She took in a calming breath and opened the door to see the blond bombshell from across the street flashing her a fake smile.

Up close, Dana appeared to be late thirties, early forties? Hot pink-painted lips, shockingly white teeth, and a dark tan. She wore a halter-top and skin-tight jeans that melted into her curvy body.

"Hi there. I'm Dana Finnegan, August's neighbor."

"Nice to meet you." Rachel put her hand out to shake. "I'm Rachel."

Dana stepped around her into the house, ignoring the handshake. She glanced around the living room as she spoke. "So I hear you're doing some housecleaning for August. That's so sweet of you." Her smirk belied her words.

Okay, it's going to be that way. Rachel didn't miss the endearing way Dana said August's name, and again she had to wonder who this woman was to him.

"It's more for Nicholas and Zachary," she said, getting comfortable with the fabricated story. "Ella had mentioned them quite a bit when we used to talk. I felt like I knew them and had to do something to help out."

"Really?" Dana pierced her with a glare. "I'm sure August would've asked for help if he needed it. I always tell him I'm just across the street, and I'd do *anything* for him."

"Right, well, I'm not trying to step on anyone's toes." Certainly not when they peeked out from her high-heeled sandals, looking freshly pedicured, painted, and rhinestoned.

"What *are* you trying to do?" Dana crossed her arms, propping up her too-perfect breasts.

"I believe I already told you." Was she dense?

"If you're interested in August, I would think again."

She gave Rachel a thorough once-over. "He's not going to be sticking around here for long. He's got bigger plans than Curlville. You know he's a musician, right? There's no way he can make decent money here."

Rachel wasn't sure why she had the urge to argue, but dang it, she did. "That may be true, but he seems dedicated to taking care of his nephews." She liked that about him. "Plus he has his practice."

"For now," Dana said. "So you might want to quit the Suzie Homemaker act. It's only going to get you so far. He needs someone more exciting and flexible. Someone who'll drop everything and move with him on a moment's notice."

"What makes you think he's moving?" Dense and delusional.

"Because." Her tone lifted to a shrill. "I mean, how long is a guy like August going to waste his talent in this dinky town? Know what I mean?"

"Sure." Rachel couldn't take much more of this ridiculous conversation. Time to get rid of her.

"Sure what?"

"Sure, I know what you mean. Thank you for your advice." Rachel opened the door. "If you don't mind, August will be home soon, and I want to make sure his sheets are fresh." *Take that!*

"Suit yourself, Suzie." She stepped outside. "Oh, I mean Rachel."

Rachel slammed the door.

Unwanted jealousy had her seething. It really, really shouldn't matter that Neighbor Barbie was after August. Bearing her claws, no less. But damn it, she couldn't help it. Dana bothered the hell out of her. Or was it the idea that August would want someone like that?

Did he?

Frustrated, Rachel yanked her hair from its ponytail and rubbed at her scalp. Suzie Homemaker? Really? First time she'd ever been accused of that.

"I need to get out of here," she mumbled. Out of this warm, cozy house that she was beginning to enjoy more and more as she whipped it into shape. And out of this town, which was also growing on her. Simple, comfortable, and inviting was what she always wanted out of life. But in this town...with August? The smart thing to do was to spend as little time in Curlville as possible.

First, she needed to find her purse. Her emergency credit card had worked for the essentials, but she'd yet to order a new driver's license and bank card. The last thing she needed was to be ticketed for driving without proper ID.

August had said her purse was in his room, so she'd check there first. She headed down the basement stairs and flipped the light switch, scanning the area to see if she could spot the purple leather.

Across the room, under his bed, she noticed it. Good. She'd just grab it and go. As she walked across the carpeting she found herself drawn to the instruments hanging on the wall, in awe that August had the talent to play them all.

He'd said he was a savant when it came to learning to play each instrument. She imagined him down here, sitting on his bed, his sexy lips creating a sexy jazz tune with the saxophone. Or a classical piece with the cello as he held it firmly between his long legs, his lean calloused fingers working the strings as his muscular arm flexed while maneuvering the bow. He'd be shirtless, no doubt. His abdomen muscles clenching with each skilled movement.

Stop torturing yourself, Rache.

She sighed and ran her fingers over the curve of the wood. Then picked gently at one of the strings.

"That one works, but it's more for looks." August's deep voice startled her. "I have another packed away safely. A nicer one."

Of course. She should've seen this coming. She spun around, trying for her best poker face. He was leaning against his doorway with his arms crossed over his dress shirt and undone tie. The corner of his mouth lifted into a sly grin.

"Want me to get it out? I didn't know you were interested."

"Sorry." She backed away from the cello but stopped when the back of her legs bumped into his bed. "I just came down to get my purse. I, uh, I guess I got distracted."

"I like being distracted. That's why I have these out on display."

He moved toward her, and with each step her pulse beat faster.

"I can pick one up and play it any time I want."

"That's convenient." She rubbed her clammy palms together.

"I'm glad I caught you before you left. I've been thinking about you." He stopped in front of her, took her hands, and wrapped them around his neck. "Nonstop."

"Oh." She couldn't resist—she leaned into him and enjoyed his warmth as he enfolded her in his arms. He was all too welcoming. Safe and secure.

He kissed her forehead and then her cheek. "Have you thought about me too?"

"Yes," she admitted, avoiding eye contact. Instead, she focused on his grinning lips. They were perfect except for a tiny, barely noticeable scar along the edge. "What happened here?" She brushed her finger over the small imperfection.

"The scar? Let's just say I talked back too much as a teenager."

"Your father hit you?" She met his eyes, searching for an answer.

"Nah, my father never laid a hand on me. My parents were amazing, but they died when I was twelve. Ella raised me from there."

"I'm so sorry. Ella mentioned that. But wait. Did Ella

hit you?"

"No," he said, stretching the word out and punctuating it with a curious question mark. "You knew Ella. She had a strong personality, but she never hurt a soul. It was her husband Grant."

"Oh, right. Of course." *Brilliant job, Rache.* "Go on. About Grant?"

"I'd gotten into it with him a few times. I gave him hell as often as I could, and he responded with force. Back then, I was a lot smaller, and even though there was only ten years difference between us, he had the upper hand. I didn't reach my potential until I left home." He winked. "I could take him now."

Rachel's fingers skimmed across his broad shoulders. "I'm sure you could. But he shouldn't have touched you. You were only a child."

"Yeah, but I was rotten." He tapped his lip. "I got this scar when he punched me for taking his Beemer for a joyride with my girlfriend at the time. I crashed it into a tree, damaging the bumper, and he split my lip open with his fist."

She smoothed her hand across his chest, wanting very much to protect the boy he'd once been, but not exactly understanding why she cared so much. "There's no excuse for abusing a child. Would you react the same way if your nephews crashed your car?"

"I'd never hit them. I'd probably want to strangle them, but only after I found out they were okay. Then I'd make them pay to repair it." He shook his head. "I can't believe I've got a beautiful woman in my arms and I'm talking about nonsense that doesn't matter anymore."

"Nothing that comes out of your mouth is nonsense, August." Wow, where had that come from? "I mean, the things you say are... They're..." She let her words fade, unsure where she was going with her muddled thoughts. Or maybe she was just too frightened to speak aloud what she was really thinking—that she was starting to care about this family. About August.

Too soon. Too much.

"Rachel," he whispered and brushed a soft kiss across her lips. "Where did you come from? I think I might be in way over my head with you." He kissed her again but didn't hold back this time.

Rachel sighed against his mouth. She hadn't realized she'd wanted him to kiss her until his lips were on hers, reminding her just how good he felt, how delicious he tasted. How easy it was to lose herself as his hands slid down over the curve of her backside and back up again. He ran his fingers under the hem of her sweatshirt, skimming them over the length of her spine.

He was teasing her, and it was working. Eagerly, she lifted up on her tiptoes and pressed her body firmly against his.

She waited anxiously for his next move, unsure if she'd stop him if his teasing hands were to unhook her bra or make their way around to massage her breasts. If he were to undress her or push her onto his bed, would she say no?

The sound of a door slamming and the brisk footsteps on the floor above decided her fate, and she tore her gaze up to the ceiling. Her mind veered from August straight to the ghost on the second floor. Had it decided to show itself?

"Damn." August rested his forehead on hers. "I guess school's out."

Nicholas and Zachary. Right. She let out a breath of relief.

"You know, if we're really quiet"—he kissed her nose—"we could continue this on the bed."

"August!" Zach shouted from the top of the basement stairs. "Dude, we're out of milk. How am I going to eat my donut holes without milk?"

August's shoulders tensed under her hands as he shouted back. "What did I tell you about yelling across the house?"

Rachel bit her lip to keep from laughing. "Looks like we've been found. I should go." The boys' entrance was just what she needed to break the spell August had her under.

He held her to him, not letting her move. "Stay for dinner. Please. I'm begging you not to leave me alone with them."

Oddly, the offer was tempting. The more time she spent in this house, the more welcome and secure she felt. Besides the mystery ghost, there wasn't a single threat to her here. Well, other than the thought of growing closer to August and his nephews when she knew she'd have to say goodbye to them. Her little scheme would only last so long before they discovered she'd lied about her friendship with Ella—lied about why she was in their home helping them. Cripes, she was an awful person.

"I'd love to, August, but I can't. This is going a little fast for me. When I traveled to find you, I had no idea I'd be so attracted to you. This sort of thing doesn't happen to me. Not this easily."

"Good. I like hearing that. So—" He dropped to his knees in front of her and over-dramatically clasped her hands to his lips. "Please?" He looked at her with radiant blue eyes, full of life. "I'll do anything. What's your favorite food? I'll either make it or order it, depending."

"August—"

"Why fight a good thing? Let's explore this chemistry we have going on. I'm not asking for a commitment."

A fling might be all he wanted, but she wasn't sure she could be the type to share her body without giving her heart. Not with how quickly she was beginning to feel things for him.

She threaded her fingers through his thick hair to save her some time, and to satisfy her urge to see exactly how silky his shaggy tresses were.

Even more than she'd imagined.

He grasped her hips and gathered her closer. "Did I mention how much I like it when you touch me?"

"Yes." That was precisely why she needed to keep her distance. She couldn't keep her hands off him. "I'm sorry." She forced herself to step away. "I'm not trying to lead you on, August. Really, I'm not."

"Wait, wait, wait." He stood and cupped her face. "No one is doing anything wrong here. We're only doing what's natural. That's why I'm attracted to you, Rache. Nothing you say or do is phony."

"You don't know me." If he did, he'd realize she was a fraud. A liar.

"I'm a good judge of character. Always have been. And I sense that you're a sweetheart. Kind-hearted. What other reason would you have to be in my house right now, helping people you don't even know?"

She was speechless. And guilt-ridden. If he only knew how selfish her reasons were.

"Stay for dinner. Are you going to make me beg again?"

"No, please don't." She laughed, loving his sense of humor...which only strengthened her guilt. If only he'd been a jerk, she'd have never allowed the first kiss, let alone a second.

"August!" Zach shouted down the stairs again. "When are you going to the store?"

"Give me a minute, kid. Hell." He frowned and let his hands fall to his sides. "Sorry."

"It's okay. I wish I could stay, but I really do have to go." Rachel eased away from the magnetic pull that kept her there and walked to the door. A third kiss could *not* happen.

"Looking forward to our date tomorrow night," he called after her.

She didn't look back. There had to be another way to help Ella, because spending another minute in August's presence wasn't an option.

~ * ~

Nicholas sat on the staircase beside Joanna. She didn't usually like to leave his bedroom but apparently their visitor, Rachel, interested her.

Joanna chewed on her lip as they both listened closely to the conversation going on in the basement. The vent in the wall let them hear most of it. But Zach's big mouth kept interrupting. Nicholas always thought his little brother was sort of like the scarecrow on *The Wizard of Oz*. If he only had a brain. Too bad Nicholas was kind of like the lion who needed some serious courage.

"Your uncle really likes her." Joanna squished her forehead up like she always did when she was over-thinking something. "Will they get married?"

"And move in here? Don't know. Why?"

She shrugged. "Rachel seems nice. It wouldn't be a bad thing, I guess. But I think she could see me if I let her."

"Really? Why do you think that?"

"Remember how you told me you see your mam sometimes?" *His mam*—Joanna's Amish-talk for mom.

"Yeah? So?"

"Rachel can see your mam too. She talks to her."

Nicholas gulped down the knot in his throat. He'd only seen his mother a couple times—in her garden he'd let die—and he hoped she'd move on to the *better place* everyone talked about. He felt bad for not talking to her, but one ghost was all he could handle. And seeing his mom as a ghost wasn't the same. Too sad.

"You think Rachel sees ghosts?" he asked.

Joanna heaved out a sigh. "No, she sees your mam, stupid. There's no such thing as ghosts."

"Right." He wasn't going to argue. "But you do think she can see you in the, uh, state you're in?"

"Maybe."

The sound of Rachel running up the basement stairs caught their attention. Nicholas heard her say a rushed goodbye to Zach right before she walked into the living room and instantly spotted Nicholas on the stairs. And then Joanna. Her eyes widened as she looked back and forth between them.

So she could see ghosts? Wow. Interesting. Nicholas thought he was the only freak in town. It was kind of cool to know he wasn't alone.

"Hi, Rachel." He broke the silence. "You leaving?"

"Yes." Her voice squeaked. "You okay, Nicholas?"

"Yep. You?" He avoided looking at Joanna and giving away the fact that he could see the ghost sitting beside him as well. He definitely wasn't ready to admit his little talent to anyone. Especially if that meant Uncle August would find out.

"I'm good. Um…" She gave Joanna another glance and then shook her head. "Well, I'll see you later. Have a good night."

"You, too. See ya."

Rachel bit her lip, nodded, and left, turning back once before she shut the door behind her.

Joanna whooshed out a breath. "*Ach!* I knew it. She could see me. What do I do now, Nicholas?"

"Nothing. It's not a big deal. Just keep hiding in my room and everything will be cool."

He turned his head so Joanna wouldn't see him smile. Whatever happened from here didn't really matter. He'd found someone else in the world that made him feel a little less alone. To think, August's new girlfriend could see Joanna. How awesome was that?

Chapter Nine

August swiveled his squeaky office chair to face the bare green wall, and to avoid the I-told-you-so expression on Loretta's face. Anything was better than seeing that. He held his phone to his ear and listened as Rachel's voicemail answered for the umpteenth time that day.

"This is Rachel. Leave a message, and I'll get back to you as soon as possible."

"Hey, honey," he said in a low voice, so his busybody nursing assistant couldn't hear him—he really needed to have his own office. "It's me again. Just checking to see if you're okay. I drove by my house this afternoon to take you to lunch, but you weren't there. I was a little concerned." He blew out a breath and hoped he didn't sound as pathetic as he felt. "Not that you need to clean my house. Not at all. I was just hoping to see you. Give me a call about tonight. I'm still game if you are."

He cringed at his dumbass choice of words before hanging up and then swiveled back around to confront the inevitable.

Loretta's smug smile stretched to her ears. "Is Casanova losing his confidence? Can't say I didn't warn you about that one. She's masquerading around here like she knew Ella all her life."

"What are you talking about?"

"Nan, the grocery clerk down the way, said that girl came in to buy some glass cleaner. When Nan tried to spark a conversation, Rachel said she's helping an old friend and wouldn't say anything else."

"And?"

"I bet my Cadillac she's up to no good. Why is she so quiet? What is she keeping a secret? And I tell you, that girl is trouble."

Hell, he couldn't deny that. Any woman who occupied his mind twenty-four hours a day was hazardous to his sanity. But he refused to admit defeat to Loretta. "There's nothing wrong with her. So she's not a busybody like the rest of you. That doesn't make her a bad person. She's helping us out. What's wrong with that?"

"Bull. The woman is lying about Ella. She's probably one of those loose women who used to follow your little music band. What are they called? Groupies?"

"Trust me, I would remember meeting Rachel. And she's not loose. Don't judge her."

"Well, then there's something else going on. I asked Dana if she recalled Ella talking about a friend named Rachel, and Dana never heard the name before either."

August felt a headache coming on. "Do me a favor and don't talk to Dana or anyone else in this town about my business." He checked his watch and figured now was as good a time as any to head home and get ready for his evening with Rachel.

Oh, yes, there would be a date. He wasn't giving up that easy. Not when he was just getting warmed up. Rachel could avoid his calls all she wanted, but she'd forgotten one important detail—he had her address in that damn purple purse sitting under his bed.

Call him desperate, but he'd felt something when he kissed Rachel. Could've just been lust or could've been more. In any case, August Kline wasn't a patient man when it came to getting to the bottom of something. Either he'd have a relationship with Rachel or he wouldn't.

Relationship? Lord, did he want that?

He supposed tonight was as good a night as any to get the answer.

"Where you going?" Loretta said.

"To find trouble. She owes me a date."

~ * ~

Rachel slipped the pale green silk cocktail dress over her head and reached back to zip it up. "I'm sorry. I just can't," she said, ignoring her ringing phone and Ella's disappointed look. The day had felt like one of the longest in her life with Ella's continual nagging.

And the phone calls from August.

She sighed when she thought of him. She hadn't realized he'd care so much if she stopped showing up at his house, but his messages were enough to melt her heart. He was so sweet and kind and gorgeous. Which made it all the more important to cut her ties with him. Even if he did wind up believing her story, dragging him and his nephews into her crazy life would only hurt them.

"I'll call him tomorrow to explain, I promise. But I can't see him anymore." And she didn't trust herself to talk to him tonight, or trust herself enough to not cave in and invite him over.

"This was the deal." Ella pointed her finger at Rachel. "You take care of my family, and in return I keep the spirits away."

"I know, but you have to understand I hadn't counted on August." Rachel pinched the bridge of her nose and clenched her eyes shut. But all she could visualize was August's sexy smiling face. Shoot.

"You're falling for him. So what?"

"If he finds out who I really am, what I am, he'll never want to see me again. It's better to end it now before we all get too attached." Too late for that.

"Simple solution. Don't tell him." Ella crossed her

arms. Stubborn.

"And how long do you expect me to continue the charade? If I could help them without seeing him, I would. Besides, you're not doing your job. There's a ghost in that house. I saw her with my own eyes."

Ella's expression tightened for the briefest moment. "There's another reason you shouldn't back out. Wouldn't you feel awful if something happened to my boys?"

"That's not fair. You said you could keep the ghosts away."

"Not that one. That one stays put." Ella's frown deepened, causing her hollowed cheeks and inset eyes to shadow.

"Wait a second." Rachel pointed at her visitor as a puzzle piece fit into place. "You know who she is? What aren't you telling me?"

"I've told you everything that's important. I'll help you pass the bar exam if you help me keep the house in order."

"And if I refuse?"

Ella threw her hands up. "I won't play this game, Rachel. Call for me when you decide you'd like to continue. But I won't wait forever." She vanished, leaving Rachel staring out her balcony door at the hospital across the street.

Getting rid of Ella was easier than expected, considering she had the power to manipulate Rachel's mind to see gas stations where there weren't any and make her car stall. Maybe this was a trick. Or maybe Ella would simply move on, forcing Rachel fend for herself.

Now that she'd had a break from the spirit visits, she hoped they wouldn't seem so overwhelming. It was always possible the visits would simply stop. She had to take that chance.

Besides, letting August rule her thoughts had a worrisome side effect. She hadn't thought about Hayes in a long time. What would be worse—an occasional panic attack or giving her heart to another man when she'd promised it only belonged to one?

She opened the end table drawer, pulled her picture of Hayes out of its photo album, and walked onto her balcony. Across the street at the hospital, several ghosts wandered the grounds. Some flitted in and out of the walls, looking confused, angry, or sad. Rachel supposed she had Ella to thank for keeping them at a distance. But how long would that last? How long until one of them noticed her?

One of the ghosts broke free of the hospital grounds. The silver-haired woman floated up toward Rachel's apartment building. Rachel braced herself for an attack—she shouldn't have made eye contact—but the ghost's serene smile calmed her. She drifted to the dusky sky before disappearing into a white glow. It would be simpler if they all went to the light, free of any earthly burden. But she supposed life wasn't that simple. Not everyone could accept death, leaving behind what-ifs and could-have-beens.

Could have been... Rachel glanced down at her picture, at Hayes's dark, charming eyes and sexy smile. She remembered her night with him and how he'd touched her in places where no other man had. How he'd gently made love to her. How she'd lost herself in him, wanting to give him everything. Her heart, her body, her soul. Everything. The memory was still there but somehow not as potent.

Oh no. She couldn't remember his voice.

Her mind raced as she tried to summon it back, but she came up blank. She could call Grayson, his twin. They were identical, but it wouldn't be the same. His words wouldn't be Hayes's words. His tone wouldn't be endearing and loving.

Tears stung her eyes. What she wouldn't give to have Hayes back. She'd cozy up into his strong embrace, kiss his firm lips, and never let him out of her sight. He'd stay safe in her arms.

The doorbell rang, jolting her from her thoughts. She wasn't expecting anyone.

She wiped a loose tear from her cheek and made her way to the door, stopping to set Hayes's picture on the coffee table. The mirror on the wall reminded her she hadn't applied makeup yet, but she didn't look too awful. After combing her fingers through her bangs, she straightened her dress and checked the peephole.

"Who is it?" she asked, but saw her answer right away.

"It's me. August." The view was skewed, but she could tell he was holding red flowers.

Her guilty pulse thrummed against her temples. She'd ignored him all day long and he was bringing her flowers? Not possible. There had to be another reason. She opened the door.

His smile broadened as his gaze swept down and back up her body. "Wow. You look beautiful."

She opened her mouth to speak but was caught off guard by the dozen ruby red roses in his hand as he thrust them toward her. They were arranged perfectly in a crystal vase.

"Roses." He shrugged. "I don't know your favorite, but I figured these were safe."

"Thank you." She took them and dipped her nose to smell the bouquet. "I love them." And now she had a chance to check out what he was wearing.

He looked impressive in a steel grey two-button sport coat over a black crew sweater. He had on dark jeans and his hair was styled, gelled back, emphasizing his handsome face. One hand was tucked behind his back. Mischief twinkled in his navy eyes.

Her heart thudded hard and low.

"I brought your purse." He pulled the purple bag from out behind his back and held it at the tip of one finger. "I hope you don't mind I looked up your address from your driver's license."

She wanted to ask why he'd gone to the trouble and why he was here at all, but her voice seemed to be stuck in her throat.

"Can I come in?"

She nodded, and he walked past her into her apartment, setting her purse on the entryway table. Instinct had her sniffing in his rich, soothing scent as he passed by. It wasn't fair he smelled so good.

She drew in another breath to clear her senses.

He made himself comfortable on her sofa, stretching his arms over the back. Confident. Sexy.

Rachel shut the door and nibbled her lip. How could this get more awkward? More important, what was he trying to prove? Sure, she'd invited him to the dinner party with her family, but she'd thought he wouldn't care this much when she didn't follow-up with directions. Or she thought he'd think she was a bitch for avoiding him, like so many men in her past had assumed. She'd never been an outgoing person. She'd always been timid and afraid to let new people into her life.

August was no different. In fact, he frightened her more than anyone before. There was nothing predictable about the man, and this random act of peculiarity proved it.

"Are you wondering why I'm here?" He patted the couch beside him.

She set the flowers on the coffee table, but decided to sit in the accent chair instead of accepting his offer to share the couch. Her hands had a mind of their own and couldn't be trusted. They itched to touch him at that very moment…anywhere, but mostly to trail her fingers down his freshly shaven jaw. Or along the muscles underneath the layers of sport coat and sweater.

Get a grip.

She clasped her hands in her lap and focused on eye contact. "I'm not sure what to say."

He drew out a breath. "I'm guessing you didn't

answer my calls because you want me to back off, right?"
He didn't wait for a response. "The thing is I'm not ready
to back off yet. I like you, Rachel, and honestly, I've never
been good at playing by someone else's rules."

"What if I insist?"

"Do you?" He leaned forward and took her hand in
his.

The scent of aftershave infiltrated her space again.
The aroma intoxicated her, as did the intense look in his
eyes and the feel of his warm, long fingers as they threaded
through hers.

"Give me a chance, Rachel. I'm not asking for a
commitment. Just a little adventure between two adults. It
could be fun."

Fun. That's something she hadn't tried in a long time,
and she imagined August could show her what she'd been
missing.

But sometimes fun wasn't worth the consequences.

"I—"

"Just give me tonight." He inched nearer so they were
face to face.

Not until then did she realize she'd moved to the
edge of the chair, closer to him. He was luring her in, and
she was doing a less than satisfactory job of resisting.

"One night," he said. "I don't care if it's with your
family. How much safer could you be? It's a first date at
your parents' home. I'll have no choice but to keep my
hands to myself."

Why? The word sat heavy on the tip of her tongue.
Why did he go through the trouble? If he just wanted sex,
he was going out of his way to get it, especially if his
neighbor was so willing to do "anything" for him.

"What about your neighbor? Dana?" She let the
question slip, despite not having a right to know the
answer. "Do you two have something going on?"

"Dana? No. Not even a little bit, honey. Is that why
you're backing off? Did she say something to you?"

"She stopped by your house. She seems a little territorial. I wasn't sure if she had a good reason."

"She doesn't. She's strictly my neighbor, never been anything more than that. I promise there's no one in my life right now. Just you."

"Oh." God, her heart wouldn't stop pounding.

"Now that we have that settled, are you ready to go? I'll drive." He didn't look like he was going to take no for an answer even if she gathered the courage to say it.

And like she'd feared would happen, her willpower was slipping.

"I don't know, August. Things are complicated. My life's a mess." She pressed her lips shut to avoid telling him everything. How she wished she could.

"I don't mind getting messy. I'm up for it. Just give me tonight."

"Just tonight?" Yep, no willpower.

"If that's what you want."

What did she want?

Him. Definitely him. If only for a little while. "I'll just grab some lip-gloss and my heels."

"I'll wait for you." His smile spread.

Little did he know he wasn't the only person who could bend her will. In fact, he was about to meet someone who held the big, shiny blue ribbon. Her mother.

"Fine." She walked to her bedroom, trying not to feel selfishly triumphant in her own right. More time with August. He was asking for it—didn't mind getting messy.

We'll see about that.

Her vanity mirror confirmed her cheeks were tinted red and her forehead was perspiring. Being that close to him did nothing for her complexion or her nerves. She picked up her compact and powdered all over. Then she glossed her lips, coated on some mascara, and combed through her hair one more time.

Nothing was out of place, but she was sure her mother would find something. *Oh, well. Just get it over with.*

With trembling hands, she slipped her heels on, grabbed her clutch purse, and made her way to the living room...to see August holding Hayes's picture.

"I'm ready." She tried to avert his attention. Why she cared, she didn't know, but there was something troublesome about August seeing Hayes, even in a photo. She didn't want the two men connected in any way, shape, or form. She strode over to take the picture from him.

"This your ex?" He held it up and lifted his eyebrows. "What was his name again? Hayes?"

"Yes." Her voice came out as a whisper. "That's the only picture I have of him."

She reached for the photo, but he ignored her to examine it again.

"He looks like he was a nice enough guy." He shrugged and made a move to drop it back on the coffee table.

Rachel grabbed his arm. "I'll take it. Just hand it to me."

His smile faded. "Here you go. No harm done."

She held Hayes's photo by the edges, careful not to smear it with any more fingerprints. Then she opened her photo album and gently slid it back in its slot. After placing the album back safely in the side drawer, she turned to August. "We should go. My mother's expecting us."

He sauntered over slowly, each step annoyingly confident. Then he brushed a lock of hair behind her ear and braced a firm hand on her shoulder, the other on her waist. "Do you miss him?" he asked, concern etched on his face.

The question coming from August brought forward a war of emotions. Sadness from the past and the happiness the man before her evoked. Each one fought to shut the other down.

"I don't want to talk about him with you. He's none of your business." She inhaled a breath to calm herself. "Sorry."

He tilted his head. "Why are you sorry?"

"I don't want to offend you."

"Honey, you avoided my calls all day, and I showed up at your house with roses, dressed to impress you and your parents. There's not much you could do to offend me. I don't mind a challenge." He grinned. "I like it."

She laughed, despite herself, and her tension dissipated. "You like a challenge, huh? I guess I'll try harder then?"

"That's the spirit." He brushed his thumb along her collarbone. "But just so you know, I plan to win this challenge. Destroy it, actually."

Every nerve in her body blazed red-hot. "Good luck with that." She tugged on his lapel playfully, pushed away from him, and walked to the door, all the while unable to hide the smile on her face.

One thing was certain. August Kline was easy to be with. Funny, sweet, soothing, and not easily scared away. And that's exactly what both of them would need to get through the evening with her family.

Chapter Ten

August drove with one hand on the wheel while Rachel held the other in her lap. She absently fidgeted with his fingers and stared out the window as they neared her parents' neighborhood. Always so affectionate. Whether she realized it or not, he didn't know.

He tried to keep his attention on the road. Apartment complexes and convenience stores dwindled and were replaced by expansive estates surrounded by manicured lawns and golf courses.

This was a different world, one far from Curlville, and even separate from where Rachel lived. He had to wonder if she missed living out here with the wealthy elite. She still dressed as if she were one of them, he couldn't help notice. Even the jeans and sweatshirts she wore seemed to be designer—high quality. But her tiny apartment was modest and lived-in. Her furniture appeared secondhand but comfortable. And the nineteen-inch television and the generic brand boom box in her living room told him she didn't splurge on the unnecessary.

He'd been happy to see she didn't live in some upscale condo. For selfish reasons, he liked that she wasn't filthy rich. That meant she wasn't entirely out of his league.

Yet, as she pointed the way to her parents' gated estate, he admitted to himself that the woman sitting beside him was altogether too complicated. That had become obvious when she'd handled the picture of her deceased ex-lover like it was an ancient relic. The sight of her carefully tucking it back in her shrine of a photo album had twisted something in his gut, something that felt a lot like jealousy. Hot-blooded, green-eyed jealousy.

Huh. He was resentful of a photograph.

What am I doing?

He liked things to be easy. Simple. *Un*complicated.

Relax, he told himself and blew out a breath. He was just having fun with Rachel—he wasn't asking her to marry him or even commit to him. True, there was something about her that prompted him to step up his game to an almost obsessive level. But he could put a lid on it if and when he wanted to.

He was not complicated. He was simple. Easy. Confident. Women liked that about him. Or they used to anyway, before he'd become the guardian of two teenage boys.

Just stop thinking, dumbass. Enjoy this beautiful woman's company while it lasts.

He slid his hand from her grasp and carefully, gently caressed her thigh. Rachel was altogether too touchable. Her skin was soft and smooth. Her flesh a nice mix between supple and toned.

Who was he kidding? He wasn't planning on putting a lid on anything any time soon. Not until the urge to be with her subsided.

A strong urge, judging from what he was doing to impress her. He'd never once made the effort to meet a date's parents. He'd avoided it at all costs, simply because the mom or dad would undoubtedly ask what his intentions were. Before Rachel, his only intention with a woman was, like him, simple.

Now?

He took her hand again and threaded his fingers through hers. Their joined hands fit perfectly in their embrace. *Oh, hell.* Was it crazy that he was thinking about how their hands fit together?

As if it were second nature, she lazily ran her fingertips over his forearm. "I have to warn you about my parents," she said abruptly, strangely cold. Her fingers rubbed more firmly on his arm.

"How horrible could they be? They raised you."

He winked but her frown only deepened. A tough audience tonight.

"It's mainly my mom. She means well, but it's difficult for her to allow things to be as they are. She likes to be in charge, for things to go her way."

"So she's a control freak?" Sounded like Ella.

"Yes." She gave him a brief smile. Gorgeous. "That's exactly what she is."

"Thanks for the warning. Anything else?" He drove up the long cobblestone drive, pulled up to the front of the gigantic three-story brick home, and put his truck in park.

She nodded slowly. "I would appreciate it if you wouldn't tell them how we met and how I'm helping you."

Ah. She didn't want Mama Spencer to know she was cleaning his house. He could understand that. "No problem. I'd like you to stop anyway. I mean, I may not be the most organized man, but I do my best. And if we're dating—"

"We're not dating. It's just tonight. One night." She looked down at their joined hands and quickly pulled hers away. "Sorry. It's easy to forget."

"That's okay. You're an affectionate person. I like that." A lot. *And yeah, we are dating.*

"No one's ever accused me of being affectionate." Her soft voice lingered on the word "affectionate" as if she were speaking a foreign language, and her lips curved up into a timid smile. "Until now."

He wanted to argue he'd never met a more touch-feely woman, and he couldn't wait to find out how that translated into the bedroom. But he figured it was time to get the whole dinner party thing over with so he could convince Rachel to agree to some alone time. He leaned over and pressed a quick kiss to her lips before leaping out of his truck and opening her door for her.

She took his hand, of course, as they walked up the red-brick paved steps to the enormous front door. Was it his imagination or was her breathing becoming ragged as she put a shaky finger up to press the doorbell.

Why was she using the doorbell? And taking a long time in doing so.

"Wait." He grabbed her hand before she could push. "You're anxious."

"Yes." She nodded. "A little."

"Because of your family or because of me?"

"Not you," she whispered and looked warily at the door. "It's silly, but they make me nervous. Being around them isn't easy."

"That's normal. Families are tough." He led her back down the steps to the driveway and around a large hedge that hid them from the house.

"Where are we going?"

"Let me give you a quick trick for handling the stress. Is that all right?"

"I don't want to be late. My mom—"

"Won't take but a minute. Look at me."

Her pretty brown eyes met his but her face was tense, her lips clamped vise-like.

"Take a moment to gain some strength. I'm going to be with you in there by your side the entire time. But before we go in, we're going to do some breathing."

"Breathing? August, we—"

"It's a tool, Rachel. One you can use when you start to feel anxious."

"This isn't helping me."

She was like the wild, unleashed version of Rachel with her quick dialogue, thick makeup, and crazy curly hair. Same sweet brown eyes, but something wicked danced behind them.

"Oh, sorry." She shrugged. "Anyway, so where did you meet Rachel? Your office? What kind of doctor are you, exactly?"

Before he could think up a good answer, Rachel interjected. "Becca, we haven't even sat down for dinner yet. Maybe we should wait for Mom and Dad until we dive into the investigation."

Becca broke out into laughter. "Gotcha." She pretended to lock up her lips with an imaginary key. "No worries, Sis. I'm on your side. You and me against the 'rents, right? Like old times."

"Sure, Bec." Rachel looked at the ground as she walked. "Like when you told the 'rents about me having a hard time studying?"

August's ears perked up.

"I'm so sorry about that," Becca said. "I didn't think it was a big deal. You know how dramatic Mom can be."

"I was confiding in you. It was a conversation between two sisters. Now I'm not sure I can trust you."

"Sorry, Rache," Becca said again, but this one didn't seem as sincere. "So you're having a hard time concentrating. So you're not perfect. Who cares?"

Rachel shook her head. "You know what? Don't worry about it. I shouldn't have brought it up."

"Right." Becca nodded quickly. "Anyway, I'll totally make it up to you. Somehow."

The conversation halted as the housekeeper led them into a room that might have been considered a living room in any other house. Two dainty white sofas flanked a glass coffee table. Another huge flower arrangement topped it, which must've made it difficult for the man and woman sitting on each couch to have a normal conversation.

Maybe they liked it that way. Note taken.

"Mr. Spencer. Mrs. Spencer," Therese said. "Your dinner guests have arrived."

"Thank you, Therese. Could you please check up on our caterer to make sure he's staying on task?" An auburn-haired woman with a pinched face and a too-perfect nose stood from one of the sofas. Her gaze quickly swept over Rachel from toe to head, stopping briefly to narrow her eyes at their clasped hands.

Rachel attempted to pull away, but August held on tight. He wasn't sure why, but he felt like he needed her as much as she needed him at that moment. She gave up and dug her fingernails into his palm.

Dang. More breathing lessons later tonight. Or he could show her other fun ways to relax.

"Rachel," Mrs. Spencer said and took a step closer. "Are you going to introduce your dinner date, or should I simply use my telepathic powers?" She let out a shrill laugh that didn't make any lines on her taut face.

"Of course. Mom, Dad," she looked to the large gray-haired man who hadn't budged or turned his frown upside down since they'd walked into the room. "This is August Kline. August"—she glanced up at him—"This is Dora and Tom Spencer, my parents."

August offered his hand to shake and the woman gave it a light squeeze. "Nice to meet you, Mrs. Spencer."

"Please call me Dora." Her assessing gaze was quick to search him out. Nothing got past this woman, he could tell. But who knew what she was looking for.

He smiled and nodded to the unfriendly man on the sofa. "Tom. Nice to meet you."

Tom didn't so much as grunt. He swirled the amber liquor in his glass and watched August with a distant interest. As if his mind was somewhere else.

Was it hot in here? His collar suddenly felt constricting around his neck. These people were the definition of uptight. Why hadn't either one of them hugged their daughter, or at least said hello?

Something.

This was going to be an aggravating evening. The less he said tonight, the better, or else he'd end up saying something he was going to regret. He thought he'd had it bad growing up with Grant and Ella. At least he'd gotten a response out of them.

"Becca said you hired a caterer," Rachel said.

"Yes, Marla Kingsley recommended him while we were at the spa the other day. He makes the best duck a l'orange."

"Duck?" Becca's vibrant voice echoed in the large space. "Mom, you know I don't eat meat, especially duck."

"Darling"—Dora's top lip twitched—"I thought we already talked about this. You'll be getting a separate vegetarian dish." She spoke softly yet sharply to Becca, and then lurched her gaze back to August. "You're not a vegetarian, are you? I'm afraid Rachel has kept you a secret. I know nothing about you. August, is it?" She didn't wait for him to answer. "I'm afraid my daughter can be quite elusive at times. Sometimes I wonder if she simply prefers to live in her own little world."

No shit. He couldn't imagine why she'd want to keep anything from these pleasant folks. He waited two beats to see if she'd finished her spiel, rubbed his thumb against Rachel's palm to let her know he felt for her, and then spoke. "I'm not a vegetarian. I'm sure dinner will be delicious."

Dora blinked as if waiting for him to continue giving her info, probably hoping for a revealing detail that would help her prove whatever theory she'd starting spinning.

He didn't budge.

Rachel's hand relaxed in his. "When is dinner, Mom?"

Dora broke her eerie stare and gave her daughter her attention. "Are you in a hurry, Rachel?"

"Of course not. I'm just curious."

"Rachel's being nice," August piped up, not able to stand it anymore. "I'm actually on call tonight." It wasn't a complete lie. In a small town like Curlville, there was always a chance he'd get called into his office, since there wasn't a hospital for miles. But he decided to leave out the small town part and the fact that he wasn't anywhere near town at the moment.

Dora cocked her head. "On call? That's right. Rachel mentioned you were a physician."

"Family medicine. I have a pregnant patient who's due any day now, and she's insisted I be the man to deliver her baby. I couldn't say no."

"I see. How...nice of you." She gave him another considerable look and tapped her finger on her chin. "Shall we head into the dining room?" She turned to her husband. "Tom? Would you lead us to the other room?"

August could've sworn he saw the old guy roll his eyes as he stood and ambled through a swinging door. Happy fella, that guy. So warm and loving, it was almost sickening.

~ * ~

Dora glanced around the table at the place settings. Everything seemed clean and orderly. Nothing out of place. No smudges that she could see. She'd made sure Therese had shined every piece of silverware. The new charger plates she'd purchased last week looked dazzling with their splash of burgundy. And the water and wine glasses didn't appear to have any fingerprints. She hoped.

She watched as the group filed in and politely gestured to where she wanted them to sit. She and Tom always sat at opposite ends of the table. For this meal, she'd have Rebecca on one side—nowhere near the guest—and Rachel and Dr. Kline on the other. She knew how flirtatious Rebecca could be, and she didn't want her ruining the evening by tempting Rachel's date.

My, how had she ever raised such different daughters? Rebecca was almost a lost cause, she'd realized at, oh, about the age of thirteen. Her younger had always been a free spirit and always, always, so loud and rambunctious. Dora could only tolerate her for a week or two before she paid for Rebecca to go on another adventure to Cancun or Brazil or wherever the wind wanted to take her that time of year. This last trip home had gone on three weeks, and they were both getting antsy.

She glanced over at Rachel, Dora's only and last hope of ever being considered a successful parent. She'd been a good girl growing up, so smart and polite. Nothing like her younger sister.

If only she weren't so nonchalant about her future. If only she had the determination and grit to either make something of herself or find a man who would help her live a civilized life. Someone with money who could take care of her. *Just like Tom has taken care of me.*

She gave her husband an adoring smile as they all sat at the dining table. Then she watched curiously as Rachel's date finally let go of her hand and unbuttoned his blazer. Holding hands. So this was somewhat serious? Not just a way for Rachel to get out of being set up with her friend Dorothy's nephew. Now there was a successful man. Nigel's impressive clientele paid a lot of money to see him. He was one of the best ob-gyns in the state. Nothing to balk at.

So what if he wasn't the most attractive man? He was wealthy enough for Rachel never to work a day in her life. Or worry about retaking that silly bar exam.

Rachel failing the exam hadn't bothered Dora as much as it had Tom. Things like that happened. Lord knew Dora hadn't been the best student in school. She'd had to rely on her looks for the most part. But beauty faded with time, and Rachel certainly wasn't getting any younger. If she needed to work to succeed in life, so be it.

One way or another, Rachel would make her proud.

"Is everyone comfortable?" she asked, to no one in particular, although she was having a hard time keeping her eyes off Rachel's date. How he inched his chair closer to Rachel's. How he whispered something into her ear to make her blush and smile just a little. How he smiled back and looked at her adoringly.

He was a charmer, obviously. A good-looking man with fair taste in clothing. At least he wasn't a complete waste of space like some of the men Rachel had dated before Grayson. She still didn't understand how Rachel had let him slip away. Although Rebecca had murmured something about an infidelity. Something about Rachel falling for Grayson's twin brother, the one who'd died in that tragic but foolish accident. But that was ridiculous.

Anyway, the past was the past. Nothing could be done about that. Yet she couldn't resist pointing out the obvious. "It's so nice for Rachel to bring home a date." She smiled at the man in question. "The last man she brought home she was engaged to marry."

Her daughter's cheeks flushed instantly, and the doctor shifted in his seat. Oh, dear. Was that cat supposed to stay in the bag?

"You were engaged?" August asked Rachel.

Interesting. So they weren't serious enough to discuss past relationships.

"For a short while, yes."

"Hayes?" The young man cocked his head and seemed to sneer the name of Grayson's twin. Serious enough to be jealous of another man, apparently. Very interesting, indeed.

Dora picked up her napkin and gingerly spread it out on her lap. "No, his name was Grayson. Grayson Phillips. An amazing young man. A bright go-getter. Everyone adored him. I believe he's doing quite well for himself now, isn't he, Rachel dear?"

"He and his wife are doing great, last I heard." Rachel looked at her date with a warm expression that spoke a thousand words. Her daughter cared for this man. "I'll tell you more about it later. It's somewhat of a long story."

"Sure. All right." August leaned over and kissed Rachel's cheek.

My, my.

"I'd love to hear the unedited version someday, too." Rebecca chimed in. "Hot twins and a sordid affair. Sign me up." She giggled.

"Becca, it wasn't like that. Can we change the topic?"

"Yes," Dora said. "Enough for now."

Rebecca loved to balk at polite conversation, throwing all decency out the window. Having her around could be quite embarrassing. Whereas Rachel remained the introvert. Why couldn't they find a proper middle ground?

At least her daughters hadn't turned out like her mother, or her grandmother. Or God forbid, her great grandmother. The craziness that had spread down through her family had stopped with her. Women who believed they had powers. Women who swore they could see and talk with ghosts. Her mother had actually claimed she could see certain aspects of the future.

The madness of it all. Sure, peculiar things had happened as a child, but Dora was always able to explain them in her head. She'd never bothered arguing with her mother, though. There was no point. She'd simply waited patiently until she was old enough to leave home, and then she'd found Tom to take her away from that foolishness.

Yes, her daughters would never have to deal with any of that lunacy, thanks to her. She'd cut ties with her mother long, long ago, ending the long line of bullshit.

She cleared her throat and tapped her fingers on the table. Where the hell was the caterer? She wasn't paying him for standing around.

~ * ~

With dessert cleared from the table, Rachel stood from her chair—a bit too eagerly, if the giggle from Becca said anything.

Troublemaker.

Rachel ignored her and waited patiently for everyone else to stand. Mother always liked to take drinks out onto the deck that overlooked the lake, but tonight was unseasonably warm and humid. Hopefully the evening would come to a close and Rachel could sneak August out before any more questions were asked.

So far he'd done a brilliant job of answering everything with just enough information to satisfy her mother. And for that, she wanted to reward him with so much more than a kiss.

If only.

The way he'd caressed her thigh under the table all through dinner had her revving for something more. His hand had been warm and calming, as had his sweet reassurances in her ear about how beautiful she looked.

Her cheeks heated and her stomach fluttered. If she wasn't careful, she'd fall hard for him. And she couldn't chance the heartache of what happens after you fall in love. After the love is taken away from you for one reason or another.

Gee, like how he was bound to run fast and hard after he discovered she saw ghosts. His *sister*, to be exact.

No way could she ever admit the real reason she'd showed up in his life. For one, he'd never believe her. So what would be the point?

Before she could stop herself, she clasped her hand in his again. He gave her a cute half grin as they followed the leader, her mother, out of the dining room and into the living room. As usual, her father hadn't had much to say throughout dinner. Rachel took after him in that sense, she supposed. They both always chose their words carefully. Sometimes with Mother, things were better left unsaid.

"Why don't we have a drink on the deck?" her mother asked. "We can talk about your next step, Rachel?"

"My next step?"

"With the bar exam of course. Or maybe we can discuss August a little more." Dora eyed him. "You have a knack for abridging your answers."

"Do I? Interesting."

He smiled and Rachel wanted to kiss those sexy lips.

"Just know that I have your daughter's best interests at heart. We haven't known each other long, but I have the deepest respect for her. She's safe with me."

Safe. That was the perfect word to describe how she felt when she was around August. But how could he possibly know that?

Her father's face softened some, like it did when he was caught off guard, which didn't happen often.

"I hope you're not the reason she didn't pass the bar." He spoke a complete sentence for the first time all night. "This girl has a bright future ahead of her. Distractions will only get in her way. Are you distracting her?"

"No, sir, I don't think I am."

"Planning to upset her in anyway?"

"Not at all, sir."

"No, Dad," Rachel said, surprised her dad cared enough to say anything. So surprised her eyes threatened to tear up. But she blinked them back. "August didn't have anything to do with that, and I promise I'll pass next time."

If she could convince Ella to return after she'd blown her off all day. What had she been thinking?

"In any case," Dora began, "we purchased a fabulous misting system for the deck, and this is the perfect time to try it out. What would you like to drink, August? I think Therese might be able to find some beer in the refrigerator."

"Yeah," Becca said, giving Rachel a don't-leave-me look over their mother's shoulder. "You should definitely stay longer. Or take me with you. Do you like to dance, August? I know this place that you two will just love."

August scratched his temple and opened his mouth to speak, but a buzzing sound from his pocket captured his attention. "Sorry. Excuse me one second." He pulled his phone out, checked his text message, and punched in a quick reply.

"Is everything okay?" she asked, hoping Nick and Zach were all right. Sure, they were teenagers who could probably take care of themselves for an extended period of time. Then again, they were teenagers, and she was well aware of how much trouble they could cause, especially after witnessing Becca's major goof-ups when she was in high school. Rachel had bailed her out more times than she wanted to count.

August cleared his throat. "Really sorry to have to end the evening but—" He waved his phone and stuffed it back in his pocket. "Duty calls."

Rachel tensed, wondering if he was telling the truth or making up an excuse to get as far away from her and her family as possible. To think he'd asked for this. He was probably regretting going through all the trouble.

"You have to leave now?" Her mother put her hand to her heart. "We've barely had time to get to know you."

"Let him go, Dora," her dad said firmly. "I can give Rachel a ride home."

"No." August gathered Rachel's hand to his chest. "No, that's okay. I'll take her home. It's on my way. But we should go." He turned to Rachel and winked, relaxing her some. "Are you ready?"

"Here's your wrap, dear." Therese appeared behind her, setting the covering on her shoulders and her clutch in her hands, as if she'd been prepared for this sudden departure. "Have a safe drive home."

"Thank you, Therese." She smiled at the quiet woman.

Without a word, Therese disappeared from the room as silently as she'd arrived.

Rachel returned her mother's air kiss and quickly moved across the room to give her father a peck on the cheek.

"Study," he said, giving her a stern look.

"Of course." She nodded and joined August's side. "Thank you for dinner, Mom, Dad. Everything was delicious. Bye, Becca." She waved to her solemn-looking sister before August tugged her arm and guided her to the foyer and out the front door.

He helped her into the truck, shut her door, and jumped in on his side. Silently, he started the engine and headed toward the main road.

"Is everything okay?" She couldn't hold back any longer. "Was it really your patient?"

"My patient?" He shook his head. "No, sorry. I didn't mean to worry you. It wasn't anything urgent. Just Zach reminding me I needed to drive him to baseball practice in the morning." He took her hand and kissed it. "I hope you don't mind me fibbing a little. I've been dying to be alone with you all night."

Alone. With nothing and no one to interrupt them. She ignored the heat rising to her cheeks. "And my mother is just a little suffocating," she reminded him, not able to say what was really on her mind—that she wanted to be alone with him too. To touch him, kiss him. Maybe more.

He chuckled. "Just a bit suffocating, yeah. I see what you meant by her wanting to be in charge. But I think she probably means well."

"You think?"

"Sure. Well, she does come off as a little cold, but it's obvious she cares about you and wants the best for you. Hell, I've never evaded so many questions in my life."

"Sorry about that."

"No problem. I didn't mind beefing up my credentials as long as you don't mind who I really am. Although, I did feel like a big ass for not mentioning Nick and Zach. I'm not ashamed of them or of being their guardian. In fact, that's probably the one aspect of my life I'm the most proud of."

"Oh, August." She hadn't meant for him not to mention the boys or to bulk up his resume. "You should be proud. You're doing such a good job raising them. Next time, please feel free to talk about them all night, if you want." She stopped and covered her mouth. "I mean, if you ever happen to see my parents again."

"Honey." He squeezed her hand but stared at the road ahead. "I want to keep dating you. I might not be the ideal man in your mother's eyes, and I'm pretty certain your dad wants me gone, but you're a grown woman. You make your own choices, and I hope you'll choose to keep seeing me."

Rachel let the conversation die, unsure what to say next. The determination she'd had to end all communication with August before had fizzled. She couldn't deny she liked him. Just being in his presence, sitting beside him in his truck, gave her a warm feeling she'd never felt before. Or in a long time. She couldn't remember, either way.

August was handsome and sexy, sure, but when she looked at him she sensed something more than just a physical attraction. There was a deep-rooted curiosity to know him better, to take a chance and maybe let him know her better. Slowly, of course. If the man could look past her mother's cold exterior and see something softer inside, maybe he'd understand what Rachel was hiding. Not that she was going to divulge any of that craziness tonight, or ever. But it was nice to know August was someone who didn't judge a person too easily.

Of course, she still couldn't quite kick the fear of falling for him, of giving her heart to someone again. But she doubted she'd be able to tell him no when they reached her apartment and she invited him in. To her bedroom.

God, could she take him there? Could she honestly let it go that far?

Her heart beat erratically all the way home, slow to fast to slow, each time she allowed herself to think of how his hands would feel on her bare skin, how much she wanted to explore his body with her fingers and her eyes, to drink in every detail.

Again, the need to know him, to truly know him, drove her thoughts.

"Do you have any tattoos?" The words left her mouth before they'd even reached her brain. What a stupid question.

He pulled into her apartment parking lot. "Rachel, you are a mystery to me, I gotta tell ya."

"Why do you say that?"

"You left me hanging back there when I told you I wanted to keep dating you. Here I thought you were sitting there thinking up the best way to let me down easy. You just surprised me with your question. It's not a setup, is it? You don't date guys with tattoos? Is that it?" He shut the engine off and swiveled to face her, a twinkle in his eye.

"It wasn't a setup. I was just curious." Her gaze drifted to his lips and her curiosity piqued. "I'm sorry I didn't respond. My mother was right about me. I tend to think too much, go off into my own little world. Does that bother you?" She hoped not. It wasn't something she thought she could change.

"Nothing about you bothers me, Rache. You can pretty much take it to the bank that I'm completely and utterly captivated by you."

"Oh." The duck a l'orange wavered in her belly.

"Can I come upstairs?" A cute smile cut across his face. "I don't have a tattoo. Believe it or not, I'm a doctor who's afraid of needles."

Rachel couldn't hold back a laugh. "Really?"

"Yeah, really. But I'll go get a tattoo right now if it'll make you want me. I'll do anything. Name it."

"Just come upstairs."

Chapter Eleven

August pressed the elevator button and breathed a sharp sigh of relief that he wasn't on his way to a tattoo parlor, letting some stranger mark his skin for eternity. The elevator doors opened, and he wrapped an arm around Rachel's waist to usher her inside.

He'd meant it when he said he'd do anything. He was falling terrifyingly hard and fast for this woman. He nonchalantly swiped the sweat beading on his brow. Yep, too goddamn fast.

But all his worries dissipated when she turned and pressed her hands to his chest. She looked up with her toffee eyes and pretty pouty lips, and all his brain cells seeped from his head and rushed downward.

To hell with everything. He was going to make love to her tonight.

He bit his tongue to keep from announcing it out loud. Sometimes his mouth got in the way of his plans by being too optimistic. Instead, he used his lips for something a lot less destructive. He leaned forward, braced her beautiful face in his hands, and kissed her. Lightly at first. Just to feel her soft lips against his, to ingest the fruity scent of her lip gloss, to revel in how perfectly their mouths fit together. To imagine those lips on other parts of his body.

Her fingers tightly gripped his shirt. He'd successfully chipped away the ice wall she'd built around her. It had cost him the price of a dozen roses, a night with her dysfunctional family, and some of his pride, but being with her now, knowing he'd be inside her soon, made it all worth the effort.

The elevator doors opened so he grudgingly broke the kiss and opened his eyes. She slowly opened hers as well and let out a small sigh. "August."

"Come on." He guided her to her apartment door, where she fumbled with her keys with unsteady hands.

The sight forced him to remember her anxiety. "Are you sure about this?" he asked. "Are you feeling anxious?"

She shook her head and leaned in closer, running a hand up his abdomen. "Not anxious, no."

"You sure?" *Just shut up, dumbass.*

"August"—she laughed—"do you want the truth?"

"Maybe. Yes."

"I want…" She paused as August hung on her words. Her smile faded. "I'm…"

"Go on." *Please don't tell me to leave.*

She glanced toward her door, her brows worried, her lips clamped shut.

"Rache?"

A shaky smile reappeared. "We should probably say goodnight."

Why did I say anything?

"Goodnight? Inside, you mean?"

"No. Sorry."

Her frown worried him.

"My father's right. I have to concentrate on studying."

August opened his mouth to speak, but no words came out. The woman confused the hell out of him.

"But I'll be at your house tomorrow. I think

129

rejuvenating the garden will help with the boys' outlook. Ella used to tell me how much they enjoyed playing in the front yard while she gardened."

"Did she now? Tell me again how you knew Ella so well." He didn't know why he asked. But something in her voice made him. Something curious. Or maybe he was just let down and feeling annoyed because she was pushing him away. Again.

"Well, you remember I mentioned she was my mentor. We used to have lunch quite a bit. She talked about Nick and Zach a lot."

"Is that right?" He believed her. She had no reason to lie—nothing to gain from helping him and his nephews. He wasn't a rich man. He had nothing to give her that she didn't already have. And he would definitely remember her if he'd ever met her before. A groupie she was not. If only. Maybe then he'd have a better chance of getting inside her apartment.

Rachel nodded and pushed her door key into the lock. "So maybe I'll see you tomorrow. I mean, if you're home before I leave."

"If that's what you want," he forced himself to say. But his hands and mouth had a mind of their own. He grabbed a hold of her upper arms and drew her to him. "Is that what you want?"

Not waiting for an answer, he firmly molded his lips over hers.

She stiffened, and then softened under his touch, giving him reason to slide his fingers along her shoulders, her neck, and into her hair. He'd been craving this all night—to taste her, to inhale her. Her hair was silk against his fingers. Her lips were sweet and incredibly supple. Fucking delicious.

He backed her against the door and pressed against her, wanting to feel the soft angles of her body against his. Just for a moment.

She clutched his coat lapel tightly.

That's it, baby.

"August." She broke the kiss. "You should go."

Damn. He released her, winded, and backed up a step, attempting to gain some amount of restraint. She wanted him to leave, and he'd kissed her instead, thinking he could change her mind. His ego would need a heavy-duty bandage after tonight.

"I…"

"I understand," he said, before she could salt the wound. "I'm going." He saluted, stupidly, not knowing what else to do with his hands. "Maybe I'll see you tomorrow."

~ * ~

Rachel touched her fingertips to her tingling lips and watched as he jetted down the hallway, passed the elevator, and took the stairs down. Not once looking back.

Clearly, he felt rejected. And probably confused.

If it weren't for the sounds coming from her apartment, she'd be in there with him now, probably in bed, definitely naked. She'd wanted that, and she was pretty sure she'd given him that impression. Up until she'd shut him down.

He hadn't heard the noises of course. The buzzing murmurs of spirits, searching for relief, contentment, an answer to a question they hadn't had the chance to ask while they were alive. Something she couldn't give them. Look what she'd gotten herself into while trying to help one of them.

Bringing him into that nightmare would have been a mistake. And who knew if the spirits would follow her if she went back home with August? She couldn't chance that either. She'd had no choice but to tell him to go.

Obviously Ella had allowed the spirits in—maybe even invited them. She'd filled her part of the bargain for as long as Rachel had. Now the ghosts were back. And she feared she needed to do some fresh negotiating.

Ella. Where are you?

Rachel unlocked her door and stepped inside. Her window was open, the curtains flapping as warm wind gushed in and out. She hadn't left it that way, she was sure of it. A forty-something year old man—a spirit—in a business suit paced in front of the window, murmuring as he counted on his fingers. In the kitchen a woman in her late thirties wearing a floral apron lurked over the stove, her eyes wide as she repeated, "Did I turn it off?" A few other spirits flitted around from room to room. Probably looking for someone or something they'd never see again.

Rachel's heart ached for them. If only they would simply move on and find peace.

Not able to help herself, she walked to the woman in the kitchen. "Yes," she said over the woman's repetitive words. "You did turn it off. The oven is off. You can leave now."

The woman stopped abruptly and peered at Rachel. "I did?"

"Yes, you did."

"How do you know? My children will be home from school soon. I want them to be safe."

"I'm sure they're fine." Rachel had no idea. She hadn't heard anything on the news recently about children being harmed in a fire. More than likely this was simply a fear that plagued this woman while she was alive, and it was strong enough to follow her into the afterlife.

"My accountant," the man by the window bellowed, "he's been stealing my money. I know it. He has to be stopped."

"Why am I here?" the woman asked. "Where are my children? The stove. I think I left the stove on."

The man flew forward, stopping only inches from Rachel's face. "You're going to find him for me, right? That bastard can't get away with my money."

Rachel should've known better. Never engage the spirits. They weren't rational. They were confused. Most of them anyway.

"Ella." She backed out of the kitchen and headed toward her front door. "Ella! You win. I'm going to your house tomorrow."

"Did you see where I put my glasses?" The elderly woman called from the hallway. "I left them on the bedside table. They're not there anymore."

"Ella!"

"It's a gas stove. I know I left it on. You have to turn it off."

"He's a thief. I should've known it all along."

"I can't watch my stories without my glasses. Did you take them?"

"Ella, please." Rachel turned the knob, but firsthand experience told her fleeing wouldn't do any good. They'd follow her. She squeezed her eyes shut, willing the noise away.

Familiar laughter filled the room, drowning out the voices.

Ella. Thank God.

Rachel spun around to see her apartment clear, no spirit to be seen. Except for Ella, of course, lounging on the sofa and twirling her hair, a smile curving every wrinkle on her face.

"I'm not sure what's so funny. Those people are obviously hurting." Like Hayes's spirit had before he'd moved on. His only goal had been to save his brother from a loveless marriage—to her. He'd been right in his attempt. Rachel hadn't loved his brother, Grayson. They'd been good friends, yes, but their desire to marry was only stemmed from their heartache over losing Hayes—a man they'd both loved and lost. And losing him twice, after he'd moved on, had been doubly painful.

She went to the photo album and checked to see if his picture was still intact after the spirits had bombarded her apartment. Thankfully, it was.

"Rachel, you really care for those souls? They drive you insane with their incessant chatter. *Where's my money?*

Find my eyeglasses." Ella laughed, lightening the tension in the room. "Honestly, am I the only bodiless soul around here with any sense?"

"*You* drive me insane." Rachel crossed her arms. "But that brings up a good question. How are you so lucid? Rational." She wouldn't give her that much credit. "*Almost* rational. You aren't repeating nonsense from a life you no longer have at least. And you can get rid of the others. How?" Hayes had been the same way.

Ella gave a blasé shrug. "My death came unexpectedly. I lost control of my car during a snowstorm as I was crossing a bridge. I banged against the side a few times before finally breaking through and falling in. Crashing into the frigid river."

"I'm so sorry."

She waved Rachel's concern away. "It couldn't be helped. But I remember knowing I was going to die and how I'd be leaving my sons behind. I remember worrying about them. I suppose it's natural that my worry transferred to my afterlife. But there are other things that need resolving too. If you keep helping me, I'm sure all will be fine in the end."

"What other things need to be resolved?" Mentally exhausted, Rachel cozied onto the opposite end of the couch, thankful the ghosts were gone.

"That's not important. What is important is my sons' wellbeing. You're starting the garden tomorrow?"

"Yes, the garden. But I want to know more about you. I think August is questioning whether I truly knew you."

"That's probably because the gossips in Curlville have too much time on their hands, and they're putting notions in his head. Loretta, in particular. She's become Auggie's second mother."

"I don't like lying to him, Ella. And I really don't like that he can't trust me."

"It's not as if you're harming him. You're helping

him."

I'm falling for him. Playing with his heart. "I don't want to hurt him."

"Then don't. There's nothing stopping you from exploring a relationship. If you like him, why not?"

"It's not that easy."

"Because you're still in love with a man you'll never see again?"

"That's harsh." Rachel wasn't going to ask how Ella knew about Hayes. If the spirit could read her thoughts, no doubt she knew more about her past life than Rachel could fathom. She wrapped her arms around her stomach and clamped her lips shut, refusing to go there.

"Harsh but true. You're no better than the ghosts who haunt you—forever stuck in a moment."

"I'm not that bad. Please stop talking about him."

Ella twisted her lips and gave a probing look.

Rachel braced herself.

"Fine. Let's talk about how your mother only wants you to be with someone who's a member of her elitist clubhouse? Is that the problem?"

Ouch. Rachel supposed she deserved that. "Not at all. I don't care what my mother thinks of August. I just didn't want her to find out how I met him."

"What does it matter? Will her judgment of you change who you are?"

"No. Not if you put it that way." Rachel sat up straight as a slew of thoughts hit her. "I've always wanted my parents to be proud of me, and I'm aware of how that's limited me. I'm aware of how I need to stand up to them. Tonight I realized something important—I'll never again ask anyone to fib or change their personality to appease my parents. August changed for my sake. He didn't lie, but he didn't necessarily tell the whole truth either. I feel awful that he wasn't comfortable enough to talk about Nick and Zach."

"Don't worry about him. He's proven to be resilient

on many occasions. I admit I don't give Auggie enough credit, but he's kind and goodhearted. And if that's what you're looking for... Is that what you're looking for?"

"I wasn't looking for anyone." Rachel rubbed her temple. A week ago she never would have believed she'd be getting relationship advice from a ghost. *Agh. I'm a mess.*

"You're fine. And Auggie could do much worse—believe me. You've seen Dana. Thank goodness he's stayed his distance from that cougar."

"She is a bit aggressive, isn't she?"

"Ppfft. Uh, yeah."

"Ella, I don't know what to do. Whether I date August isn't even the biggest issue here. If I'm going to continue this masquerade, I have to give him more of a reason to keep letting me into his home and life. If he doesn't trust me, we're both out of luck."

"I see what you mean." Ella tapped her finger on her chin. "If you're worried about August not believing you, what you need to do is to make yourself less of a mystery to him, but mostly you need to stop the gossip chatter. If the ladies in Curlville don't know every detail about you, they don't have a problem filling in the blanks with whatever suits their fancy. Before you know it, you'll be the most infamous axe murderer, slash money launderer, slash husband stealer in town. And they'll tell Auggie."

"How am I supposed to talk to them? I don't know them."

"That's easy. You want to make an appointment at Dolly's Hair and Nail Salon."

Chapter Twelve

The garden was looking up. And it had only taken Rachel one week to find and purchase the exact arrangement of flowers Ella wanted and another week to weed, mulch, plant, fertilize, and water her way to meet the control freak's approval. Not bad.

What do you think? she asked Ella, careful not to speak aloud. Dana had a nasty habit of glaring at Rachel from across the street. No point in creating more controversy. Rachel hadn't gathered the nerve to visit the hair salon yet, so whatever the women in town thought of her was more than likely twisted into a tangled web of sticky gossip by now. Or at least that's what Ella continued to point out.

Not that it mattered. August had kept his distance since the night she'd invited him to her apartment and then abruptly told him to leave, as if she'd had a bad case of bipolar PMS. Geez, how embarrassing.

It wasn't surprising he hadn't made any lunchtime visits or left his office early like he had before. And last evening when she'd stayed late to snag a glimpse of him, she sort of understood after he'd abruptly excused himself to the grocery store, saying he'd needed to pick up things for dinner. But it did hurt that he wouldn't make eye contact. For two weeks, he'd avoided her.

He probably thought she was playing mind games—hard-to-get to the extreme. But if he wanted her out of his life, he hadn't directly told her so. Nor had he given her any more reasons to think he still wanted to be with her.

None of that should make a difference in the long run. Because, on the bright side, she'd had plenty of time to study.

It's just that she kinda *missed* him. A lot.

Missed his voice, his laugh, his smile, his touch. And his amazing lips. Sweet mercy, the man could kiss.

"The garden is nearly perfect," Ella said, while sniffing one of the sweet peas. "The bulbs you planted will brighten it up so much when they start growing."

Rachel checked the time on her phone. If she stayed a few more minutes she'd see the boys bound off the bus, stop to say hi, and then rush inside all pink-cheeks and vivacity. Their energy was infectious. She adored them.

Is there anything else you want me to do? she asked Ella.

Ella stood from smelling the flowers and smirked. "Just stay. Make them dinner. They'd love that."

Why don't you ever stay to see them?

"I wish I could. But I have a strong feeling Nicholas can see me."

"Do you think so?"

Ella nodded.

"Wow. Yeah, that would be difficult, wouldn't it?" And devastating for Nick. A thought occurred. "Do you think he can see the mystery ghost inside?"

Ella turned sharply toward Dana's house.

A man, wearing sunglasses and a baseball hat, slowed in front of Dana's house and pulled into her garage.

"Damn it." Ella glared as the garage lowered, concealing the man's identity.

Who is that?

"No one. Just don't let him in this house. Not ever, under any circumstance. Do you understand?"

"No, I don't. Tell me who he is." She glanced at Ella, only to discover Ella was no longer there.

Rachel sighed and swiped a patch of dried dirt off her wrist. There were too many secrets in this town, starting with the Amish girl who lurked inside the house. Yes, it was possible Rachel had brought the ghost with her, but she didn't think that was the case.

If Nicholas saw ghosts, that would explain a lot about his taciturn behavior. Sweet kid but very guarded, and maybe for a good reason.

Poor guy. They'd have to have a talk, and soon. She couldn't imagine life as a teenage medium. And when it boiled down to it, she supposed that's what she'd become. A medium.

Ever since she'd communicated with Hayes's spirit, this strange otherworld had split open, allowing her to see too much. He'd been the one to crack the door open to this bizarreness. And now she couldn't seem to shut it.

She hoped Nick wasn't plagued by multiple crazed spirits, like Rachel was when Ella wasn't keeping them at bay.

What would she do when Ella no longer had a use for her? Hmm. Better question was what would she do if Ella wanted to use her indefinitely?

Rachel pushed those thoughts away and walked up to the house to wash off the rest of the dried dirt. A couple of her fingernails had broken off in unfortunate areas. The gardening gloves hadn't helped much.

She glanced up at the stairs on the way to the kitchen. This mystery ghost seemed to be fairly well-behaved. Of course she'd been a child when she'd died. She was probably terrified and utterly confused.

Rachel made a note to research the death of a teenage Amish girl in the area. She'd also ask August about the man across the street...if she ever got him alone again.

She washed up at the kitchen sink, taking her time and hoping she'd get to see Nick and Zach for a few minutes. She wasn't sure what they thought of her. She was a stranger for the most part. And here she was standing in their home.

The bus wheels squeaked, and Rachel peeked out the window to see the boys racing to the front door. She smiled at their youthful spirit, the brotherly love. The way she and Becca used to behave back in more innocent times.

A knot lodged in her throat as she remembered how she and Becca used to talk about what they'd be like as grown-ups. They'd both admitted they wanted to find an occupation they loved, along with having a family. And they'd pinky-sweared that they'd give their children a loving, comfortable home. Affection and laughter would be a priority, rather than objects and wealth.

Somehow that goal had gotten clouded over the years.

Rachel moved away from the window and opened the bag of cookies she'd bought at the grocery store. Ella had wanted them to be homemade, but Rachel didn't trust her baking skills. Plus, the oven wasn't working properly.

She poured the cookies onto a plate and held her breath as the boys sprang into the kitchen.

"Hey," Zach said, always in his exuberant tone. "I thought that was your car out there. I knew you'd be here. Nick thought maybe you weren't going to come around anymore, since Uncle Auggie gave you the slip last night."

"I didn't say that." Nick's cheeks flashed red. He picked up a cookie and fumbled it between his fingers. "I saw the garden. Thank you for doing that."

"You're welcome. I'm glad you like it." Her heart beamed. "Shouldn't be too difficult to keep it going all summer and into the fall."

He almost smiled. Almost. "My mom used to work out there a lot. She loved that garden. It was kinda sad when it didn't grow back the way it used to."

"Yeah." Zach nodded with a solemn look. "I

remember. It's cool that you fixed it up. Thanks, Rache."

"No problem. I'll even teach you two how to do upkeep for when I'm not around anymore."

"Sure, that would be okay," Zach said, shoving a cookie in his mouth. "Are you going to stop coming? I mean, did Auggie screw up or something?"

"Zach," Nick scolded.

"What?" Zach rolled his eyes. "It's a decent question."

"Don't worry," Rachel said. "Your uncle didn't do anything wrong."

"Cool." Zach grinned. "Hey, Rache, can you make that chicken dumpling stuff again?"

"Zach, dude, shut up."

"What? I'm hungry."

Rachel laughed. "It's okay. I don't mind making dinner." She just hoped August wouldn't mind her continuing to barge in on his family. "How about something different? Do you like spaghetti?" Therese's spaghetti had always been a staple Spencer dinner.

Both boys nodded.

"Good. Maybe you two can help me prepare it after you've done your homework?"

They looked at each other, dropped their backpacks onto the table, and began to pull out books and papers.

Ella would be proud.

"Great. I'll run to the store and get what we need."

~ * ~

August didn't make it home for dinner. But at least he had a good reason, Rachel discovered, as she listened in on a phone call between Nick and Loretta. August had gone into the hospital in the next town over to deliver a patient's baby. From what she could understand from Nick's conversation, it sounded as though he'd left in the morning.

"No, we're fine. We just ate," Nick said to Loretta. "Uncle Auggie's girlfriend helped us make spaghetti and garlic bread."

A pause.

Nick glanced at Rachel, his eyebrows bunched. "Sure, I guess. Hold on." He handed her the phone. "Loretta wants to talk to you."

"Okay." *Cripes.* "Thanks."

Zach shot a thumb over his shoulder. "I'm going upstairs."

"Fine," Nick said. "I guess I'll do the dishes this time, but you're doing them next time."

Rachel bit back a smile, watching as Zach zoomed out of the room. She put the phone to her ear. "Hello, this is Rachel."

"And this is Loretta. We finally get to talk. I've been wondering when we'd get the chance. You're the girlfriend now, are you?"

"Just someone helping out the family, actually."

"Really? That is so very kind of you. I have to say you're going way out of your way for someone who barely knew Ella. That's what August tells me—that you were friends with Ella. Is that true?"

"We had lunch together several times. Ella was somewhat of a mentor for me, since I'm studying to become a lawyer." She repeated the rehearsed story, but felt a huge sting of guilt, knowing Nick was listening in.

"I find it peculiar Ella never mentioned you. To anyone. Ella loved to talk. She shared everything with me."

"I was thinking the same thing when August mentioned you two were good friends. Ella never spoke of you. Mainly we discussed family law, since that was her area of expertise." Rachel patted herself on the back. Good one.

"Well, that is odd." Loretta huffed.

"You know"—Rachel checked her jagged fingernails—"I was thinking of making an appointment to get a badly-needed manicure. Would you recommend Dolly's?"

"Dolly's?" Loretta's voice perked up. "Dolly and her beauticians are the best in Indiana, if you ask me. Of course I recommend them."

"Great. Maybe we can have a girl's day of pampering soon? We could get to know each other better, if you like."

"Pampering? I wouldn't mind that."

"It's settled then," Rachel said. "When do you suppose August will be home? I can stay with the boys until then."

"That's not necessary. The boys are fine on their own for a few hours."

"It's no trouble. I insist." If only to see August. She'd been disappointed when he hadn't come home again. "So when do you suppose?"

"He could be home any minute or hours from now. There's just no telling. He was out the door here at nine with a rushed goodbye. I had to shout into the parking lot to find out what he was up to. The boy has no sense of how to run a business."

Rachel stirred in her seat, not liking how August's employee talked about him. "I'm sure he had a good reason to rush out. Anyway, we'll set up a date for Dolly's soon. Sound okay?"

Loretta agreed, and Rachel said goodbye, turning toward Nick. The quiet teenager was busy scrubbing spaghetti sauce off a plate.

"Do you want me to help you with that?" Rachel asked him, hoping to start a conversation.

"Sure." He rinsed the plate and set it in the dish drainer. "So you knew my mom pretty well?"

"I liked her a lot." She grabbed a dishtowel and dried the plate, trying to think of a way to discuss ghosts without seeming abnormal or scaring him away. "Do you like to watch TV, Nick?" She could mention one of the popular ghost hunting shows.

"Our TV broke a couple weeks ago."

"Oh." Poor kid. Rachel had a good guess what had

happened to the TV. "You know, I have an extra one at my place. I'll bring it over." She didn't need one in her bedroom anyway.

"Thanks." He kept his gaze down, focusing on cleaning a pot. "Our dishwasher doesn't work either."

"I noticed a lot of the electrical equipment in the house isn't working. Did you have a power surge?" Rachel knew otherwise. The ghosts were the reason she kept her electronics unplugged when she wasn't using them.

"I guess. Something like that." He glanced at her. "It happens a lot."

"Why do you think that is?" She urged him on. Maybe he was ready to tell someone.

He gulped and set the pot in the drainer. "Rachel?"

"Yeah?"

"Do you believe in ghosts?"

"Yes, Nick. Yes, I do." What a relief.

He cracked a smile. "Yeah, so do I."

A couple moments of silence passed before Rachel got the courage to ask, "Do you want to talk about that?"

He shook his head. "Maybe later. I gotta go upstairs." He wiped his hands dry and turned to go.

"Wait, Nick?" She had to find out if he was okay.

"Yeah?"

"Is she nice to you? The ghost?"

Another shy smile appeared. His cheeks reddened. "She's okay. Just annoying sometimes. Like when she's alone for too long." He gestured toward the kitchen door.

"Right. Just let me know if I can help you. You can always talk to me. About anything."

He nodded and gulped. "Okay. Thanks. Um, bye." He darted from the kitchen. His footsteps thudded against the stairs as he hurried.

At least she'd made some progress. He knew he wasn't alone. And he knew he wasn't insane. Rachel supposed that was a comfort for herself as well.

She finished drying the dishes and then went to pace

in the living room. August might be home soon, and she needed to figure out what she planned to say to him. He was probably upset about the other night. She'd led him on and then abruptly turned him away. If that hadn't deterred his feelings for her, the condescending questions from her mother all through dinner probably had.

The sound of his truck pulled her out of her reverie. She drew in a breath and waited for him to come inside. Because meeting him on the porch would be weird, right? Of course she looked perfectly normal standing in the middle of his living room, stiff and unsure.

She shook out her tense shoulders and tried to relax. All she wanted was to see him, to get her fix. Maybe get close enough to smell his scent, touch his warm skin, kiss him once more.

The door opened and he stepped in. A sight for sorely desperate, slightly stalkerish eyes.

"Hi," she said, taking him in. He looked good in black slacks, a blue dress shirt, and striped tie. His hair was ruffled, probably from running his hand through it. He'd had a long day.

"Hey."

He grinned, and her heart stalled. Still no eye contact though. Oh, dear.

"I made dinner for Nick and Zach. I hope you don't mind."

"Not at all." He slipped off his tie and hung it on the coat rack. "Thank you for taking care of them. Loretta said she'd stop by."

"She called. I told her I'd stay with the boys until you got home."

"Rachel, you didn't have to do that." He loosened the top buttons on his shirt. A somber frown formed. Not an expression he wore often. "I'll say it again, you don't have to keep helping us. I appreciate it, I do, but…" He sighed.

"I didn't mind at all. There are leftovers. Spaghetti." She tried to sound upbeat.

"I ate, but thank you."

"Loretta said you delivered a baby today. How did that go?"

His hand slid through his hair. He seemed to be stuck in the spot by the door. When he didn't answer, she resisted the urge to go to him, to wrap her arms around him, to help him forget whatever ailed him.

"Do you want me to leave?" she asked instead.

"No." He finally made eye contact—the simple act breaking the wall lodged between them. "You're not going anywhere. Not until we talk."

"Okay. Let's talk." She wasn't sure whether she should be relieved or worried.

"I'm going to say hello to the boys, change out of these clothes, and then we're leaving for a walk."

"A walk?"

"Yep. It's a nice night. I need to unwind, and you need to explain a few things to me. All right?"

Fabulous. What did he mean be that?

"I can do that." She hoped, but worry set in, making her anxious.

She freshened up as best she could in the downstairs bathroom while waiting for August, changing into the extra set of clothing she'd brought with her—a pair of white-cotton shorts and a soft-pink fitted T-shirt. Working in the garden all day had pinkened her cheeks and disintegrated her makeup.

At least she looked healthy? Her eyes sparkled in the too-dim bathroom, where only one of the two light bulbs glowed. Her pulse paced faster than normal as anticipation thrummed through her.

What does he want me to explain?

She tugged her hair loose from the ponytail, brushed through the knots, and dabbed on some lip-gloss.

Nothing more could be done. Her mother would be horrified to see her like this. But Rachel didn't care.

She opened the door just as August ran up the stairs

from his bedroom. He'd changed into a casual polo shirt and jeans that hugged him in all the right spots.

"I'll be back soon, boys," he yelled up to the second floor and got a mumbled response.

"Ready?" He grabbed her hand but didn't smile.

She gripped tight, relishing the feeling. "Yes."

They walked hand in hand down one street, and then the next, without saying a word. The crescent moon and muted light of the antique lampposts didn't do a great job of lighting the way. And the mature maples, poplars, and weeping willows cast shadows here and there.

But she felt safe with August. Safe and calm. Despite his obviously crummy mood.

Her free hand slid over his muscled forearm as she leaned into him, sniffing when her nose caught a whiff of the fresh cologne he must've applied when changing. Being close to him like this was addicting.

"Rachel"—he glimpsed at her from the corner of his eye—"where do I start with you?"

"What do you want to know?" She only wished she had nothing to hide. She imagined it would be refreshing and fulfilling to pour her heart out to August. He seemed like the type of guy who could be a best friend. Her best friend.

"Start with your panic attacks," he said. "How many have you had?"

She sighed, trying to think how to word this. "Just a couple. I'm not worried about it though. I've been under a lot of stress, you know? I bombed the bar exam, and my parents spent so much money on my education. I felt like a failure." Her chest tightened just thinking about it.

"Don't do that." August's voice rumbled low, surprising her. "You're smart, kind, and beautiful. Don't let anyone make you feel different."

"Thank you." She bit her lip and dipped under a tree branch hanging low over the sidewalk. "I think the same about you. Handsome, smart, all-around good guy." She dared a glance to meet his quizzical stare. "You're a catch."

He rubbed his forehead and chuckled uneasily. "Thanks. I have to admit I have a helluva time trying to read you."

No kidding. "Well, let's talk more." She tried for a light-hearted tone. "What's your philosophy on life, Dr. Kline? What do you want the most from it?"

"Good question. I'm always telling myself I want an uncomplicated life, but the complications keep building up. And sometimes I'm not sure if it's a good thing or a bad thing. One moment I'm in a fast-paced, high-pressure career that allowed zero personal time, the next I'm moving out of my upscale bachelor apartment that I never got to enjoy and moving in with three roommates, so I can join an eighties tribute band and start dating questionable women."

"Questionable women?"

"Let's just say monogamy wasn't a priority for them."

"Ah."

"Next thing I know I'm living in a small town, raising two teenagers, wondering if I'm screwing them up. Trying to maintain a family practice. And then I meet you." He squeezed her hand.

August Kline, meet the Queen of Complicated. "If only life could be simpler."

They turned the corner onto Main Street. The sidewalks were deserted, and the road was sparse with cars. Downtown Curlville consisted of several quaint buildings with flower boxes at each window, bright-colored trim, and redbrick pathways.

Rachel drew in the fresh scent of late spring. The evening was unseasonably warm and perspiration prickled at her neck and temple.

"What do you say we lighten the mood?" He pointed to the building across the street—Main Street Wine & Spirits. "Thirsty? Curlville's most popular store, but don't ever let on. I say we grab something strong and take it somewhere private."

"I'm game." She was somewhat of a lightweight. Drinking any alcohol would mean staying the night in Curlville. Whether that meant spending the entire time with August or not didn't matter. She didn't want to leave him just yet.

With his hand on her back, they crossed the street and entered the charming building that sat snug between a deli and an ice cream shop.

The bell rang above the door as they stepped inside.

"Doc Kline," a handsome Hispanic man called from behind the counter. A small television blared the sports channel on the counter in front of him. "What can I get you on this fine evening?"

August shook the man's hand and motioned to Rachel. "Rachel, this is Hector. Hector, Rachel. Hector's a good friend of mine. He organizes the adult softball league I play in."

"Nice to meet you." Rachel shook his hand, feeling comforted by the man's warm smile and kind eyes.

"Actually," August said, "Hector is a man of many trades here in Curlville. He owns this place, he teaches math at the high school, and he's the track coach."

"And," Hector said, "they've asked me to step in to teach music."

"Really? Do you know anything about music?"

"Not a thing." Hector winked at Rachel and shot a thumb at August. "This guy, on the other hand, would be perfect for the part, don't you think?"

"Definitely."

"Whoa." August waved a hand at Hector. "First, no winking at my girl. Second, I couldn't find a spare moment to teach even if I wanted to."

"Think about it. You're a musical genius, and you know how to handle teens. The school would be excited to have you, you'd make some extra cash, and you'd be giving back to the community."

"Handle teens? Me?" August shook his head. "Look, all I want tonight is a cold, strong beverage and some time alone with Rachel."

"Gotcha." Hector chuckled and pointed to the refrigerated section. "Start there."

"Great." August turned to Rachel. "What's your poison?"

"I'm *your girl*, huh?" She lifted a brow, pretending to tease when the simple sentiment had butterflies swandiving in her belly.

His lips curved up to a half grin. "Sorry. I got a little territorial. Forgive me? You're not going to run away, are you?"

"Not a chance." She hid a smile and strolled ahead of him down the aisle. Her fingers traveled lightly over the bottles of liquor. "What about a rosé wine?"

"Yeah? That's an idea."

"Something sweet and cold to drink." She glanced over her shoulder to see his gaze lingering on her derriere, where the white cotton fit somewhat snugly. "What do you think, August?"

His stare journeyed along her back, slowly, until he made eye contact. "I was thinking something stronger actually."

"Stronger?" Her voice squeaked, and she had to look away from his intense stare. She hurried down the aisle, trying to hide the blaze of her cheeks as heat burned her skin. "I'm okay with vodka."

"Okay." He leaned into her as he grabbed a small bottle of vodka off the shelf behind her. His other hand skimmed her back. The light touch sent tingles down her spine. "Straight vodka?"

"Maybe club soda. And cranberry juice too."

"Both strong and girly. Is this what you call compromising?"

She smiled. "What about glasses?" This impromptu date was sort of exciting.

"I think Hector has some plastic cups up front."

"And ice?" This close to him, she couldn't resist pressing her hand to his chest. Solid. Secure.

"Ice. Right. This wasn't the best laid-out plan. We might have to get creative. I have an idea. Come on."

Chapter Thirteen

After a long day, August hadn't felt much like playing *Guess What's Going on in Rachel's Head*. Was she here simply to fulfill her benevolent-but-strange need to help him and the boys, or was there something more? The uncertainty and constant push-and-pull had forced him to take a step back the past couple weeks.

But when he'd walked into the house tonight and saw her standing there all sweet and unsure and just so fucking beautiful, he hadn't been able to summon the desire to ask her to leave. In fact he'd liked that the first thing he'd come home to was her face, her voice. Just having her in his presence did wonders for his mood.

Watching her walk ahead of him in the liquor store had been another bonus. She had a fascinatingly sexy and elegant sway to her hips. Her pink lips, pale skin, and coppery hair made her appear delicate, as well as the soft curves of her cheeks, nose, and jaw. Then there were her entrancing honey-brown eyes that both blocked him out and invited him in, depending on the moment.

Which led him back to square one. Did she want him or not?

Her body language told him yes with a curvy capital

"Y", so he was going with that. He led her across Main and down Jefferson, and all the while, she held onto his arm, leaning into him like they were on a lover's stroll and not simply a friendly walk.

An unnerving craving in him wanted to be the guy she could lean on. To trust. But he didn't let on, worried about the effect of his words and actions. Look what had happened the last time he'd kissed her. She'd suddenly tensed up and sent him home, leaving him spiraling both physically and mentally.

When stripped to the core, the main reason he'd avoided her was the fear of losing her for good.

He didn't want to screw up whatever logic she had going on in her head compelling her to show up at his house every day. And every moment spent together proved that when he pushed, she retreated.

What also troubled him was the growing doubt that she was hiding something from him. Something unexpected. Something he couldn't ignore. Loretta's warnings weren't completely unreasonable. How had Rachel met Ella? Had she truly been friends with his sister? And what were Rachel's intentions?

In the past days, he'd had time to think.

He'd had his share of loss, and he didn't look forward to going through the grief involved with cutting someone special from his life. Seeing that Zach and Nick were intertwined in this whole situation, August had to take heed.

Like Loretta warned him to do. Damn the woman.

So tonight he'd ask Rachel a few questions. Maybe the vodka would loosen her tongue.

Or maybe he didn't need to know what was resting in her Pandora's box, ready to spring open. His dad used to say sometimes it was best not to bother the cobwebs in the basement. Usually he'd said this right after an argument with Mom, sitting on the front porch of their old house, staring up at the moon and the stars.

His dad had been a wise man. And August didn't plan to push Rachel. Too much. He'd hope she was in his life for the reasons she'd stated. But first he'd ask what needed to be asked.

"August?" Rachel's voice tore him from his thoughts. "Are you going to tell me where we're going, or is it a secret?"

She kept her gaze forward, but he could see the arc of her lips sloping into a smile. The dim lighting from the street lamps played softly on her skin.

"No secret at all." She could trust him. "Right this way." He came to a stop at the locked gate outside the Curlville public swimming pool. Tall leafy hedges surrounded the fenced area, so Rachel could have no idea what was on the other side.

"We're at our destination?" She motioned toward the cheap lock that kept trespassers out.

The heated pool on the other side would be open to the public next week, right before the beginning of the kids' summer break. Until then the high school swim team used it on a daily basis, preparing for their upcoming meets.

He knew all the details. *The Curlville Daily* never failed to mention the particulars of the high school sporting events. Not much else happened in this little town.

Rachel released his arm when he reached for the lock and twirled in the combo.

"I'm more than curious," she said. "How do you know the combination? And what's on the other side?"

"I was a volunteer weekend lifeguard last summer. They never change the lock. And that should answer your question about what's on the other side."

"A swimming pool. Interesting choice." She didn't sound thrilled, nor did she sound anxious.

"Yep, Curlville is a happening town. We got it all."

"I think it has just enough," she said warmly, surprising him. "I like this town."

"Do you? Is that the reason why you keep coming back?" He kept his tone light, trying not to seem overly eager to hear her answer.

"One of many." She licked her bottom lip and leaned against the fence, her gaze fixed on the lock as he pulled it open.

Good enough for him. He cleared his throat. "It's a heated pool. I figure we can dip our feet in while we talk. There's a freezer inside the snack bar. I'm betting they stock ice in there. See?" He pushed the gate open and held it for her. "I'm a resourceful guy. You gotta like that about me, at least."

She laughed. "How could I not?"

He caught her scent as she slipped past him. A hint of something fruity. Subtle and elegant. Very Rachel. Unbelievably sexy.

"I'll get the ice if you want to get comfortable," he said, but saw she was already disposing of her sandals.

Her gaze took in the space as she found a spot by the pool. "It's well taken care of. I'd like to see what the garden over there looks like in the daytime."

August scanned the surroundings. Besides the large lap pool, there was a diving area and a hot tub to the side. Stacked against the fence were various lawn chairs and recliners. And over toward the back were a kiddie playground and a walking garden with a thatched wooden gazebo. On summer nights, the gazebo lit up with thousands of tiny white lights. The residents used the common area to barbecue and socialize.

This part of small-town life wasn't so bad. Zach and Nick liked it. Well, when Nick wasn't being antisocial, anyway. What was up with that kid?

August tried to put that worry on the back-burner as he collected two cups of ice and made his way back to Rachel. Long lean legs stretched as her feet dangled in the pool. She leaned back on her hands, looking relaxed.

"This was a good idea, Auggie."

She used the nickname he'd grown to hate, but somehow it sounded provocative rolling off her tongue. Wouldn't it be great if he got a taste of that tongue tonight?

"Auggie, huh?" He poured some vodka in the cups, filled them with club soda and a splash of cranberry juice, and handed one to her.

"Sorry. You don't like that, do you? I hear the boys call you Auggie sometimes. I thought I'd give it a shot." She paused as a thought crossed over her face. "Grayson, my ex-fiancé, liked it when I called him Gray. The shortened version sounded less cold, he'd say. And I've always had a problem following social cues. I've been told I sometimes come off as a little icy." Her shoulders slumped as she sank into herself.

Who the hell was this guy? "Tell me more about good ole Gray. Your mom brought him up a few times at her dinner party. She seems to think it was a mistake for you not to marry him."

"My mom is misguided. Unfortunately she doesn't know all the facts, or refuses to accept them."

"Enlighten me." He tossed his shoes and socks to the side.

"We weren't in love, August. Gray was Hayes's twin brother. When Hayes died, Gray and I clung to each other for support. But from the beginning, we knew we weren't meant to be."

"Because you thought Hayes was the one?" August wasn't sure why he'd let that slip. He didn't want to hear the answer. Grinding his teeth, he rolled up his pant legs and plunged his feet into the pool.

"I was in love with Hayes, yes." She shrugged her shoulders. "But I think you already knew that. So tell me what happened today."

The sudden change of subject didn't go unnoticed.

"No." He tried to tamp down the ridiculous jealousy boiling over, but failed. "Those two names, your exes, I don't want to know any more about them—as long they're both out of the picture." He turned toward her. "Are they out of the picture?" Did the treasured photo of Hayes prove otherwise?

"What do you mean?" She sipped her drink, glancing away.

"I need to know if you're over Hayes." Of all the doubts he had about Rachel, this one was foremost on his mind.

She bit her bottom lip, not responding. His jealousy grew horns. Big ugly green horns. Over a dead guy.

"I want a relationship with you, Rachel." The words ejected from his lips like ash from a volcano. "A commitment," he added for good measure.

She set her cup down and swiveled toward him, her lips partially agape, her eyes giving him nothing but the glisten of the moonlight. Damn, she was hard to read.

Any other woman, any other time, he'd be thankful for an opportunity to back pedal. But—nope. His mouth wouldn't give up. Time for the lava to flow.

"Did you hear me, Rache? I want a relationship with you. But I have to know if you want the same or if you're looking for something else."

"I heard you." Her gazed dropped hard and fast to the water. "I just…"

"Don't leave me hanging, honey. I like you. I'm attracted to you. I think you like me too."

Still nothing.

"Rachel, look at me at least." When had he turned into a masochist?

"I, uh. Yes," she said to the water. "Okay, yes." She looked up, cheeks flushed, lips pressed together. So damn pretty in the moonlight.

"Yes? Meaning you want to start something with me and forget about any other guy? Because I need to know for sure. I may like a challenge, but I don't like guessing games."

"August." Her brows scrunched together cutely as she hit him with a perplexed stare.

She reached for him, pacifying some of his worry. Her hand smoothed over his jaw. Her fingertips slipped into his hairline. Damn, his body broke out in goosebumps. The woman had an insane effect on him. He set his cup down and thought about kissing the answer out of her. But he had to know now.

"Am I your guy, honey? Tell me you're over him." He pushed, probably too hard. But he was too selfish to share her heart. If he was going to dive into a relationship with Rachel, he needed to have all of her. Every part. Because if he didn't, he'd go more nuts than he would if she left and didn't come back.

Okay, maybe not that bad.

Still, she stayed silent, though her expression told him she was trying her best to come up with something. Maybe to let him down easily? Or to tell him the dead guy wins.

"Wait. Just wait." He stood. Panicking, he glanced around for an escape from her next words. The pool. Right. He held up a finger. "Hold that thought."

Hoping he didn't look like a lunatic, he yanked off his shirt and tossed it onto the ground. Next he unbuttoned his jeans and pushed them down, leaving only his boxers.

Rachel's gaze ran down his body. "What are you doing?"

"Going for a dip." To cool off. To gain some levity, some self-control. Maybe he'd find his self-respect too.

He dove in. Even though the pool was heated, the water shocked his body, sending a welcoming surge to his clouded mind. He stayed under, swimming the width of the pool and back again, until emerging.

Swiping the water from his face, he had to blink a few times to spot Rachel. And realized she'd disposed of her top as well.

His pulsed jumped, and the pounding at his temples traveled down straight to his groin. Her milky skin contrasted from her lacy black bra. Her pert breasts filled the cups nicely, and even several feet away, he could see the roundness of her rosy nipples. God, he loved lace.

"I can't let you have all the fun." She crossed her arms over her lean waist, showing a brief lack of confidence that contrasted with her words.

"No, you can't. Come in with me." He slicked his hair back and held out his hand for her to take.

"I should probably—" She unbuttoned her shorts and slid them down. Her hands noticeably trembled.

White lace panties sculpted over her thin yet curvy hips. And August's cock hardened.

"I don't match. I wasn't expecting—"

"Come here, Rachel. Please."

Chapter Fourteen

Trespassing onto land that may or may not be considered school property. Was that a Class D Felony or a Class A Misdemeanor? Rachel couldn't think with her head fuzzy and her body heated. But she was sure a number of crimes were being committed at that very moment.

Including indecent exposure.

Oh, cripes.

She glanced down at her mismatched underwear and imagined what her mug shot would look like.

What was she thinking? How could she think when August was beckoning her?

"Maybe this isn't a good idea." She crossed her arms, wishing she hadn't gone with the foolish gut instinct to strip. A familiar child-like shame gnawed at the very part of her gut that felt guilty for her near-nakedness. But she couldn't quite understand why, despite her shame, she moved slowly toward the edge of the pool, continuing what could possibly turn out to be a very bad life choice.

"Water feels nice. Come in." August's deep voice was grounded by the pool, giving the illusion of them being in a private cocoon. Crickets chirping was the only other sound for what seemed like miles. No traffic. No passersby.

The gnawing eased and she allowed her arms to drop. The gorgeous vision before her wasn't hurting either. The moonlight hit August in ways that danced on the drips of water skimming down his toned, tanned body and cast shadows under his midnight eyes. He slicked his hair back from his face and held out his muscled arms, waiting for her to join him.

Committing criminal acts had never felt so tempting.

Not that she'd ever committed a crime. She'd always been attracted to the allure of bad boys but had never done anything remotely unscrupulous with them. Yet after she'd seen August undress and dive into the pool, she'd found herself doing the same—wanting to join him.

Stop thinking, Rache.

I can't help it.

Her guard had dropped for a nanosecond, and now she was standing on the edge of a public swimming pool that high school kids used during the day. *Kids!* This could be considered a sexual offense. She'd probably be labeled a sex offender for the rest of her life.

A sex offender!

"This is a bad idea." The cricket sound gave a synchronized hiccup, breaching the peaceful cocoon. Was someone out there? She quickly glanced up to check if any buildings surrounded the pool, above the hedge line. Thankfully there were none to be seen. No peering eyes watching them from a window.

Of course nothing could stop someone from entering through the gate just as they had.

"How many people have the combination to that lock?"

"To the gate?" He lifted a brow. "Honey, don't worry. I promise no one is going to bother us. Even the sheriff is at home sitting in front of his TV, drinking a beer. This little town has a zero crime rate."

That didn't make her feel any better. *"We're* committing a crime." What was Ella going to say about this? She'd wanted Rachel to help August, not do jail time with him.

He dropped his hands, one covered his mouth as he attempted to hide his smile. But she saw the flash of teeth, the curved lips.

"Are you laughing at me, August Kline?"

"No." He moved to the edge and grabbed her ankles before she could retreat to her pile of clothes. "I'm not laughing at you. I think you're damn adorable, but I'm not laughing."

The feel of his rough wet fingers rubbing along her skin made her shiver. And almost, almost, forget what she'd been worried about.

"Come in with me. It'll be fun."

She could only imagine how fun it would be to slide into his arms, wrap her legs around his hips. Kiss him. The man had a remarkable body. Muscled and lean in all the right places. She wondered what he did to keep in shape. More so, she wondered how it would feel pressed up against his wet and nearly naked frame.

His smile twisted to a sensual smirk as his hands ran up and down her calves. "I dare you to come in."

"You dare me, huh?" She tried to sound playful as her stomach flip-flopped.

"Forget about the millions of worries flurrying through that beautiful mind of yours and get in here with me. I won't let anything bad happen to you, Rache. You have my word."

Misdemeanor. Nope, couldn't be more than a misdemeanor.

"All right."

"Yeah?"

Rachel nodded and lowered herself as carefully and gracefully as possible, considering she was down to her undergarments.

Her mind didn't have time to wander too far as August slipped his hands up to her waist. He lifted her and drew her down, taking control of her body.

The water was cool against her fevered skin. She draped her arms around his neck, taking a moment to run them over his strong shoulders. Goosebumps erupted as he surrounded her with a full embrace, as skin-against-skin as they'd ever been. Her breasts felt full against his solid chest.

She'd always been thin, too thin, but with his hand boldly rounding over her ass, along her hip and waist, she felt curvy. Sexy and desirable. His hands reached her thighs, and he lifted her against him, urging her to wrap her legs around his hips.

Out here. Where anyone could see them.

It was exhilarating. Exciting. All the things she'd felt with Hayes.

Don't think of him. Not now.

She closed her eyes, rested her cheek against August's five o'clock shadow, now more like nine-ish o'clock, and held on as he walked her deeper into the pool. His hands gripped her flesh, holding her securely, as his lips skimmed her neck, her jaw, her earlobe.

She shivered against the light sensual contact. He was breathing quickly too, she realized, as she arched into his kisses. The otherwise quiet night gave their passion away, seemingly silencing the crickets, but she couldn't bother to care. Her eyes rolled back as she reveled in how his hands glided along her wet skin. She curled her fingers into his hair and squeezed her legs around his hips. Heat teased her core, met firmly by his solid erection. Boxers and thin panties the only barrier.

A moan breezed from her lips.

She wanted him badly.

But like this? Here?

He backed her against the wall of the pool. Then his mouth was on hers, taking her. She parted her lips and his tongue swooped in, determined and skilled. The cranberry gave his natural flavor a sweet tang, and she found herself slipping her tongue along his, tasting more and more, drinking him in. She couldn't get enough.

The kiss lingered on, lazy and delicious. And all she could think about was the here and now. The man knew what he was doing. Or maybe it was their enigmatic chemistry. Either way, she could continue this dance for hours. Days. Maybe even years.

No, I can't go there.

He pulled back then. "Rachel, tell me you want more." His eyes were heavy, his voice so deep it pulsed down her body.

"I want more." So much more.

"That's all I needed to hear." He guided her to the stairs and lifted her out of the pool.

Her legs dropped down, finding the ground, but they didn't do her any good as they wobbled beneath her. Thankfully he held her close.

"Come with me." He bent to scoop up his jeans and led her to the side of the redbrick building he'd disappeared into earlier to retrieve ice.

"Where are we going?"

"Somewhere private, where I can guarantee no one will interrupt us." He pushed open a door and flicked at a light switch, but the light didn't turn on. "They must've cut the fuse box. Let's see if the water's still on." He grinned impishly and led her into the room. The sheen of the moon glowed through the high windows.

The water? "Are you testing me, August? You want to see how far I'll follow you?"

"No test, no games. I just want to be with you, Rachel. Do you trust me?"

She nodded hesitantly, still unsure what he was up to. She glanced around the shadowy room, seeing that it was good-sized with metal lockers covering two walls. In the corner was a large shower with several shower-heads. In the center stood a toolbox, buckets of paint, and various carpentry equipment, all piled neatly. She smelled the scent of fresh construction—cut wood and newly painted walls.

"They finished remodeling a few days ago. Looks like they haven't cleaned up the tools yet." He gave her a reassuring smile that didn't do anything to ease her nerves.

"August, I have a confession," she blurted, her anxiety hitting a peak. "I admire spontaneous people. I'm attracted to them. To *you*. But I'm not spontaneous. Not in the least. So you should understand I'm incredibly wary right now."

He tugged her into another embrace and kissed her, making her legs weak again.

"We can leave, but I don't want to say goodbye yet. Where do you want to go? I'll take you anywhere. I just want to be with you."

His raw honesty was refreshing. And stunning. So much so that he left her speechless. Her mouth went dry, and the fluttering of her heart upgraded to a temple-pounding pulse.

She was falling so very hard.

So what now? Take the plunge and prepare for heartache?

Her entire body leaned toward him as if to answer her own question. She didn't have a choice. No matter how much she tried to deny their attraction, the draw was too strong.

"I want to make you feel good, honey. So I'll ask you again—do you trust me?"

Absolutely, yes. She nodded again. If she weren't utterly in lust with the man coaxing her forward, she'd leave and go somewhere safe and familiar. Somewhere well-lit where she could see a ghost coming at her from a distance. Somewhere that wouldn't get her booked and fingerprinted, hence ruining her law career before it began.

Ella had better be on duty tonight. Or this budding relationship with August would end before it began.

He dropped his jeans on a wooden bench and led her to the showers. Her body trembled as he turned the knob to the faucet and waited as the water heated.

Okay, they were going to shower together. That would be nice. She'd never showered with a man before. In fact her experience with men—one man—was limited. No, spontaneous she was not.

Just relax. Breathe.

To ease her anxiety, she directed her full attention to August. Which wasn't difficult. His wet cotton boxers clung to his skin, and Rachel let herself admire his athletic physique as he tested the water temperature. The tightness of his muscled legs, the just-right roundness of his ass. The way his lean waist sculpted up to a broad back and wide shoulders.

"I like the way you look at me." He caught her staring and returned the favor, searching her body with his heavy gaze. A heated moment passed before he waved her over. "Come here."

Steam rose from the tiles, playing with the streams of moonlight pouring in and clouding the air around them. She dropped her arms to her sides and moved toward him.

She liked the way he looked at her too—eager and hungry. That and the misty ambience lightened her mood and allowed her to pretend she was more impulsive than she gave herself credit for.

She was here, anyway. Down to her underwear in a locker room of the public pool in Curlville, Indiana, two hours from home.

Just go with it. Be fearless, like Becca. Her sister would be impressed.

Heck, she was impressed with herself.

She followed his lead as he dipped under the shower and let the water stream down his head, over his muscled chest. He looked so damn good she couldn't help but place her hands to his pecs and let them travel slowly down his abdomen.

He drew in a sharp breath and tugged her arms around him, taking her mouth again. The kiss was wet and lush but didn't last long as his lips found their way along her neck, over her collarbone. Then to her breast.

Her lower belly pulsed.

His fingers glided up her arms to her shoulders, where he eased her bra straps down. One hand slipped around to unclasp the back. The lace hit the floor and his hand covered one breast. One bare breast.

Oh wow. She hadn't been touched in so long. The sensations sparking through her were almost overwhelming. But he caught her gaze and held it—the look in his eyes both inspiring and soothing.

"You have a perfect body, Rachel." He massaged her lightly, rubbing his thumb over her nipple. "Every inch of you…" He let his words fade and bent to take her nipple into his mouth.

Rachel almost lost her footing. But his hands gripped her waist and held her secure. "August." She couldn't think of what to say. So she clamped her lips shut and just enjoyed the moment.

The shower water trickled between them, heating her already feverish body. He moved to her other breast as his thumbs slipped into the sides of her panties and tugged them down, down.

They fell to the tiles, and August's fingers slid between her thighs and found her heated spot.

Catching her breath, she gripped his shoulders. He released her breast and found her mouth again, covering her racing breaths. Something about his taste calmed her. Though the calm didn't last long. Not when his fingers worked her in spots that'd been starved for so long.

Yes, right there. Oh, yes.

She rocked against his hand as the beautiful pressure built. Smoldering hot, the sensation climbed until…wow. She moaned against his mouth as the waves rolled through her. Shattering her. Shaking her to her core.

When she finally sank back to earth, she realized his arm was around her in a tight embrace, one that had allowed her to completely give into the pleasure while remaining on her feet. His other arm slipped around her as well.

He held her like that until her body stopped trembling, and then he reached behind them to shut off the water, only leaving her for a moment.

"Did we just do that?" she asked, her mind still fuzzy.

His chuckle was low and heated against her cheek. "Absolutely, positively the sexiest orgasm I've ever heard in my life."

"Heard?" Geez, what had she sounded like?

"Oh, yeah. I want to take you home and discover what other responses I can get out of you."

Her cheeks burned so hot she thought he must feel it against his skin.

"Don't say no," he said against her ear.

"What about the boys?"

"They'll be in bed upstairs. They'll never know. Besides, they're not little kids anymore. Zach has been giving me shit about not having a girlfriend in a long time. You'd be saving my reputation if they did happen to find out."

She felt his smile against her forehead before he pressed his lips there.

"What would Ella say?"

He paused, tensed, and Rachel fought the urge to tilt her head up to see his expression. Whether the gossips in town had gotten to him or not, maybe now—as she stood there naked in his arms—wasn't the best time to mention his deceased sister. But she couldn't help it. Ella was still very much a concern, even if August didn't realize it.

"I'd like to think Ella would want me to be happy." He relaxed his tense body and lazily ran his knuckles along her jaw. "You make me happy, Rachel."

She couldn't remember when she'd felt this happy.

And being in August's arms all night would be a fantasy come true. She wasn't sure she could fall much harder than she already had. How would that even feel?

"Okay."

"Okay?"

"Yes." She wanted to spend the night with him. No matter the consequences.

The next few minutes passed by at warp speed as he quickly dried them both off with towels found by the showers and gathered their items to dress.

Her mind was still in a haze when they started on foot back to his house.

"Did you lock the gate?" she asked as an afterthought.

"Yes."

"And you're sure it'll be okay if I spend the night?"

He chuckled and brought her hand up to kiss her knuckles. "Yes. Nothing to worry about."

Just as he uttered the sentence, a police car turned onto the street and headed their way.

"Oh, no." She took a sharp step back, tripping over her own feet.

"It's all right." August helped right her balance. "I know this guy." He gripped her hand and held securely as the police car pulled to a stop.

A middle-aged man, grey hair and thick black glasses, waved to them. "Dr. Kline, miss."

"Hey, Sheriff Moody. How are you doing tonight?" August walked up to the car window, forcing Rachel to go along with him. At least the two seemed friendly.

"Sheriff, this is my girlfriend, Rachel." He gave Rachel a sexy grin as "girlfriend" exited his lips, and her heart alternated to a different beat, a different excitement. "Rache, this is Sheriff Louis Moody. He's been keeping Curlville safe for a long time."

"Much too long." The sheriff chuckled. "Nice to meet you, Rachel. I've heard a bit about you from the

169

ladies in town, including my wife, Dolly."

"Nice to meet you, too, Sheriff. Hopefully I'm not disturbing the peace too much."

"Not at all. I think it's kind of you to help a family out. And any friend of our sweet Ella is a friend of ours." His tone was genial, but his scrutinizing gaze didn't miss a thing. Either he was ignoring August's and her damp hair and clothing or he was thinking of a way to bust them. It was obvious they'd just come from the pool.

"Thank you." The less said the better.

He nodded and veered his gaze to August. "You locked the pool back up, didn't you?"

"Yes, sir." August squeezed her hand. "Just taking a dip. We left everything as is."

"That's fine. Just want to make sure we keep it secure with all the young children running around."

"Of course. It's all secure."

"Good." The Sheriff leaned out the window more. "Hey, August, I need to warn you about something, and I'm not sure you're going to like it too much."

"Oh? What's that?" August rested a hand on the car and leaned in, concern on his face.

"It's the damndest thing, but I've had a report of someone seeing Ella's ex-husband driving around town. Ole Grant Golding. The person who reported the sighting says it's either him or someone who has a strong resemblance. You aren't expecting him, are you?"

August took a step back and wiped a hand down his face, dropping her hand in the process. "He's in town. Shit."

"Is everything all right?" Rachel hoped so.

"Zach and Nick's biological father," August said, looking perturbed. "He called me the other day and said he was interested in seeing the boys."

"Well, that's a shame," the sheriff said. "He never was much of a father to them. And the way he left town and didn't return—" He shook his head. "He should stay gone, as far as I'm concerned. He did nothing but stir up trouble when he was here. Those boys are lucky to have a stable father figure like you to step in."

"Sheriff, I appreciate your support," August said, but still looked a shade too pale.

"Of course. Ella always spoke fondly of you. And you've been an upstanding citizen since you've moved here. A splendid addition to Curlville. Not to mention Dolly won't stop talking about how you've been helping her with her carpal tunnel issues."

"Thank you, sir. Your wife's an ideal patient. She actually listens to me." August's smile eased the moment. Did he have any idea how he affected people? How he affected her?

"Dolly's happy to have a doctor who's actually studied up on the subject," the Sheriff said. "Dr. Williams was somewhat old-fashioned, God bless his soul."

"I'm happy to help."

"Good, good." Sheriff knocked his knuckle on the car door. "Say, if Grant does anything funny like trying to take over custody, you let us know and we'll stand up for you. We'll put in a good word. Got it?"

"Moody, that means more than you know."

"Any time. I'd like to have a word with him too, so if you happen to see him, give me a holler, would you?"

"You bet. Anything wrong?"

"Just have some questions for him about an old case I got a hunch about. Nothing time sensitive though."

August put an arm around Rachel, gathering her close. "We'll keep an eye out, and I'll let you know if I hear from him again. If he's in town to get Nick and Zach back, he's going to have a fight on his hands."

The sheriff drove off, leaving them to finish their walk home.

"Do you think he'll fight for custody?" Rachel couldn't help but ask. Grant Golding didn't sound pleasant.

"I don't know why he would after all this time. Narcissists don't tend to care about anyone but themselves. That's how I remember him, anyway. And he hasn't proven me wrong yet."

She squeezed August's hand and rubbed her thumb against his palm. He seemed on edge, judging from his acid tone and the taut angles of his face.

"I'd stand up for you too, August." She stopped in front of him, forcing him to face her. "In case you wanted to know. I think you're a wonderful father."

"You're sweet to say that. I sometimes wonder if they'd be better off with someone else."

"I think it's normal to feel that way. I'm sure a lot of biological parents could probably relate. But you heard what the sheriff said. And I agree. Those boys are lucky to have you."

His gaze warmed as he reached up to caress her cheek. "I'm the lucky one."

The odd heart flutter began anew. "I'll have to agree with that. You are pretty lucky. Want to go home and test that?"

"God, yes. What are we waiting for?"

Chapter Fifteen

Bounce. Scoop. Catch. Bounce. Scoop. Catch.

The noise wouldn't stop. Nick rolled on his side and glanced at the clock on his nightstand. It was just past midnight. *Not cool.*

He glared at Joanna's somber moonlit profile. "Joanna, I gotta get some sleep. I have a chemistry test tomorrow."

"That woman is in the house with your uncle. Don't you care?"

"Why would I?"

"It's a sin. They should be married before they lie in the same bed."

"Oh, man. This is why you're upset? Get over it, Jo. Not everyone has the same beliefs as you. Ever heard of live and let live?"

"Bad things happen when you behave like a heathen."

"Bad things happen, huh?" Nick sat up. "Give me an example."

Joanna made cryptic comments like this all the time. It was annoying that she didn't just come out and spill what had happened to her before she died.

"I'm too ashamed." She let the ball drop and watched

it roll away.

Very dramatic.

"Like I'd care what you did years ago. Everyone makes mistakes. Get it off your chest already. Maybe then you can move on to heaven, like you talk about all the time."

She gathered the ball and jacks and pushed them under his dresser where she liked to keep them. "It's not that easy... But you should know."

"*What's* not easy?" he said, feeling grumpy. If he didn't get some sleep, he wasn't going to be able to concentrate at school tomorrow. Yet he couldn't help but ask. At least he might finally find out what'd been eating at Joanna for so long. And what'd been keeping her from moving on.

Not that he wanted her to go all that bad.

"It's about your dat." *Dat.* Must be her Amish word for "dad."

Dad?

"My dad?" A cold chill flushed through Nick. Hearing anyone mention his dad always gave him the creeps, but he never let it get to him. He remained composed, shaking off the ugly feeling.

"Yah. Your dad." She switched her pronunciation. "He did bad things." She spoke so fast that Nick had to process the words a little longer than normal.

Then he got it.

"Whatever," he said, both dreading and wanting to hear what Joanna had to say. So she'd known his dad? So what? "I definitely don't care about him. Why should I? He never cared about me." Nick jumped to his feet and paced at the foot of his bed.

Joanna clamped her lips shut.

"Well?" He waved his hands. "What the hell did he do?"

"You shouldn't curse like that."

"Tell me, Joanna."

"Shh. You'll wake Zach."

"He falls asleep with his head phones on. Just tell me already. You can't bring up my dad and then act all righteous. What did he do? Did you know him?"

"Yes, I knew him." She picked at a thread on her dress. "I knew your mam too."

My mom. Nick gulped, his eyes instantly stinging like they did whenever someone mentioned his mom. But he repressed the sadness and replaced it with anger. "What the hell, Jo? You knew them in real life? Like not as a ghost?"

"I'm not a ghost. And I did know them. I did." Her eyes brimmed with redness, but Nick couldn't stop being mad.

"Why the hell didn't you ever tell me?"

"Please stop cursing."

He clenched his fists and tried not to freak out. Although he was close to losing it. She'd never told him she'd known both his parents in real life. He'd always assumed she'd died years and years ago. Look at the way she dressed, with her long brown dress and bonnet. The way Amish girls dressed hadn't changed in centuries. At least he didn't think so, since it was against their beliefs to dress in modern clothing. They always wore plain handmade dresses in dull colors.

He thought back to when he first saw Joanna but couldn't remember. She'd always been there. First in the shadows, watching him at times. But she'd never fully showed herself until a couple years ago, when they'd started to be about the same age.

"So when did you die?" He tried his best to mellow out his tone. Otherwise, she'd never tell him anything. Though he wasn't quite sure he wanted to know where this story was heading.

"Why do you always ask me that? I don't want to remember."

"But you do remember. So might as well tell me.

We're friends, right?"

She rolled her eyes and nodded. "You don't understand. Your dat…" Her mouth scrunched up, pouty and mad.

"Joanna," he began carefully, going with his first hunch. "Did my dad hurt you?"

She got that stubborn look on her face, the one that told him she was done talking. A watery wall of tears brimmed her pretty eyes, and one broke free, snaking down her cheek. He felt bad for her, but he needed to know.

"Jo, you can't leave me hanging like this. Did he hurt you?"

She swiped at the tears and then crossed her arms. "I saw him with the neighbor woman," she whispered so low Nick almost didn't hear her. Almost.

"Dana?"

"Yah. The worldly, godless woman who lives across the street. She's no good."

"What do you mean you saw them? What were they doing? Talking?"

She shook her head. Her cheeks darkened in the moonlight.

"Were they kissing? Making out? What?"

Her entire face beamed red as she continued to whisper. "I came over early to help your mam prepare supper for you. But she wasn't here. I heard noises upstairs."

"How did you know my mom?"

"I helped her. She paid me to watch over you and Zach and to help her clean the house some times. She was busy with work. And she had to drive to Indianapolis almost every day. Sometimes she stayed the night there so she didn't have to drive."

"Holy crap." Nick walked to Joanna and stood above her slouching body. "You used to be my babysitter?" Flashes of old buried memories sprouted from somewhere in his mind. He remembered her as she used to be. A real live person. "I sorta remember you."

She stood and re-crossed her arms. "You were so little. I couldn't let you see what your dat was doing in your home, so close to you. You and Zach were playing in the room next door. Just playing like good boys. I couldn't believe your dat would leave you alone and go do something so evil. He was not a good man. He was not a good father."

Nick swallowed and pressed his hand to his racing heart. "What happened then?"

"I'm only telling you because you need to be careful. He's back again."

"Who's back? My dad?"

She nodded.

"Shit." She couldn't be serious. Besides, she never left the house, so how would she know?

"I do too leave this house," she said. "Just never when you're here. I need to protect you from him. Now that he's back, now that you've become a man, you should know everything. You must be careful and help me protect Zach."

"Okay, fine." He'd play along. He wasn't sure he could believe whatever she was about to confess, but he'd pretend he did. If only to find out what she'd been hiding for so many years.

"I don't lie."

"Right. 'Cause it's a sin. I get it. But there's this little thing called lying by omission. Ever heard of that?"

She shook her head, looking toward the floor. "I didn't learn that in school. What does that mean?"

"Never mind," he said, frustrated. "Just spill it, Joanna. Like you said, I'm a man now. I can take it."

She pushed a lock of stray hair back into her bonnet and cleared her throat. "I knew what they were doing. It's adultery. And that's—"

"A sin. Right. Then what?"

177

"I saw you boys alone, all alone. And I heard the noises in the next room." Her cheeks flared anew. "Like the noises my mam and dat used to make when they were alone in the bedroom. But I didn't hear your mam. I heard another woman. She yelled your dat's name, and I knew right away he was sinning." Joanna's face blazed a shade darker.

"Who was it?"

"You were only five and your brother just three, and you were left alone in your bedroom. You were so good, caring after Zachary. But I got angry. I'd seen the way your dat had looked at that woman before. The neighbor lady."

"Dana Finnegan? Are you sure?"

Joanna twisted her lips, her disgust apparent. "Yes, that's the one. And I'd seen how she looked at him, how she'd touched him like only a wife should. So I knew it was her in there with him." She paused as her expression tightened.

"Go on, Jo."

"Fine. I got mad and I opened the door. It was wrong of me to intrude on your dat's privacy, but I couldn't help it. I lost my temper, and I marched in on them, and I yelled for him to stop it right that instant."

Nick would've laughed—Joanna had the worst temper—but he didn't like where this story was going. Especially because Joanna stood here now as a ghost, not a living breathing person.

Something bad had happened.

"Then what?"

Her red-rimmed eyes widened, glossy. If she could get any paler, she did just that.

"Joanna, please tell me. It's okay."

"Your dat sent the woman home. He looked angry. I was glad, but a little bit scared too. I used to get spankings from my dat, but he'd never looked at me like your dat looked at me that day. Not with so much hate."

"I don't remember that. Sorry. I don't remember

much about him at all."

"You're better off not knowing what he was like." She reached out to touch Nick but seemed to think better of it. "Anyway, I got you and Zach cleaned up, and I made you supper. I did my job just like your mam wanted me to. She was running late again. Your dat was supposed to go to work at the sugar factory—they were shutting it down for good that week. He always left at seven, but he didn't leave that day. He waited in his room until after I bathed you boys and put you in bed."

Nick's head started to get dizzy so he sat on the floor against the wall and brought his legs up to his chest.

He always knew his dad was a jerk. What kind of person would just up and leave his family? But Nick never thought his biological father would turn out to be a monster. What would that say about Nick?

"So what did he do? Was it an accident?" He chanced a sliver of hope.

"No, it wasn't an accident," she said, anger rising in her voice. "That was no accident. I was going back downstairs to clean up before your mam got home, and he pushed me. He came up behind me and pushed me hard. I couldn't stop myself from falling down those steps." She swiped at a tear. "I hit my head on the last step, and I hurt something awful. All over. But not for long. I went right to sleep."

"Joanna. Are you sure?" Nick's heart fell to his stomach. The stairs were steep and dark when the lights were off. Maybe Joanna had fallen.

"I told you I don't lie," she bit out, and Nick's alarm clocked blinked.

"Okay, okay. I believe you. But shit. That's pretty messed up if it's true."

"It is true. And that's not all he did. He's evil, Nicholas. An evil, evil man."

"Jesus. If he murdered you, what could get worse than that?"

"I woke up later, but I had to leave my body." Her eyes glossed over. Her face crinkled. "I rushed inside to see if you and your brother were safe. Nicholas—"

"What?" He felt cold. Chilled.

"You were the only one who could see me. Even then you saw me. So I stayed. And waited." She sat back against the dresser, as if the story had taken the breath out of her.

"I'm so sorry, Jo." What more could he say? "Did anyone find out what happened?" Stupid question. He would've heard about this at some point.

"When my dat came over looking for me, your dat told him he thought I ran away. He said I'd borrowed a suitcase and clothes from the neighbor lady." Joanna swallowed hard and a flood of tears broke loose. "My dat knew I'd been talking to an English boy, the same boy who had left for Florida a week earlier. Michael had wanted me to go with him and I'd told him neh. I would never leave my family. I'd never be shunned from my church for any reason. But my dat had seen the two of us talking in the barn. He'd seen the boy kiss me."

"And your dad believed that you left to go to him?"

"Yah. And I couldn't use my voice to tell him it wasn't true. He couldn't see me like you can. He was sad I would leave, but he believed I would go."

"I'm so sorry, Joanna. I'll tell the cops. I'll tell your dad. I'll tell everyone about what really happened."

"No." She sniffed back more tears. "You have to be careful or he'll hurt you too. All your dat wants is the money, and then he'll leave."

"Wait. Money? What money?"

Chapter Sixteen

August didn't have time to worry about the loaded laundry basket he'd hidden under the piano. Rachel had his entire attention. Her hands were everywhere. His shoulders, his chest, his stomach...lower.

Damn. He was going to lose it before he had his pants off.

He walked backwards, kissing her soft lips while leading her to his bed. No noise from upstairs meant good news. But he'd made sure to lock his door just in case Nick or Zach came down and decided to pop into his room.

Only question was why the hell was he thinking about his nephews when a sexy, beautiful woman was eagerly unbuttoning his jeans and slipping her hands inside?

"Rachel. You're turning me on, honey." He smoothed his hands down her back and gripped her ass, lifting and swiftly laying her on his bed.

She laughed and cradled his jaw. "I love being with you."

"Same here." He wanted to say more but couldn't seem to get anything else past his lips. He'd already laid his heart out for dissection earlier and was still waiting for an answer.

"Really. I'm comfortable with you." Her smile disappeared into something more somber. "That's rare for me. To give and to trust."

What did that say about her other relationships? Probably wasn't the best time to bring that up. Again.

"I'm glad to hear it." He slipped his hand into her hair, still damp from the pool. "I've already told you how I feel about you."

Tell me I'm your guy.

"I know. Thank you."

Thank you? Not what he wanted to hear.

But he wasn't going to ruin the moment. He had her right where he wanted her. In his arms. About to be naked.

He kissed her lips and began working on her top, slipping it up over her silken skin. Her hands got back to work as well. Together, they had each other's shirts off in no time.

In the low lamplight, August took a moment to appreciate her soft, pale breasts contrasting against her rosy nipples. So damn beautiful. She'd left her bra off to dry. And her panties. She'd draped them over the piano bench before she'd attacked him. Which was all good with him. The less clothing the better.

He unsnapped her cotton shorts and pulled down the zipper. She lifted her bottom, and he tugged the shorts onto the floor. Immediately his eyes went to the juncture between her thighs. A pretty triangle of reddish blond hair covered her mound.

How could any woman be this perfect?

Her knees clasped together and he could tell she was getting shy. *Uncomfortable.*

Think of something funny to say.

No! Not funny. Save funny for later. In fact, don't say anything at all.

He'd never been this nervous before. Could be because it'd been a while since he'd had sex. More likely because he'd never felt this strongly for a woman.

Don't overanalyze, he told himself as he held up his finger for her to wait and then finished undressing. His mad dash to yank off his jeans seemed to make her smile. Then her gaze fell to his erection, hard as could possibly be, and she bit into her bottom lip.

"I just need to..." He let his words fade as he reached into his pocket to pull out his wallet and then a condom.

Before long he was beside her again, drawing her into his arms, and kissing her as though she might disappear if he didn't do it just right.

Her slim body molded into his. Her hand grasped his jaw. Her lips and tongue moved with his, tasting and enjoying. Flesh against flesh, he was in a blissful state of heaven.

He ran his hand along the curve of her waist and along her soft belly. His fingers slid lower over the soft hair of her mound, then into her wetness. She was ready.

A soft moan vibrated from her throat as he delved one finger into her. Her legs spread for him as she lay on her back, cluing him in that she wanted to get to the really good stuff.

August moved on top of her, wedging himself between her long legs and lean thighs. She was trembling, and he remembered she'd said she'd only been with one man. Which made him want to do everything possible to erase that memory from her mind and replace it with a new one.

Just him. No one else.

Call him selfish, but this woman was his.

In the low light, he watched her expression as he inched inside of her. Impassioned brown eyes stared up at him with an intensity that gave him chills. Her pretty lips were slightly agape, and her cheeks flushed. She lifted her hips in motion with him. Perfect harmony. *My God, she's incredible.* He contributed to the rhythm by grasping one hand to her ass and driving in deeper and faster.

She was snug and warm. Perfect.

His.

Their lips lingered and gave lusty, slow kisses, as they drove each other to a crescendo. He felt her body tense, her muscles growing tighter and tighter.

"Let go, baby."

Her head fell back against the pillow and her mouth gaped open, her eyes clenched shut.

"Oh, wow." She breathed. "Oh, wow. Oh, wow. Oh, wow." Her voice grew louder with each "wow."

August would've smiled—even her orgasms were sexy-adorable—but he was coming to a fast release as well. He gripped her ass harder and thrust forward again and again.

Her fingernails dug into his back as her inner muscles contracted around him. Intense pressure built until he couldn't last another moment. Then he let go, a rush of bliss—of heaven—as he came into her. His body dropped onto hers, and she wrapped her arms around him. Her lips pressed against his cheek.

"August," she whispered, her body no longer tense under his.

He sighed and nuzzled her neck. Lord, he was a goner.

They lay like that for several minutes until August figured he'd better relieve her of his weight. But she grabbed his shoulders and held him down for another kiss.

"Thank you," she said, looking way too serious. "That was wonderful."

He couldn't stop a grin. "No need to thank me. We can do it again in about ten minutes. My treat."

She laughed, raspy and sexy, successfully lowering the ten minutes to oh, about, zero. He eased out of her, trying to hide the effect she had on him.

"I'm not kidding." He grinned wider, cuddling her naked body to his. "In fact, you can be my sex slave for the rest of the night. I'll bring you food and water, but you're not leaving this bed."

"That sounds kind of nice."

Holy shit.

"Let me get the handcuffs," he teased. "I think I left them upstairs."

"Go get 'em."

Her poker face was killing him. And left him no choice but to play along.

"Oookay. You asked for it." He slowly got out of bed—hating that he was moving from her sexy body—and disposed of the condom.

He pulled on his jeans while she snuggled up in his bed, getting comfy with his blankets and pillow. Like she belonged there.

"Not scared?" he said, feeling a pit growing in his stomach.

He could tease and joke all he wanted, but this thing between them had become much more than the casual affairs he'd had in the past.

Rachel's lips twisted into a small smile. "Can you bring me an apple while you're at it?"

Ha. Very cute. "How 'bout a whip and chains? A flog?" He lifted an eyebrow in challenge.

"How about whipped cream and strawberries? I play nice."

He dropped his head back, staring at the ceiling, silently thanking whatever mysterious force of nature had brought this woman to his bed—to his life.

"August?"

"Yep. I'm here." He adjusted his jeans and appreciated the relaxed, just-had-sex, satisfied look that had settled on her face. "So whipped cream and strawberries. Do we, uh, have those?"

"We do." She nuzzled her head deeper into his pillow. "I made the boys strawberry shortcake for dessert. There are leftover strawberries and half a can of whipped cream. Hurry up before I fall asleep. Your bed is comfy."

He watched her for a moment too long, revering in

185

how the soft pale curves of her body intertwined and contrasted with his dark navy comforter. Damn, he wished he had a camera.

"Is something wrong?" She planted her head on her hand, looking somber again.

"Not at all. I'll be right back. Don't move." He winked, swallowed down whatever the hell was stuck in his throat, and tore up the stairs.

~ * ~

Strawberries and cream. Rachel still tasted the sweet flavor as she licked the last of the stickiness from the corner of her mouth. She fisted the blanket as she thought about how the whipped cream mess had gotten on her lips in the first place.

In the dark of the room—in the company of August—it had been easy to allow herself to be intimate. Passionate.

Too easy, as if she'd transformed into an entirely different person. Carefree and playful. Desirous and desirable.

She'd wanted August with an enthusiasm she'd never felt before.

But now, as August's arm wrapped securely around her waist, his slumbering body naked against her backside, she was back to her usual self. The passion had subsided, they'd snuggled up close, he'd fallen asleep...and her mind had renewed its exhausting goal to finish the never-ending race of worry and anxiety.

So she'd had sex with him. Twice. Incredible, toe-curling, wowing sex. And it was her own fault. She'd known it would change her...*them*. She'd known she'd fall harder for him. And yet she'd nearly torn his clothes, shedding them, so she could get closer to him. To touch him. To know him that way. Any and every way. Like she was obsessed, which she supposed she was.

Her grip on the comforter tightened and her shoulders started to pinch.

Now what? Tell him the truth about why she'd bombarded his life?

No.

She'd lose him. She'd lose Nick and Zach too. Somehow she'd grown to care for them in different ways. Spending day after day with them, in their home, hadn't helped. Now she couldn't imagine never seeing them again. How painful would that be, saying goodbye? Worse, not being able to say goodbye?

If August discovered her little secret, he'd want her gone. And she wouldn't blame him. No sane man would invite such craziness into his life, whether he believed her or not.

God, what was Ella going to say about this night of temporary insanity? Rachel—the woman who was supposed to be caring for Ella's family—was breaking laws and having food-play sex with her brother.

Okay, so maybe the whipped cream had been kind of fun...

"Rache, you dreaming?" August's sleep-heavy voice by her ear startled her.

"No," she said too loudly, and then lowered her voice. "No. I'm awake. I thought you were sleeping."

"Mmm. Can't. Figure I better keep one eye open in case my sex slave tries to escape." He shifted, giving Rachel the chance to turn and face him, the comforter bundled safely between them.

"I wasn't going to leave," she said truthfully, tamping the urge to push a lock of his hair away from his forehead. The dim light coming from the basement window did nothing to stop her obsession to touch him.

"Good. I'm glad." He ran his knuckles along her cheek. "Anything wrong? Your body was tensing up."

"Nothing's wrong. I'm fine." Time to change the subject. "You never told me how your day went. With the delivery."

"Right." He rubbed his jaw and yawned. "I need to

leave early to check up on them. In a couple hours."

"Is the baby okay? Did something go wrong?" Rachel gave into her need to touch him. She moved the comforter out of the way and snuggled into his body heat, hoping she was comforting him as much as he soothed her.

"No. Nothing like that. Mom was a pro, laboring for only a few hours, and the baby was healthy." He swallowed. "They named him August."

"That's sweet. You must be so proud." She squeezed his hand.

"I am."

"You don't look happy about it. Afraid they'll call him Auggie?" she teased.

Expecting his warm chuckle, she got a frown instead. "That's not it."

"Tell me then." She inched back just enough to read his expression.

"I had an epiphany, Rache," he said, looking hesitant. "The baby arrived and started crying, and I couldn't stop smiling. My entire body warmed, and I experienced this feeling of euphoria I'd never felt before."

"That's good, right? What was the epiphany?"

He kissed her forehead. "You want to hear this? Aren't you tired?"

"You can't stop now, August. My curiosity is piqued."

Finally, a smile curved his lips. "Thing is, honey, I realized the reason I felt so much was because I knew this family well. I cared about them. I'd never really had that chance before. To know my patients on that level. In New York, I'd burned out hard. In the practice I was in, volume was more important than time with the patient. The waiting room was always packed, and we were booked back-to-back every day. I was tired all the time. Always worried I'd miss something abnormal on a lab report or order the wrong test. The reward of helping an occasional patient didn't outweigh my nerves or seeing some patients get sicker and sicker. I didn't want to simply prescribe a drug and send them out the door, but at times that's all I could do."

"That sounds incredibly stressful."

"It was, and delivering this baby brought back some of those feelings."

"Were you worried about the delivery?"

"Yeah, I'll always have that in me. It isn't smart to be overly confident."

"Makes sense."

"But helping a family I knew was different. My stress wasn't so much about what I thought I might miss. It was more pressure of making sure everything was okay for them."

Rachel traced his jaw, his scruff soft against her fingertips. "So being a family physician in this small-town environment brought out a new side of you. An unexpected side effect."

"So it seems." His hand slipped over her hip, pulling her closer. "Ella would be happy. For the first time, I got a rush out of being a doctor. I'd always thought I'd quit medicine once the boys weren't dependent upon me anymore. Now I'm not so sure."

Rachel yawned, content as August wrapped her up in his arms. "It's a lot to think about."

"Agreed. Good thing I have time."

"You do. And Ella would be proud of you no matter what. Nothing mattered to her more than family, and you're her brother." It wasn't a lie. Ella's spirit wouldn't still be around if she didn't care deeply for her family.

"Do you think so?"

"I have no doubt."

"Good to hear, honey."

"Is there anything I can do?" she asked. "I mean, to help you decide?"

His hand moved slowly down her thigh. "Having you naked and against me is about all I could ask for."

"I think I can do that." She laughed and playfully

flung her leg over his hip.

"Much better." He skimmed his hand over her bottom. "I can't deny I haven't been thinking about teaching music at the high school. I could look into it. You know, as a part time gig. Or maybe set up my own teaching studio out of the house."

"To appease your passion for music?"

"It couldn't hurt. If the boys don't mind, that is. I don't want to tarnish their reputations."

"Their cool uncle who used to be in a rock band? Teaching music? Somehow I don't think they'd mind."

"You think I'm cool?"

"Mmm hmm. And sexy." She brushed a soft kiss to his neck...a neck that strangely no longer smelled like Hayes. Just August. All August.

He cleared his throat. "What about you? Are you ready to fall into your father's footsteps?"

"Oh, I'm going to pass that damn exam. Mark my words."

"Determination on you is pretty hot. I like it."

"Good." She just wished she was as certain about what she'd do after the bar.

"And after you pass?" The man was a mind reader.

She sighed. "Honestly, I'm not sure. Not at all."

"Whatever you decide, you have my support."

"I'm glad. August?"

"Yeah?" His fingers skimmed along her jaw and combed into her hair. The touch sensual and possessive.

"Let's skip the serious talk until later."

"I can do that."

"Mmm…" She nearly purred as he pressed his growing erection against her center. "Are we giving up on sleep?"

"Definitely."

Chapter Seventeen

Showered and ready to tackle whatever Ella ordered, Rachel headed toward the bedroom door. She'd slept in until nine, surprised August or the boys hadn't woken her as they'd dressed for the day.

"He left a note for you." Ella appeared, blocking her path.

"Where've you been?" Rachel lifted her chin, trying not to appear guilty.

"Around. He taped it to the door so you couldn't miss it. What a sweetheart."

"He is a sweetheart." Rachel slipped past Ella, feeling protective over the man she'd spent the night making love with. She snatched the paper off the door, daring Ella to say anything remotely bad about August.

She read:

Rache,

Strawberry shortcake tonight again? How about dinner first? I want to take you somewhere nice.

Auggie

Rachel's cheeks heated.

"Funny." Ella eyed the note. "I always thought he hated when I called him Auggie."

Rachel shrugged. "Maybe he likes it now."

"Maybe he likes *you*. A lot. When I suggested a relationship, I didn't mean this." Ella pointed at the bed. "Having premarital sex with him under the same roof where my children sleep. I thought you were different." She crossed her arms. "I thought you were a prude."

"Are you serious?" Rachel couldn't tell. Ella's sense of humor bordered on dry. Parched, really.

Either way, her guilt doubled. Maybe she shouldn't have spent the entire night.

Ella tapped her finger on her arm, perusing Rachel as if she'd just been sentenced to purgatory. A look she knew too well.

"You can stop staring at me like that. My mother has dibs on my guilt." Rachel's chest squeezed at the thought. She hadn't returned her mother's deprecating voicemails from last night and this morning, demanding to know where Rachel was spending most of her time. Instead she'd replied with a quick text, fibbing that she was studying at the library.

Lying like a teenager trying to escape punishment. Cripes, what had she let her life come to?

She rubbed at her tight chest. *Relax.* She thought of the breathing technique August had showed her. She closed her eyes, breathed in deeply through her nose, feeling her diaphragm move up into her ribcage, her belly extended outward. She pushed the breath out through her mouth, releasing her tension and worries.

"Are you okay?" Ella said. "I was only giving you a hard time."

Rachel opened her eyes to cast a dirty look the spirit's way, but kept breathing. Deeply in and out.

Ella sighed. "Honestly, do you remember what I told you? Deal with what's making you anxious, and you won't have a need to be anxious anymore."

"I tried that," Rachel blurted, forgetting about her technique. "Helping you was supposed to be easy and quick. But you won't stop fussing. Everything needs to be perfect. The house needs to be perfect. The garden needs to be perfect. August needs to be perfect. Don't you get it?"

"Calm down. You're going to give yourself another panic attack."

"No, I'm not. I'm fine. It's you who needs to loosen up. August has been doing his best. In fact, I can't imagine your sons being in better hands. He's warm. He's funny. He's kind. He isn't holding them on a tight leash. He's letting them have their space but keeping them in sight at the same time. You could learn a little from the way he's raising your sons."

Ella's shadowed cheeks sank in a little deeper. "Are you calling me a control freak?"

"Ha! To say the least. You need to back off, Ella. They're doing just fine without you." As soon as the words spewed out, Rachel wanted to suck them back in.

"Is that so?"

"That's not what I meant to say."

"I know what you meant." Ella crossed her arms. "And if that's what you think, I guess you don't need me either."

"I'm sorry, Ella. I shouldn't have been so harsh."

The doorbell rang, ratcheting up the tension with its loud dong.

"I'll be right back," Rachel said. "Don't leave. We're not done talking."

She ran up the stairs as the doorbell rang a second time. The only other visitors she'd had during the day was the pastor of the local church who'd asked her to come to Sunday service since she "seemed to spend so much time in town."

And Dana.

Please anyone but Dana.

Rather than peek through the peephole, she swung to door open, like ripping off a bandage.

And there she was.

The buxom blond with a pink glittery halter-top and a short white mini-skirt. Her lips, which perfectly matched her top, sneered and lifted into a forced smile.

"Hi there."

"Hi, Dana. How can I help you? August isn't home."

"Well, duh. I knew that. I'm here to talk to you."

Rachel's shoulders almost touched her ears, so she wiggled out the tension and gestured inside. "Would you like to come in?"

"So nice of you but no thanks. Actually, I was wondering if you'd like to go to Dolly's? Loretta mentioned you want to go and asked me to ask you."

"Oh?"

"Yeah. So let's go."

"You mean right now?"

Dana's thickly mascaraed lashes flittered as she gave Rachel a long look. "Unless you want to change first?"

Rachel glanced down at her jeans and fitted T-shirt. Nope, this was all she had left to wear. She'd need to return home and replenish her wardrobe—maybe add in some less casual pieces. Until then, she had to make do.

She briefly thought about turning Dana down, but knew she had to get this over with. The women in town wanted to get to know her. So they'd get to know her— and she'd get to know them. Like Ella had suggested, she needed to face what makes her anxious in order to conquer the anxiety. Right.

"No, I'm ready," Rachel said. "Just give me a second." She closed the door and ran downstairs to apologize once more. But Ella was gone, probably upset. "Damn." She'd simply have to find some way to make it up to her.

Rachel drove separately to Dolly's and parked midway between the salon and August's office. A man was outside his office door, scraping the words off the window. The old physician's name flaked to the sidewalk.

August was finally having it removed.

Yes. Good for him. He was moving on with life—life as he now knew it. Rachel was happy for him. Proud of him.

She was sure Ella would be proud of him too.

Which only reminded her that she could really use Ella's help at the salon. The women undoubtedly wanted to interrogate Rachel about her relationship with their long lost friend.

Ella? Rachel closed her eyes and tried to summon her. *Ella, Ella, Ella. I'm so sorry.*

Nothing.

Okay. So she was on her own. Which was totally fine. She could do this. She was friendly, smart, and sometimes funny.

She could make August laugh, anyway. Picturing his smile in her mind calmed her nerves. She kept it there as she climbed out of her car and walked across the parking lot to Dolly's.

Dana stood at the entrance, talking on her cell phone. "You didn't find it? Why don't you look some more?" She twirled her finger through her hair and stared at the ground. "You have issues... Okay, whatever. The salon's closed anyway."

Her hushed tone made Rachel pause, along with hearing that the salon was closed.

"What's going on?" Rachel said as Dana slipped her phone into her purse.

"What?" Dana swung around, clearly startled. "Oh." She straightened her bunched brows and thumped her palm against her forehead. "You're not going to believe this. Duh. The salon doesn't open until another two hours today. I totally spaced it."

"Really? Shoot," Rachel said, trying to sound convincing. "I was looking forward to getting to know you better." Or finding out what that phone call was about. Whatever it was had left Dana off balance.

"Right." Dana shrugged. "Well, I guess we need to postpone our little pampering date."

"What about Loretta? I thought she'd be here too."

"Loretta? No, she's working."

"I thought the point was to—"

"Look," Dana snapped. "It doesn't matter. We'll just do it another time."

"Okay. Fine with me." What was up with this loon?

"Are you going home too?" Dana said, almost as an afterthought.

"I'm not sure what my plans are yet. Why?"

"Just wondering. You're spending a lot of time at August's. Spent the night last night, didn't ya?"

Rachel didn't respond, too flabbergasted by the woman's nerve.

"Your silence says it all." Dana glared. "So are you going home to Indianapolis anytime soon? Coming back to August's? Or what?"

"Why do you care, Dana?"

"Geez. Don't get all snippy. I'm just curious." Dana adjusted her purse over her shoulder. "See ya around."

"Bye." Rachel scratched her head as Dana strode purposefully back to her car, cranked the engine, and zoomed off. *What the heck was that all about?*

Guess she had the next few hours free since Ella was ignoring her. Rachel glimpsed at August's truck sitting in the parking lot in front of his office. He was already back from the hospital. Baby August must be doing well.

She smiled and wondered how Adult August would react to a spontaneous visit. She needed to talk to him anyway.

And seeing him wouldn't be too awful either. Her stomach fluttered.

Butterflies. When was the last time a man had given her butterflies?

Hayes.

Yep, she needed to talk to August.

~ * ~

Dana shot down Main Street, not thrilled she'd spent her morning trying to play nice with August's friend—a friend that managed to spend last night in August's bed. She assumed anyway. What sane woman would waste all that time cleaning the man's house and not get some booty action out of it?

And August's booty was prime. So Dana couldn't really blame Rachel for the effort. The good thing was now Dana knew why August hadn't responded to any of her advances. Hot blonds weren't his type. He liked redheaded runway-model-thin women. If only she'd known. She could've dieted and had Dolly do her magic with some red tint.

But whatever. Dana pulled into her driveway and cut her engine. Inside her house, she plopped her purse on the kitchen counter and caught sight of Grant sitting at the table.

"So no luck, huh?" she asked, still not sure what exactly he'd been searching for in August's house.

Yesterday, after giving her one of the best orgasms of her life, Grant had asked her to somehow lure Rachel out of the house this morning. He'd planned to look for something Ella had left behind. Something he thought was owed to him.

"Hello?" She hated being ignored.

He raked into his hair as he stared, eyes glazed, at the wall.

"What's up with you?" She remembered he'd mentioned something weird on the phone. Something about hallucinating and wanting to get the hell out of that house. Crazy talk.

"Nothing. I'm fine. But I'll need to get back into that house."

"Good luck with that. The boys will be in and out of there all weekend." She tapped her fingernail on the table. "Unless you want to see them?" He hadn't mentioned them in a while, and Dana began to wonder if they weren't the real reason he was in town.

"Monday, then," he said, dodging the question, a severe look of determination on his face.

"Why didn't you just keep looking today?" She knew better than to ask any more about Nick and Zach. Grant never had been *Father of the Year* material.

"I told you why. I got freaked out. Felt like someone was watching me the whole time. And it was fucking cold in there. I had chills the whole time. And—"

"What?" The man was losing it.

"I thought I saw someone. Someone who's been dead a long time."

"A ghost?" Dana laughed. "Darling, you need to lay off the weed and whiskey."

"I wasn't— Never mind. Shit. You think I'm losing it."

"No. I think you have a whole lot of history in that house. Did you think you saw Ella?"

"No." His face paled two shades. "Nobody important. Nobody that will stop me from getting what I need from that house."

"Are you ever going to tell me what that something is?"

He turned toward her, his lips curving into a smirk. "You sure you can keep a secret with that sexy mouth of yours?"

Dana grinned. "I was able to get the redhead out of the house today, wasn't I?"

"You did good, baby. We're a team."

"So tell me." She slipped onto his lap and kissed his cheek, hoping to warm him up.

"I'm looking for money. A good deal of money."

Dana snorted. "In that house? Is it August's?"

"No, and let me finish. There's a story behind my suspicions."

"Well, go on then. I love a good story."

"You ever heard the reason Ella and I moved to Curlville?"

"Hmm. Sounds familiar. Go on," Dana said.

"We moved here after one of Ella's clients, a woman going through a divorce, mentioned she used to live in my old house." He pointed out the window toward August's. "The woman told Ella some tale about her marriage and family being strong while they lived there. It was all happy times, but as soon as they moved away, apparently everything fell apart. The husband lost his job and started cheating on her. Their son was diagnosed with Leukemia. Their daughter got in a car accident. The works. So the woman tells Ella she wished she'd never moved away from here."

Dana rolled her eyes. "Curlville never did nothing for me, that's for sure. But I remember that family. They weren't so perfect. The wife could have lost about twenty pounds, the kids were snotty brats, and the husband stuck his nose up at everyone."

"Yeah, well, Ella was so entranced by this woman's story she started to do research on this town and that house. She saw the house was for sale. She printed out pictures of it and fell in love with the idea of living here. Then it just so happened I lost my job. We needed to downsize and quick. The house in Curlville was hugely reduced and in foreclosure, so she talked me into moving here. Said it was serendipity."

"I guess I recall Ella telling me this story," Dana said. "What does it have to do with what you're looking for?"

"Before Ella died, I came to see her at her work. Nobody knows this so you need to keep it quiet."

"Of course. Go on."

"We argued, like old times. She yelled that I was an SOB for disappearing and never coming to see the boys. I'd said I was trying to reach out now, and look what it got me—into yet another yelling match."

"You two always fought so much."

"Do you want me to tell you the story, or not?" Grant said, delivering a mean look.

The man needed to have his blood pressure checked. She nodded and Grant continued.

"I'd told Ella I'd start paying child support, and she told me she didn't need my damn money. She had enough money tucked away to pay for the boys' college education and then some."

"Wow. What did she mean?"

"I was shocked too, so I asked her how she got this mystery money. After dilly-dallying around, she finally admitted the previous owner, that divorcee I was telling you about, had given it to her. The woman had gotten her luck back. Her husband came back to her. The son was in remission. The daughter got a huge settlement from the car crash she'd been in. And, you're not going to believe the next part."

"What?" Dana clutched his shirt.

"The woman won the freaking lottery and became a multi-millionaire."

"You're kidding?"

"Nope. The woman visited Ella and wanted to show her appreciation for all Ella had done for her during the divorce. Apparently Ella had listened to the woman cry and sympathized with her, yada, yada. She'd helped the woman through a rough spot. She'd also heard Ella had moved into her old house, and she wanted to help with the maintenance, getting the place all shiny and new. So she gave Ella fifty grand cash, just like that, in a box, wrapped with a bow. Said it was a gift."

"No way. Ella never told me."

"She never told anyone. She never even had the chance to put it in her will, because she died a week later— one day after I talked to her."

Dana stood, feeling a rush of excitement. "You think the fifty grand is inside the house?"

"It has to be. It never showed up in her bank

account. I'm sure August would have mentioned it to someone in town. Doesn't sound like that's the case."

"No, I definitely would have heard about something like that," Dana said.

"I've been thinking about where Ella would hide her valuables. One time I noticed her lifting up a loose plank under our bedroom dresser all secretly so I wouldn't hear her—but I saw her. I looked in there later and found a small case with about two-hundred dollars and this family heirloom necklace she'd gotten from her grandmother."

"The one she told everyone she lost?"

"The same one. I knew she never trusted me, but I let her keep that little secret. Until now. Now she owes me for all the fights, all the nagging, all the secrets. For having to raise her bratty brother. She owes me."

"What would you do with the money if you found it?"

"I told you. I'd take you out of Curlville. We'd get married, go on a nice honeymoon."

"Ooh, that sounds incredible." Dana sat back down in his lap, buzzing with a new type of enthusiasm. Maybe August wasn't the guy for her. Maybe she needed to give Grant a chance.

"Don't get too excited. There's a small amount of debt I owe some bookies. Nothing huge. Just whatever's accumulated in the past couple years or so."

"Oh." Her buzz dulled. "How much?"

"Nothing you need to worry about." He gave her that mean glare again. "You'll get what you want. You just need to help me get that money. You understand?"

"Sure. Like you said, we're a team."

~ * ~

"Stay hydrated," August said to Mrs. Lepsky as he guided her out of his office.

"I understand." She waved the prescription for antacid in her hand. "I'm sure these will help a lot."

"But remember..." He paused when he noticed

Rachel standing in front of Loretta's desk, handing over a clipboard and a check. A check? What was going on here?

"Remember what, Dr. Kline?" Mrs. Lepsky pulled on his sleeve.

"Keep working on the natural remedies. Replace your morning coffee with green tea once in a while. Lessen your meal portion size." His gaze strayed to Rachel turned toward him. *Damn, she's sexy.* "You know, Mrs. Lepsky, the weather's warm lately. Taking a little stroll with Mr. Lepsky every evening will help wonders with both of your heartburn woes. The pool is opening soon too." He grinned. "Swimming is good exercise."

Rachel's lips parted as her cheeks flushed pink. She quickly looked away.

"We'll try anything, Dr. Kline. Thank you." Mrs. Lepsky waved to Loretta. "See ya, Loretta."

"See ya, Connie. Don't forget you're bringing your famous chili to Bunko tomorrow night. The spicier, the better."

"Oh, well—" Mrs. Lepsky sent August a horrified look. "Sorry, Dr. Kline, I signed up for chili a while ago."

"Smaller portions, Mrs. Lepsky," August said, "and you'll be fine." He patted her hand and opened the door for her.

Mrs. Lepsky admired the new name on the door—his name. "Good job," she said, smiled, then left.

August nodded at his retreating patient, waiting until she was out of earshot before he turned. "Chili, Loretta? Are you here to help me or be a pain in the ass?"

"Help you, of course." Loretta batted her eyelashes with feigned innocence. "Anyway, your next scheduled patient is running late. And Ms. Rachel Spencer is here for a follow-up."

"Hey, honey," August said, his anger diminishing as Rachel walked toward him.

"I hope it's okay that I barged in like this."

"Isn't it sweet she actually paid for her visit this

time?" Loretta said.

August ignored the tyrant and kept his sights on Rachel. "You're not barging. You don't need an appointment. And you're not paying to see me either. That's ridiculous." He led Rachel into the examination room, bellowing, "Tear up that check, Loretta, and then go to an early lunch," as he shut the door.

"Are you sure?" Rachel asked.

"Don't ever encourage that woman." He backed her against the exam table, all the while trying to keep his hands off her body—the same body he'd kissed and studied into the early morning hours. "You okay? Anything happen?"

"I'm fine. I just wanted to see you, to talk to you. Last night was pretty intense. In a good way," she added.

"I agree." Damn, it was hard to hold back what he really felt.

Then he thought to hell with it and did what he'd wanted to do since he'd left her that morning. He tilted her head up and kissed her. Her stiff lips softened for him immediately. Her arms reached around his shoulders, holding on. The kiss lingered, passionate, deep.

Until she sighed sweetly and broke away. "I feel guilty taking up your time."

"Believe me, having you in my arms is the highlight of my day. I'm looking forward to taking you to dinner."

"That's part of what I wanted to talk to you about."

"Go on." He braced himself.

"I can't go to dinner tonight. But let me explain." She lifted a finger as he opened his mouth to protest. "First, I wanted to ask you... At the pool, do you remember saying you wanted to be in a relationship with me? Is that still what you want?"

"Yes, definitely." He was glad she was bringing this up and not the other way around. "You have an answer for me?" Let it be a good one.

"I want that too. I want you." She swallowed and

fiddled with his tie. "And no one else. Just you."

"That—" He cut himself off before he bared his entire soul. "That's good to know," he said, dialing down the urge. A tight breath released.

What the hell was wrong with him?

Probably the fact that he was so damn in love with this woman.

"But you can't go to dinner?" he asked, shaking his head.

"I want to, but I need to go home and take care of a few things. My mother has been trying to get ahold of me. And I need fresh clothes. All I have with me is the clothes from yesterday and what I'm wearing."

"That you look incredibly sexy in."

"Funny, August."

She smiled, and he lost the rest of his senses.

"Okay, come back tonight and bring all your clothes with you. Bring everything. Move in with me." *Did he just say that?*

"What?" She laughed softly. "You're joking, right?"

"It's a nutty idea." Big time. "I get that. It's also foolish to deny what we have going on. We're still learning about each other, but I love what I know about you so far."

Her gaze fell to where she had a grip on his tie. She loosened her hold and flattened out the wrinkles. "August," she said, slowly, "we don't know each other that well. There's more than a few things you need to learn about me."

"Maybe. But you can't deny our chemistry, our connection. I can't stop thinking about you."

"I think about you too," she said, sounding hesitant. "August, what if I disappoint you? I may not be the woman you think I am."

"You mean a woman who's sweet, beautiful, smart, and just happens to have a voracious appetite for licking whipped cream off my body?"

Rachel cracked another smile, releasing a soft laugh.

"I'll add sense of humor to the list," August said. "Honey, there's been a lot of things I've been unsure about in my life. You're not one of them. My gut, my heart, my mind, is yelling at me to grab onto you, hold tight, and never let go."

Her eyes widened as she looked up and met his stare. If he didn't shut up, he'd scare her away for sure.

Only he couldn't stop. "I need you to know something about me."

"What?" Her voice lowered to a whisper.

"Too many times I've regretted not telling the people I care about how I feel about them. Before it was too late. I need you to know I care about you more than you probably realize. Anyway—" He stopped himself, knowing he sounded desperate. Too serious.

The woman was attracted to "bad boys." And he was pretty sure bad boys didn't profess their undying love in less than a month of meeting a woman.

"Anyway?" Her hands splayed against his chest as she waited for him to finish.

"Move in with me. It's too time-consuming and dangerous for us to travel so far to see each other, and I like waking up and having you beside me."

"Oh."

"You can study all you want at my place," he added, sensing her hesitation. "You can turn Ella's room into an office. Or we can move into Ella's room, and you can use the basement. I'm open. Just think about it. Okay?"

She gulped, but thankfully didn't run. "Okay. I'll think about it."

Chapter Eighteen

Rachel's largest tote bag, clenched tightly in her hand, was full of necessities to last a week, maybe two. A tote bag wasn't as obnoxious as a suitcase. Definitely not as permanent.

If August changed his mind, she wouldn't feel as rejected. She'd brought only the necessities, not her entire life's worth of possessions. No, those were going into storage—after her lease ended at the end of the month. So if this turned out to be temporary, she wouldn't be homeless. And if it lasted longer than a month, she'd find a new place—this time in her own name, paid for out of her own bank account with money she planned to save while working somewhere in Curlville. At least until after she passed the bar. After that, she'd rethink what to do next.

In any case, she had nothing to worry about. She'd thoroughly thought this through. She had a backup plan for a backup plan.

And the ghosts? As long as she kept her bargain, Ella would help her. She hoped.

Besides, the only ghost inhabiting the Curlville vicinity was in this house. And she was a quiet one. Rachel could deal with that. Plus, Nicholas seemed to have the spirit under control for the most part.

She shut the door behind her and decided to test the theory. "Hello?" She glanced up the stairs, hoping for no paranormal activity.

Given that the boys were at school and August was at work, no one should answer.

"Hello? Anyone home?" she said a bit louder. No response. Not even a bouncy ball.

Good start.

She marched toward the basement door, focused on her objective: find space for her necessities and unpack. August had promised to have half of his closet and dresser cleared out, which was sweet. In fact, he'd been nothing but accommodating and reassuring since she'd agreed to this move.

Her mother, on the other hand, hadn't stopped calling and texting. Even going so far as video-calling at one point, trying to get her point across that this was too soon, Curlville was too far, and August was not the right man for her.

But for the first time in Rachel's life, she stood firm. It was past time to grow up and take charge of her own destiny. Following the path that made her happiest seemed like the most sensible choice, no matter what her mother said. And the thought of spending time with August, Nick, and Zach made her smile.

How could this be wrong?

Several doubts popped into her head, answering that question in various ways. The biggest doubt was the fact that Rachel wasn't being completely truthful with August about why she'd entered his life. And the why wasn't something she felt comfortable sharing. Sharing that bit of info would land her back into her apartment and out of August's life.

Was she being selfish? Probably. But she wanted this. She wanted normal and comfortable. More so, she wanted to fall into August's arms every night and wake up to this family she'd grown to love. Love. She loved them all.

Yes, she was being selfish, but for all the right reasons.

With a refreshed state of mind, she unpacked without a hitch, neatly folding her clothes, placing them in the appropriate drawers, and hanging a few blouses and one cute sundress she'd chosen. Maybe next week she'd bring the rest of her wardrobe.

"You two should get married." Ella's voice startled her out of her reverie.

"Ella, you can't sneak up on me like that." Rachel stashed the tote into the closet and turned to face her visitor.

"Sorry." The coy grin on her face said she was anything but sorry. "Now we're even."

For the hurtful words Rachel had said last time she'd seen Ella. "I'm sorry about what I said."

"Water under the bridge. What you should be worrying about is marrying my brother before moving in with him. Set an example for the boys. Think about what you're teaching them."

"That's a little old-fashioned." Rachel folded her arms in front of her. If she could stand up to her mother, she could win this argument with Ella. "Many couples live together before deciding to marry. It's the smart thing to do."

"So you do want to marry him?" The lawyer in Ella was still alive and thriving, it seemed.

"I didn't say that, Ella. We're simply getting to know each other better without having to drive across the state to see one another."

"Fine. No need to get defensive." Ella extended her arm to feign a nose poke. "To be truthful, I'm glad you're here. My family needs you. And you need them. It's meant to be."

"Wisdom from the otherworld?"

"Just observations. August is a different man from

when you first met him. More focused, less confused. And the boys seem happier, particularly Nicholas."

"I'm glad." She didn't know how true that was, but the sentiment made her proud.

The doorbell rang, chiming from the upstairs.

"It's Dana again," Ella said, her smile flatlining.

Rachel returned the frown. "My new favorite neighbor."

"She comes with the territory, unfortunately. Whatever you do, don't let her get to you. She's an energy sucker. I can see that more clearly now than ever."

"Twenty/twenty hindsight?" Rachel offered as a joke.

Ella didn't look amused.

"Sorry. I'll go see what she wants." She started upstairs. "Unless you already know?"

No answer told her Ella had left or hidden or did whatever it was that she did when she disappeared.

The doorbell chimed again as Rachel made her way across the living room. The energy-sucking vamp was persistent today. This should be entertaining, at least. She straightened her blouse, took a breath, and answered the door. Sure enough, Dana was on the other side. Her hot pink lips stretched into a tight smile.

"Rachel, right?"

Oh, puhleeze. "That's me. Short term memory problems? I heard that can be an issue for menopausal women. How can I help you, Ms. Finnegan?"

Dana's mouth gaped open. "I am not—" A growl rumbled past her too-plump lips. "Never mind." She glanced past Rachel, inside the house. "You all by yourself?"

What, no comeback? No Suzy Homemaker comment? Something about Dana's demeanor seemed off. "Why do you need to know?"

"Silly me. The boys are at school, right?"

"They are. What's going on, Dana?"

"Nothing much." She leaned against the doorjamb,

her gaze still searching the living room. "I saw your car out there and thought I'd stop by. I feel bad about the other day. You know, how the salon was closed, and we didn't get a chance to hang out. I thought we'd try again." She finally met Rachel's eyes. "What do you say? Let's go get those nails done. They can't be looking too hot with all this gardening you've been doing."

"I don't think—"

"You should go with her." Ella's voice whispered in her ear.

Rachel gasped but quickly converted it to a cough. "Excuse me."

"Come on, hon," Dana said, obviously oblivious to Rachel's startled behavior. "It'll be fun. I promise not to bite. And the salon's open this time. I checked."

"Nothing to be afraid of." Ella's somber voice chilled Rachel's skin. She really had this ghost persona down. "Everything will work itself out."

That's slightly cryptic. What's to be worked out?

"Hello?" Dana snapped her fingers too close to Rachel's face.

"Um, yeah. Sounds good."

"Forgive me." Ella moved into view and swatted at Dana's face, her hand slicing through—through—the blond head. "I needed to do that. Now go with her. It's important."

Dana took a step back and rubbed her arms. "Wow, I just got the chills. Weird." She shook her head, and Rachel bit her lips to keep from laughing. "Anyway, are you coming or not?"

"Sure." She stretched out the word, completely unsure of her decision. But she'd trust Ella, who had yet to lead her in the wrong direction.

"Great!" Dana squealed. "Grab your purse."

~ * ~

Rachel drove her own car again, wanting an escape route. And from the way Dana was acting, she'd bet her designer mother-approved wardrobe she wasn't going to want to drive back home with her new neighbor.

Dana pulled her late-model convertible sports car up next to Rachel's, her cell phone to her ear. Her cheeks were flushed as she animatedly threw up her free hand and forcefully pressed the phone shut. She shook her head and exited the car, instantly switching on her smile. *Strange woman*, Rachel thought as she met Dana at the rear of her car.

"Any problems?" Rachel asked, hoping to get the scoop. "With whoever was on the phone?" she added when Dana looked confused.

"Oh, that. No. Just boyfriend drama. Honestly, sometimes it's not worth the trouble." She mumbled the last part.

"I didn't know you had a boyfriend. Who is he?"

"No one you'd know. He's from out of town."

Out of town. Rachel bet she'd hear more about this mystery man once they were inside the salon, so she let it drop and followed Dana inside.

The salon wasn't what Rachel had expected. Instead of stepping onto the set of Steel Magnolias, it seemed she'd walked straight into a metaphysical fair. Himalayan salt water lamps and multi-colored crystals were placed strategically at every workstation. To the right at the front of the shop stood a small table with a deck of tarot cards on top.

A sixty-something woman with round pink cheeks, a bright-teal muu muu, and long black hair bellowed from her workstation. "Hey there, Dana. Who do you got with you?" She held up a steaming curling iron, pointing it at Rachel. Bracelets jangled from her wrist. "Is this the woman causing all the hullabaloo in town? Why, you're just a tiny one. Perfectly harmless. Come on in, darlin'. You're welcome here anytime. My name's Dolly, like the sign says."

This was the sheriff's wife? Interesting couple.

"I'm Rachel." Just in case there was any doubt. "It's nice to meet you." Rachel wasn't sure what else to say, but Dolly's vibrancy did make her feel welcome. She smiled and followed Dana's lead, sitting next to her at the manicuring station.

"Nice to meet you, sweetheart." Dolly wrapped the curling iron around her client's silver lock of hair. "This here is Mimi, my mother-in-law." Dolly shot a surreptitious look Rachel's way, explaining just how she felt about her mother-in-law. "Mimi's a little hard of hearing, so she doesn't like to talk all that much. Isn't that right, Mother?"

The elderly woman looked up from her magazine for the first time since Rachel arrived. "What?" she yelled, and then stuck her nose back in her rag mag.

"Anyway"—Dolly swerved Mimi's chair around so she could face Dana and Rachel—"what brings you two in today?"

"Rachel needs a manicure." Dana lifted her hand, admiring her own painted fingernails. "And maybe I'll get a new color, something not so flashy."

"Look at you being all subtle." Dolly's infectious laugh filled the salon. "What about you, Rachel? Going to go practical or something sexy for your new man?" She winked. "I saw August at the market over the weekend, and I swear that man's aura was radiating."

"Radiating?" Rachel slunk down into her chair, her face heating. There went any chance her relationship with August was a secret.

"Now that I see you in person, I understand why he's acting like a lovesick teenager. Your aura is quite lovely."

Her aura. What an unusual compliment, but who was Rachel to judge someone else's behavior?

She opened her mouth to thank Dolly, but Dana's obnoxious coughing fit stopped her.

"So sorry," the blond said, beating at her chest. "Something went down the wrong pipe."

"Oh, please." Loretta strode from the back room, her hair pulled up in an impressive beehive. "Only time Dana has an exaggerated coughing fit is when she thinks someone in town might take away her Ms. Curlville crown."

"It's *Miss* Curlville, Loretta." Dana waved her hand, shooing away Loretta's statement. "And I highly doubt Rachel, here, wants to compete against me. Please."

"No, darlin'," Dolly said. "Rachel would be in a different age bracket altogether."

Loretta laughed as she took a seat in Dolly's second hair station. Rachel couldn't resist chuckling along. These women were straight out of a Lifetime movie.

"You know what I find funny?" Dana sat forward, invading Rachel's space and peering into her eyes. "You claim to have been friends with our friend Ella, yet Ella never once mentioned you. Can you explain that?"

Here it comes. The third degree questioning Rachel had been expecting. "Maybe Ella had a life beyond Curlville? She never mentioned you to me, either. It's not absurd to think the topic just never came up."

"Not absurd at all," Loretta cut in. "You know what I think is strange?"

Rachel turned to the woman, ready to answer whatever question she had lined up. But Loretta wasn't looking at Rachel. Her scrutinizing glare was centered on Dana.

"Why are you looking at me?" Dana huffed and jabbed a thumb toward Rachel. "She's the one we're questioning. Remember?"

"Someone seems a little defensive." Dolly set her curling iron down and gave the conversation her whole attention.

"It seems so," Loretta said. "Makes me wonder if you're hiding something."

"What would I be hiding?" Dana's blushed cheeks took on a darker pink hue. "I'm an open book."

Rachel's guard dropped, and her ears perked up. What was this all about?

Loretta crossed her arms, not taking her gaze off Dana. "Word around town is Grant's back. Have you heard from him?"

"Of course not," Dana answered too quickly, and then tried to backtrack. "You mean Grant Golding? Ella's ex-husband? Why would I have seen him? Of all people." She snorted. "Ridiculous gossip."

"I hope you're telling the truth, Dana." Dolly shook her head. "That man is bad news."

Dana rolled her eyes. "He's no worse than anyone else around here."

"Possibly," Loretta said. "But everyone knows his abrupt departure from town and his family was highly suspicious. Who does that? He didn't even leave a Dear Jane letter for poor Ella. Just up and left without any warning."

Dolly's mother-in-law, Mimi, suddenly dropped her magazine and squinted her face as if trying to hear. "Are you talking about that man who took off with the Amish girl? What was her name? Jolene?"

"Joanna." Dolly scrunched up Mimi's curls and sprayed it with a wall of hairspray.

Rachel's skin tingled. Why did that name sound familiar?

"Or he killed her," Loretta offered, making Dana gasp. "Maybe it was an accident, or maybe it wasn't. All we know is they both disappeared at the same time. Just like that." She snapped her fingers.

Killed? Rachel's head buzzed. Killed as in dead, as in the Amish girl could possibly be the ghost. And if Grant had murdered the girl, it would explain why she haunted August's house. An unsolved murder would make a spirit want to hang around. But Rachel couldn't assume. She had to find out more.

"How old was this girl?" She tried to appear casual,

staying in her seat when the urge to stand and pace consumed her.

"A teenager." Loretta sighed. "Maybe sixteen at the most. A young thing."

"Pretty little blond girl," Dolly added. "Her family thought she'd run away with a boy her age."

Pretty little blond teenager. That described Nick's ghost perfectly. *Oh, no.*

Dana shifted tensely in her seat as Loretta continued. "She helped Ella with housework and taking care of the boys. My, they must've been toddlers at the time."

That would explain why she stuck to Nicholas's side. What a mess this was. More questions filled Rachel's mind.

"Grant couldn't have murdered anyone." Dana's brows wrinkled high and close together as she finally spoke. "He wasn't perfect, sure, but to accuse him of killing someone is just silly. And that Amish girl wasn't very pretty at all." Her face burned redder by the second.

"Why are you getting so upset, Dana?" Loretta smirked. "Unless you're worried we're going to start talking about your old shenanigans with Grant? Everyone in town knew what you two were doing while Ella was making that long commute home from Indianapolis."

"Oh, really?" Dana shrieked, face flaming, eyes glazed with anger.

Wow. Yep, a huge mess. Rachel wondered if Ella knew about this rumor. A new thought sprung to mind as she remembered when Ella had that strange reaction to the man who'd driven into Dana's garage.

"Dana, who's the man who visited you the other day?" The question spilled from Rachel's mouth. "The one who'd pulled into your garage and parked his black sedan there?"

"You"—Dana pointed a finger at Rachel—"are a nosy one. It's none of your concern who I keep company with."

Rachel ignored her, too fired up. "Was it the

boyfriend from out of town you mentioned before we walked into the salon?"

"This is outrageous." Dana stood and strode to the door. "I refuse to be talked to this way. You people need to realize who you're dealing with." The door swung open and Dana stormed out to the parking lot.

"Well, that was fun." Loretta smiled. "Dolly, make sure you let your husband know Grant's staying at Dana's house." Loretta turned to Rachel. "Dolly's husband is the sheriff. He's been wanting to question Grant about that girl's disappearance for a long time now."

"Oh, I'll get right on that." Dolly laughed, shaking her head and reaching for the phone. "Nice detective work, Rachel. Welcome to the neighborhood."

Chapter Nineteen

Nicholas ran as fast as his legs would allow, his heart racing with the beat of his pounding feet as they hit the pavement.

He's there. He's in the house. You have to make him leave.

That's all Joanna had told him when she'd appeared in his math class, but her teary, frightened eyes said so much more.

Someone bad was in his home. Someone she knew.

His dad?

The thought fleeted through his racing mind as he jumped his neighbor's fence, taking a shortcut through their backyard. Almost there. Almost.

Hold on, Joanna.

He'd left class as soon as Joanna disappeared after one last frenzied plea. Faking a stomach ache to ditch class would probably land him in detention but whatever. Helping Joanna was more important. He'd never seen her so distraught—and she rarely left the house. So something had to be up.

After hopping another fence, he landed in his backyard and quickly ran around to the front. Nothing about his house seemed out of place from the outside,

217

except the front screen door was ajar. Rachel wasn't here. Her car wasn't parked where it usually sat, which was a relief. He wondered if it also meant the supposed intruder knew Rachel was out of the house.

Nick bound up the porch steps and stopped himself from going inside. He needed to settle down, to be as quiet as possible. If someone was inside, he didn't want to be seen.

He shook off the nerves, waving his hands and taking a few deep breaths. He thought about calling the cops, but what would he say? My ghost warned me about a burglar?

No. He'd just have to see for himself. Hopefully, the person was long gone.

With a light touch, he turned the door knob. It was unlocked, but that didn't mean much. Most folks didn't lock their doors in this town. But if Rachel had been the last person to leave, the door would've been dead-bolted. She was always warning them to be safe. Coming from a big city, she'd said she was in the habit of securing the doors and windows before leaving.

Nick looked closer. The lock didn't appear broken. No signs of forced entry. Weird.

He slid inside and surveyed the living room, listening closely for any sounds. He didn't hear anything, but the couch cushions were tossed onto the floor, along with the books from the bookshelf. Someone really had been here. But—

"He's gone." Joanna floated down the stairs, answering his next question. Her eyes were red-rimmed and her cheeks were puffy.

"Shit. What happened, Jo? Who's gone?" He met her halfway and reached out to her, only to stifle the urge to pull her into his arms. Or to try, anyway. It was easy to forget she wasn't real. Not fully, just her spirit.

"Your dat was here again." Her lips trembled.

"In this house? Again?" He hadn't really believed it when she'd told him the first time. Didn't seem possible.

218

She said she'd scared him away with her ghostly ways, and Nick hadn't wanted to take her seriously. But now he wasn't sure he had a choice.

"Yes. He was looking for the money again."

That familiar kicked-in-the-stomach feeling forced him to take a step back. It was a different kind of sad than when his mom had died, and later when he'd seen her spirit. It was harsher than when his old baseball coach had told him not to show up at the next game, after he'd missed too many practices because of Joanna. Nope, this feeling deserved a category of its own. Which sucked big time, considering dads were supposed to care about their kids. Not trash their houses.

"Asshole." He clenched his fists tight, needing the anger to go somewhere besides his gut. "Is that all he cares about?"

"I'm sorry, Nicholas. He's an evil man. Not good enough to be your dat."

Nick sniffed, his eyes burning. "I'm so pissed."

"At least he didn't get the money. But the upstairs is torn apart. He kept pulling up the floorboards until I blasted the radio in your brother's room. Then he got scared and started yelling at me. Calling my name and your mam's name and cursing at us. I got so mad. When he started back down the stairs, I pushed my body through his, trying to show him how it felt to fall down those stairs. He didn't budge, but he knew I was there. He screamed like a baby and ran out."

Good for her. His dad deserved it, but why was he calling his mom's name? "Was my mom here?"

"No. Just me."

His heart pinched, like it did whenever he thought of his mother. "What do I do now?" he asked, mostly to himself. There wasn't much Joanna could do outside of haunting. "I should just give the money to Uncle Auggie. I don't know why I haven't done it yet. He'll know what to do with it."

Joanna had showed him where his mom had hidden the fifty grand—in a metal game box underneath the floorboard where Joanna kept her jacks and rubber ball. What a sneak she was. All that time Nick had had no idea the money was there. Apparently no one else did either, except for Joanna. It was a secret that had died with his mom. How many more did she take with her to the grave? Sometimes he wished she'd show herself to him so he could talk to her. He missed her so much.

"Keep it hidden for now, Nicholas. It's safe where it is. At least until your dat has given up and gone away."

"You think so?" Nick wasn't so sure. He'd dug a deep hole in the garden late one night and buried the box there. With the digging and gardening Rachel had been doing, the upturned dirt wasn't noticeable. He hoped.

"Yah. If your uncle has the money, it'll only put him in danger. I scared your dat pretty good." A quiver of a smile lifted her lips. "I don't think he'll be coming inside this house again. Let's wait to see what happens."

"All right. Fine." Nick just wished he had someone to talk to about this besides Joanna. He glanced around at the mess his dad had made. "I'll get the hammer and nail these boards back in."

~ * ~

"Are you going to tell August about Grant Golding, or am I?"

Loretta only needed to ask the one question before Rachel stood and darted out of the beauty salon, heading to August's office.

Warn August about Grant Golding? Yes, she'd do that. Tell him about the ghost living in his home? She couldn't see any way around it. Not anymore. Not when it was highly possible Grant had something to do with the girl's death. She'd been able to keep it a secret, like Nick had, but now there was more at stake than losing August.

Please let him understand.

Or at least not have her committed. That would be a

start.

Her heart skipped when she saw him through the glass window as she made her way to his office door. He was handsome and focused as he sat at his desk, typing on his computer keyboard, a stack of papers to the left. He was busy with paperwork, but this couldn't wait. Waiting any longer would only prolong the inevitable. Why did she ever think she'd be able to have a relationship with him when her world was so convoluted? Her heart squeezed. Because she was in love with him and didn't want to lose him.

"Hello?" She peeked inside the door.

August was at his desk, typing on the keyboard. Earbuds plugged his ears as he hummed something that sounded like "You Might Think" by The Cars.

Rachel stepped inside and waved, gaining his attention. He yanked the earbuds out and stood. His navy blue dress shirt and matching tie deepened the hue of his eyes, immediately drawing her in further. Everything about him was welcoming.

Maybe he would understand.

"Rachel." His forehead wrinkled with apparent worry as he approached her. "Everything okay?"

Frowning probably wasn't the best way to start this conversation so she evened that out and met him for a hug.

He kissed her cheek. "Did I leave you enough room for your clothes?"

"There's something else." She grabbed his hand and led him to the waiting area where they sat side by side.

"Did I forget to make the bed?" He grinned. "I'm sorry, Rache. I was a bachelor for so long, but I'm trying to get better at straightening up."

"You're fine. Really. But I just found out something that might concern you."

He brought her hand to his lips and kissed her knuckles. "Give it to me. Nothing could be as bad as the look on your face is making me feel. You're worrying me, honey."

She drew in a shaky breath. "August, we have a good reason to think Ella's ex-husband Grant has been visiting Dana, possibly living at her house."

His expression pulled taut, jaw clenched, eyes narrowed, lips curled into a scowl. Pure anger—at just the sound of the man's name. Yes, this Grant character was bad news, if he could engender this type of response from August. "Why would you think this?"

Rachel gave August a summary of what had happened at Dolly's salon. His brows rose as she came to the last of it.

"So what do you think?"

"I think you're right to suspect Dana is hiding something. You said Dolly called the sheriff?"

"Yes. He's on the way to Dana's house to check it out. But with the way Dana bolted out of there, I'm betting she's going home to warn him. Or something. I'm not sure what to think of Dana. She seemed shocked by the accusations. Did you know about the Amish girl?"

He shook his head, but then held up a finger. "Wait. I vaguely remember meeting her when I visited them during a break in school. It was my first Thanksgiving after I'd left for NYU. I didn't hear about her going missing, though. You said it was the same time Grant disappeared?"

"That's what I heard at Dolly's. Loretta and Dolly both seemed highly suspicious of Grant's role in the girl's death. I don't blame them. I think they might be right to suspect Grant of wrongdoing. Possibly of something incredibly heinous and evil."

"They think he killed her?" He cocked his head, his gaze holding a suspicion of its own. "*You* think he killed her? Why?"

Rachel stood. Her heart beat too fast to sit still. She needed to pace. And to avoid that stare. "I have to tell you something else, August. You might not believe me, or you might think I'm insane. Probably both. In any case, you're going to be upset with me."

"You can tell me anything, Rache. I thought you knew that."

"I do. You're incredible. And kind. And accepting. And that's why I knew I had to be completely truthful with you. You deserve that." She was talking too fast.

August sat back and braced his arms over his chest— a protective gesture. His expression was also guarded as he waited for her to go on. So she gulped against the painful knot in her throat and continued.

"The Amish girl Loretta and Dolly described—" Oh, boy. This wasn't going to be easy. "She's a spirit who's been living in your home. I've seen her." Rachel thought about mentioning how Nick could also see the girl, but decided that was his secret to reveal. She wouldn't betray his trust. She couldn't.

August leaned forward, intelligent blue eyes on full alert. "What are you talking about, honey? Is that a metaphor of some sort? Her spirit?" He shook his head. "I don't get it."

"She's a ghost." A cold flush swept down her face and chest as the damaging words broke loose. "I see ghosts, August. I have for a while."

"What? Ghosts?" He rose from his rigid sitting position and gripped her shoulders. "Rachel, what sort of medications are you taking?" He eyed her just as any physician would, gauging her with concern and scrutiny. "Name them all. Everything."

"I'm not taking anything stronger than multi-vitamins. I swear I'm being completely honest with you. You need to believe me. The Amish girl is dead. I see her spirit as a teenager. She's exactly how Loretta described her, and she's living in your home." There was no going back now.

August snorted. With a quick movement, he swept

her purse off her shoulder and opened it. "You're hallucinating, Rachel. What are you on?"

She let him search her purse, knowing the only medication he'd find was a sample size of ibuprofen and her daily vitamins. "The only drug I have in my possession is a sedative my doctor prescribed to calm my nerves. They're in my nightstand. They made me drowsy, so I stopped taking them. If you don't believe me, I can show you the bottle. There're twenty-eight left of a bottle of thirty."

With a reluctant move, he handed her purse back to her. "What's going on here, Rachel? I'm obviously not going to believe you see ghosts. That's ridiculous. So what are you doing? Either you're not in your right mind or you're messing with me. Which is it?"

"I'm not—"

"You want out of this relationship? Did you change your mind and think 'Hey, why not make August think I'm a nut ball so he'll end it with me?' Is that what this is about? 'Cause if it isn't, I'm worried about you, honey. Did Dolly have alcohol over there? Is she still smoking weed? Moody warned her about that." He gripped Rachel's shoulders again and peered into her eyes. "They're not dilated, not bloodshot. They're normal."

This wasn't going well at all. It was a disaster, in fact. Her mind raced. If she didn't backtrack, she'd end up in the psych ward by dinnertime. Why did she think he might understand, might believe her nonsense. She barely believed it herself.

"You're right." Her eyes burned as she realized what she had to do. "I'm a coward." She attempted to blink back the tears flooding her eyes. "I'm so sorry. I'll get my things out of your house. I just…"

"You what? So this is you breaking up with me? You want to do it this way?" He shook his head. "No. You were just joking, right? This was all a joke. Only it's a little late for April Fool's Day."

"I'm sorry, August." She pulled away from his tightening grip, walked around him on shaky legs, and grabbed her purse. "I'll go. You deserve better than this."

"No, no, no." He gripped her arm before she could open the door. "You don't get to end it this way. We need to talk it out. You could've just told me the truth—that you're scared. That you don't love me. That you think you can do better. Please stay and talk to me."

If she stayed, she'd break down, and he'd have no choice but to think she was unstable. No, she had to find another way to make him believe her. Her words weren't enough. But first, she needed to get away from him.

"I can't stay." She couldn't look at him, not with how badly his hand was shaking as he held her hostage. How badly she was hurting him. "You've seen how I am. I'm a nervous wreck. I guess I was trying to save myself from another panic attack, making up a stupid story. If a ghost lived in your house, I couldn't live there." She sounded like raging lunatic.

"A stupid story," he repeated. "I'm so confused. You're making my head swirl, honey. This morning you were moving in with me, starting a life with me, and now you're making up shit just to get away from me. It doesn't make any sense." He dropped his hand finally. "You can't even look at me. I let myself fall in love with you, and now you want to run from me."

Oh, God. I love you, too.

A loud clang startled her, and she jerked her head to see he'd kicked the chair.

"August, I should go."

"Yeah. Shit. Sorry. I lost my cool. You should definitely go. Just go."

Rachel swiped her tears off her cheek and sped out the door toward her car, determined to make this right. Determined to find a way to make him believe, and to help Nick and Zach too. She couldn't leave them with this unsolved mystery, knowing their father could be a danger to them.

She dropped into her car and started the engine. "Ella. Ella, please. You have to help me."

Chapter Twenty

Dana slammed her front door and scanned her living room. "Grant! Where are you?"

Nothing. Just silence. Damn man thought he could come and go as he pleased, expecting her to keep him a secret. Well, look what happened? Everyone in this nosy town knew he was here anyway. Not only did they know, they were accusing him of foul play. He had some serious explaining to do.

"Grant!" She stormed down the hall, checking the rooms. She'd always reckoned he was trouble, but she had no idea he was wanted for questioning in a murder. A murder! The missing Amish girl had been a mystery, sure, and Dana had strong suspicions that Grant had something to do with her disappearance. But she'd thought the worst scenario was Grant wooing the girl into running away with him. He'd been charming, younger, and temptingly good-looking back then, so she hadn't given much thought to any other suspicions.

Especially after... Memories of the day that nosy girl had found Dana in bed with Grant flooded her mind. It had been right before they disappeared. The girl's rage had seemed personal—as if *she'd* been cheated on, rather than

Ella. And that was why Dana had so easily assumed the two might have been having an affair. The sting of Grant's betrayal had been too overwhelming. Dana had thought she'd been his only mistress. But was she?

No. She'd shrugged off that anger a long time ago. She hadn't wanted to believe Grant would leave Ella and her without any explanation. Not for a pretty little Amish girl, of all people. The teen hadn't even worn makeup. She'd worn bland long dresses that covered her curves. There'd been nothing special about her except for the fact that she was young and forbidden.

But what if... What if the anger the girl had shown that day was something else besides jealousy? What if the girl had been angry on Ella's behalf?

Which would've given Grant a very good motive for wanting Joanna dead. Because showing that sort of loyalty to Ella would've only meant one thing—that Joanna would've told her about Dana and Grant. Ella would've found out.

Damn. Did he kill that Amish girl in the heat of the moment? After all these years, the thought seemed plausible. She gulped. His weird behavior since he'd been back didn't help her doubts.

Had she been unknowingly harboring a murderer?

She shuddered before stopping at the garage door. If his car was gone, she'd change the combination to the garage door opener, and then he could find somewhere else to stay—probably the jailhouse. If his car wasn't gone... Her pulse raced as she cracked the door open. A cluttered mess came into view, but no car. She walked into the garage, thankful he was gone.

He'd left a reminder that he'd been there. The metal shelves that had stored her tools, gardening supplies, left-over paint cans and whatnot had been toppled over onto the concrete floor. It looked as if there'd been an earthquake. Paint splattered everywhere, with no signs that Grant had tried to clean it up or put any items back where they belonged.

No, he'd done this on purpose. As if he'd lost his temper in a fit of rage. Why the garage though? Had he been looking for something?

Dana scanned the area, taking mental notes on what might be missing. She wasn't always the smartest woman in the room, but she had a decent memory. And she was neat and tidy. Everything had a place, making it easier to find what she needed.

Her gaze roamed over to where the lawn mower sat. The shelving above it hadn't been touched, but something was off. Something was missing. *The gas can.* The mower was gas powered, and she kept a five-gallon container handy for when she needed to refill the mower. The can had been empty, and sitting in its usual spot, ready for her to take to the gas station to fill up. She was sure she'd left it there.

But why would Grant take that, of all things? He wasn't nice enough to help her with the lawn, that was for sure. He never helped her inside the house, not even rinsing out his own dishes, so why would he go out of his way to mow the lawn?

Huh.

The doorbell rang, making her jump. This whole ordeal was fraying her nerves. D*amn you, Grant,* she thought and made her way to the front door. Peeking through the peephole, she saw the sheriff on the other side and breathed out a sigh of relief.

She'd tell him everything he wanted to hear. About Ella's money, about how Grant planned to find it. As long as her good name wasn't dragged into the muck with him, she'd bear her entire soul. And hopefully the sheriff would show her some mercy.

~ * ~

August sank down in his desk chair. "Unbelievable," he muttered, unable to fully comprehend what had just happened. His hands still shook from the shock. He pressed them flat against his desk and tried to clear his head.

Despite his confusion, one absolute raced through his head. He should've fought for her. He shouldn't have let her leave—shouldn't have told her to leave.

She'd caught him off guard, though, with her story of seeing ghosts—all of it as a ruse to turn him off. What had she been trying to prove? He still had so many questions, and he feared he'd never have closure without stripping her mind down to the core. Only she was gone, getting her things and heading back to Indianapolis.

Maybe he'd pushed too hard, too fast, insisting she turn her world upside down and move in with him. He'd have dropped everything and relocated to Indianapolis if it hadn't meant taking the boys away from their home. They'd been through too much already. Moving them would have been a mistake. He knew that, yet he couldn't help but analyze every single angle of what he could've done differently.

But the cold hard truth couldn't be ignored. Rachel didn't want him. At least not enough to advance the relationship to a deeper level. Hell, she probably took another look at her precious picture of her dead ex and changed her mind.

Shit. Was it possible Hayes was the reason behind the ghost story? Did she think she saw him?

August dropped his tightly coiled shoulders and pushed out a breath. The mind was complex. Complicated. And who knew what type of medication her doctor had prescribed for her anxiety?

But a ghost in his house? A dead Amish girl, to be exact, who was somehow related to Grant's disappearance?

"Rachel, what were you thinking?"

The office phone rang out as if in reply, making August instantly wonder if Rachel was calling him to make some sense of this all. He quickly dismissed that idea, thinking she'd call his cell phone rather than the office phone.

He shook his muddled head and picked up the receiver. "Dr. Kline. How can I help you?"

"Dr. Kline, hello! How are you today?" a spirited voice rang out on the other end.

August recognized it as Miss Levitz, the school counselor, who he'd had several meetings with since becoming Nick and Zach's guardian.

"This is Miss Levitz," she confirmed. "Sorry to have to call you at your office." She sighed.

"Is everything all right, Miss Levitz?" The last time she'd called him, she'd informed him that Zach had ditched two days in a row. The kid had been sick, and August had forgotten to call in for him, so the issue had been cleared up quickly with a stern reminder for August to excuse all absences. But as far as he knew, both boys were in school today.

"I'm afraid not. I was informed that Nicholas complained of a stomach ache, but after his teacher sent him to the nurse, he was seen leaving the school grounds. He hasn't returned. He's missed second and third period. Do you have any idea where he might be?"

It was times like this August was grateful he lived in a small town, where the school paid attention to the coming and going of the students. Of course, he had a feeling Nick and Zach sometimes got special attention. The community had come to their aid on more than a few occasions since Ella had passed and he'd taken over.

"I bet he went home." August ran his hand through his hair, wondering if Nick might run into Rachel as she collected her things. "I'll call his phone to see what's up. Thanks for the phone call. If he's truly sick, I'll give the school a call to excuse him. Otherwise, he'll be back for his last couple of classes."

"I appreciate it, Dr. Kline. I hope everything is fine."

"Thank you." August hung up and dialed Nick's

phone. It went straight to voice mail. Hell, probably broken again. That clumsy kid went through so many phones. He called the home landline, but there was no answer.

Loretta swept in then, hair bigger than ever, an odor of aerosol breezing in with her. "Hey there. Did Rachel tell you about Grant? Can you believe he's been gallivanting around with Dana? The nerve that man has. The sheriff headed over there to ask him some questions."

"About the missing Amish girl?" August stood, overcome with dread.

"She did tell you then. Good. We need to be real careful until Grant is found. I never trusted him, and who knows what's going through his mind?"

"Loretta, will you please call and reschedule my afternoon appointments?" August grabbed his keys and wallet.

"Well, I don't think it's necessary for you to go over there too, Sherlock. The sheriff will take care of things."

"I need to find Nick. He left school without permission. And Grant Golding better have nothing to do with that."

"You don't think—"

August didn't wait for Loretta to finish. He hurried out the door and to his truck.

Nick. You better be okay.

~ * ~

Rachel jolted to a stop. An empty police car sat across the street at Dana's house, but all seemed calm in the neighborhood. Dana's curtains were drawn, not allowing Rachel to glimpse inside. She could only assume the sheriff was questioning her. And possibly Grant, if he was there.

There was no way of knowing for sure. And apparently Ella wasn't willing or able to help. She hadn't appeared, no matter how many times Rachel had tried to summon her.

Fine. She'd deal with this on her own, call upon

Joanna's spirit, gather some sort of evidence to solve the girl's death, and win back August's trust. Most important, she'd save this family from further harm or emotional distress. They'd been through enough.

And there was no time for an anxiety attack, she told herself. She had to fix this.

With one last deep breath, she sprinted up to August's front door—her front door—and pulled her keys from her purse.

Wait. The door was ajar. That's odd.

She listened closely. No voices. But she did hear a strange banging sound, as if someone were hammering wood.

What the heck?

No time to guess and ponder, she shoved the door open and called out. "Hello? Who's here?"

The banging stopped. The sound had been coming from upstairs from one of the bedrooms.

"Hello?" she called again.

"Uh, yeah?"

Nick's voice eased Rachel's rising panic, but now she was consumed with curiosity.

"Nick?" She ran up the stairs. "What are you doing…?" Her words faded as she scoped out the mess. Several hallway floorboards had been yanked up.

She rounded the corner into Nick's room to see his mattress toppled over and his dresser askew. Joanna sat primly next to Nick, who was holding a hammer in one hand and a floorboard in the other.

"What happened?" Rachel eyed them both.

"It's complicated." Nick's cheeks flushed as he shrugged. "I'll clean it up." His puffy red-brimmed eyes belied his teenaged nonchalance.

Rachel wasn't fooled, and she wouldn't let Nick take the blame for something he didn't do. There was something else going on here. "Who did this?" She directed her gaze to Joanna. "Was it you?"

"I knew you could see me."

"Of course I can. And I want to help you." The many spirits who'd haunted Rachel in the past year would have loved to hear those words, but Joanna simply narrowed her eyes and pouted her lips.

"She's a little shy." Nick rolled his eyes. "What do you mean you wanna help?"

"First, tell me how this happened?"

"It was his dat," Joanna blurted, as if she'd been holding the words hostage at the tip of her tongue. "He was here, searching the house."

"Jo? What the heck. I thought we weren't telling."

Rachel took a step back. "His dad? You mean Grant, your biological father? He was here in this house?"

"Yah," Joanna said, as Nick shook his head. "That man is evil. He needs to be sent to prison, far away from Nicholas and Zachary."

Rachel glanced at Nick, who crossed his arms and scowled. "Please tell me everything you know, Nick. I promise you'll feel better once you do. And I have a good feeling you've been holding a lot in."

He shot his thumb toward Joanna. "She's the one with all the big secrets."

"Is that true?" Rachel masked her worry with concern and empathy. "Maybe it's time to finally let it go. And to move on," she added.

"To heaven?" Joanna smiled, her pale ghostly face brightening, showing a sweet innocence. She'd been so young when she'd died.

"You've been waiting a long time," Rachel said. "I can only assume the reason you've stayed is because you have unfinished business here."

Joanna glanced at Nick. "I needed to protect the boys. They were in my charge."

Nick looked away, his cheeks pinkening.

Rachel couldn't help a grin. This spirit had always had the best of intentions, and it showed. "You did a wonderful job, Joanna. Look at how happy and healthy they are."

"But I always knew their dat would be back. He's not a good man. He'll hurt them."

"He killed Joanna," Nick said, matter-of-factly. Blunt and exactly what Rachel needed to know. "He pushed her down the stairs and then just left town like nothing happened. Like he didn't commit murder, like he didn't have a family."

Her heart sank. She reached for Nick, but Joanna stepped in the way in a protective gesture. "I'm so sorry. For both of you."

Nick turned and stared out the window, quickly swiping at tears. "He's an asshole. Now he's back to find some money my mom left behind. But Jo and I hid it so he can't find it. I won't let him have it. Not after all that selfish prick has done."

Money Ella left behind. Why hadn't Ella told her?

"Nicholas, don't curse." Joanna fisted her hand. "You know better."

"I don't give a crap, Jo." Nick turned back to face them, anger making him look years older than he was. "That jerk isn't my dad. He's just some guy who was once in my life. He hurt you and he needs to pay."

"Nick is right, Joanna." She was proud of him for finally expressing his feelings. "Grant needs to be punished for what he's done. You said he's after money. What money?"

"Joanna saw my mom hide a large amount of cash under one of the floorboards. We got it out before the jerk came and tore the place up. It's hidden in a good place for now."

"If he didn't find it, he might be back. Might still be in town." Rachel shivered, and Joanna and Nick glanced at each other. "Nick, I made the mistake of telling your uncle I can see ghosts, and about Joanna being here."

Nick snorted. "He didn't believe you."

"It's not his fault. I sprang it on him. But I think we can convince him of our…ability."

"Ability? Huh. Like a superhero or something."

"You're definitely a hero." She wanted to hug him. "What do you think? We can help Joanna move on. She first has to realize that you're safe. How can we do that?"

Nick looked at Joanna. "How, Jo? How can we put Grant Golding away?"

Joanna sighed and shook her head. "I don't know. Maybe I can show you something."

Her remains. The morbid thought popped into Rachel's mind. Joanna never received a proper burial, not if Grant Golding murdered her. Not if no one knew she was dead.

"Will you take me to the place?" Rachel said carefully, unable to imagine what this situation was like for the young girl. Rachel hoped this was the way to finally put Joanna's soul at ease.

"Just you." She pointed at Rachel. "I don't want Nicholas to see."

"Why not?" Nick threw up his hands. "You're dumping me?"

"Nay." Joanna caressed her ghostly hand to his cheek. "I just don't want you to see me that way."

"Oh." Nick's mouth gaped. "You mean where you're buried."

Joanna nodded.

"That's a good idea." Rachel tried to deflate the tension in the room. "The police will need to see that area to investigate. I'm sure they'll find something to convict Grant."

Nick let his shoulders drop. "Okay, fine. What should I do then?"

"Is it close?" Rachel asked.

Joanna nodded again, her eyes brimming with tears.

"I'm so sorry," Rachel said. "Thank you so much for looking after Nick and Zach all these years. Your family would be proud of you."

"Do you think so?"

"Of course."

"I'm proud of you too." Nick pulled her into a hug. Though their bodies didn't meet tangibly, they seemed pleased with the airy connection.

"We should go," Rachel said, wary of the time it would take to find the remains. "Nick, stay in the house. I'll lock the doors. The sheriff is across the street at Dana's house. If you hear anything strange, I want you to call 911."

"It's okay. I have Sheriff Moody's cell number." Nick shrugged. "Small town. Messed up kid," he said as an explanation.

"All right." Rachel sighed and looked to Joanna. "Ready?"

Chapter Twenty-One

August wasn't sure whether to be relieved or angry when he saw Nick standing in the living room, holding a hammer and looking guiltier than when he'd blown up the laptop August bought him for Christmas. The boy was destructive, and he seemed to be the common denominator for the electrical failures in the house. Whenever he was around, something blew up.

And now the kid was ditching school, caught red-handed with a hammer.

August shut the front door and crossed his arms. "Explain," was all he dared to say as his temper flared.

"It wasn't my fault. I was trying to fix them."

"Fix what?" God, his head hurt. He couldn't afford to replace anything else in this damned house.

"The floorboards. Look—" Nick gulped and held his hands up in a protective gesture "I promise to explain that later. What's important is that Rachel might need our help. She told me what she told you. You should believe her. It's true."

The pain in August's head pulsated to the organ *du jour*—his heart. "I'm not sure what you're talking about, Nick. Rachel isn't being herself. I'm a little worried about her." *And now you.* "Did she seem disoriented? What'd she say?"

Now more than ever, he wished he hadn't let her go. Was she really having a psychotic episode? He'd been too wrapped up in his own ego and self-doubt. Maybe she *hadn't* been trying to break up with him.

"She seemed normal, Uncle Auggie. The way she always is." Nick heaved out a teenaged-sized sigh. "She went to look for Joanna's remains. She probably needs our help, especially with my dad on the loose."

"Who the hell's Joanna?" August said, louder than he should have, as shock hit his system. Remains?

Nick dropped the hammer on the floor, looking as freaked out as August felt. "Joanna's the girl my dad murdered before he disappeared."

Was he joking? 'Cause this wasn't funny. August waited for a "just kidding" but nothing came. Fuck.

"Did Rachel tell you to say this? Did she tell you some eerie ghost story?"

A knock on the door stopped the conversation short.

"Don't move. We're not done." Not even close. Jesus, how much more therapy was Nick going to need after this episode?

"Find out who it is first," Nick said. "It might be my dad. We don't want to let him in. He's dangerous."

"Fine." August peeked out the window to appease the kid. "It's Sheriff Moody. We're safe."

"Okay, good." Nick blew out an anxious breath.

Hell. Definitely going to need some therapy.

August swung open the door. "Sheriff, how can I help you?"

"August, we need to talk."

The phrase of the day. Though it must be serious. The sheriff rarely called him by his first name. Great. Welcome to the party.

"Come on in." August rubbed at his temple, hoping this had nothing to do with Rachel.

"Nicholas, how are you?" The sheriff nodded at the boy. "Short day at school?"

"No, he's ditching," August said, anxious to get to the point. "What's going on, Sheriff?"

"I don't know if it's a good idea to talk in front of Nicholas. Perhaps we should go in the other room."

"It's about my dad, right?" Nick stepped closer, stumbling over the hammer he'd dropped. "I want to hear."

Sheriff glanced at August. "Probably not a good idea."

"Please." Nick clumsily kicked the hammer again. "I can take it. Whatever it is, I've heard worse. Believe me."

"Is it about Grant?" August picked up the hammer and put it safely on the coffee table. His mind swirled with all he'd heard that morning and from the accusations flying around. Murder?

"Yes." Sheriff cleared his throat.

"All right. I'm not sure why, but Nick's already had an earful, so let's hear it."

The sheriff pulled a notebook from his back pocket and flung it open, silently skimming over the page. "I just came from Dana Finnegan's house. She's been harboring Grant Golding."

Rage in the form of heat merged with the pulsing in August's head. "How long?"

"A few weeks. He's been lying low over there for some reason. I'd like to bring him in for questioning. Have either of you spotted him in town?"

"No," Nick and August said in unison.

Sheriff scribbled in the notebook. "He's missing again. I put out an APB on him and his vehicle. According to Ms. Finnegan, he's been acting strange. Have you had any intruders?"

"No," August said, as Nick said, "Yeah."

August shot Nick a questioning glance. "What are you talking about?"

"He was here today. He was looking for something." Nick bit his lips, a telltale sign he was holding something back.

"Go on," the sheriff said.

"I didn't see him. But I know it was him." Nick gestured at the hammer. "He'd pulled up some floorboards and moved around some furniture. I was cleaning it up when you got here."

"How do you know it was Grant Golding, son?" Sheriff asked in his usual cool demeanor that August admired.

He was anything but cool and collected at the moment.

"I just know. Who else would it have been?"

The sheriff scribbled some more notes. "I'll have a couple of deputies come over and swipe for prints and such. Is there anything else either of you would like to share?"

"I've been hearing about the missing Amish girl," August said. "Do you think Grant had anything to do with that?"

"I wouldn't give too much credit to rumors, mind you, but I would like to question Mr. Golding about the girl since they disappeared from town at the same time, and she'd been working here as a nanny. The girl's family is Amish, and there have been other instances of young adults in their community running away. The difference in this case is this girl never came back, not even a whisper from her. The family has stuck to the belief that she ran away with an *English* boy her own age. Another possibility is she left with Mr. Golding."

"English?"

"That's what they call folks who aren't Amish. In any case, the family shunned the girl, as the Amish do when a family member leaves the religion, so talking to them about her hasn't exactly been helpful."

"That's bullshit," Nick said, his hands fisted and his

cheeks instantly going red.

"Nick," August said, warning him. Though he didn't want the kid to close up on them now. Not when he suspected a lot more was going on inside his head. Did he know the reason why Grant had trashed their house—and what he'd been looking for? Hopefully the police could make sense of it.

"Sorry. But that is bullshit."

"No need to get upset now, son." Sheriff Moody shut his notebook and gave Nick his whole attention. "Like I said, he's only wanted for questioning at this stage—"

"I wasn't talking about my dad. I don't care about him." Nick's taut expression revealed years of bottled up anger.

August's heart hurt for the kid. Goddamn Grant.

"I was talking about the shunning," Nick said. "They shouldn't do that to family, not when the shunned person hasn't done anything bad. It's stupid. Family is supposed to care about you."

Sheriff Moody nodded. "I happen to agree, but that's the way of their people." He turned to August. "The bottom line is the coincidences have always bothered me, and I've been waiting for a chance to question Golding. Nothing may come of it. Of course, if we find out he trespassed on your property, you have every right to press charges." He shot a guilty look toward Nick.

"I'm fine with that." Nick's face hardened.

The sheriff's phone rang, and he detached it from his belt clip. "Sheriff Moody here… Uh-huh… Don't do anything yet. I'll be right there… Right."

He hung up, his usual poker-face expression a bit more tense, making August wonder what the phone call was about.

"I have to go," the sheriff said. "If you spot Golding, you have my number. I'll also make sure the school knows, in case the man gets any ideas about approaching Zachary."

"I appreciate that. Is there anything we need to worry about?"

"Just hang tight. Everything will work itself out, like it always does."

August shut the door after the sheriff left and spun around. "Tell me what's going on, Nick. How did you know your dad was here?"

"Joanna told me." He stiffened and tilted his chin up, stubborn like Ella used to do.

"Joanna the missing Amish woman? Do you mean to tell me you know where she is and you didn't tell the sheriff?"

"No, Joanna the ghost who's been haunting this house. She came to school and told me my dad was here. That's why I ditched and ran home."

"Oh, hell." Now Nick was acting strange. "Did Rachel tell you to say this? Did she put this in your head?"

"Rachel didn't do anything but make me feel like I wasn't a freak for seeing a ghost. 'Cause she sees Joanna too. And I think that's cool, so you better not break up with her because of it."

This is out of control. "Where did Rachel go?"

"Joanna's showing her where my dad—Grant, I mean—buried her body."

"Body?" August took a breath. "And where is that?"

"You don't believe me, do you? Why do you think everything in this house breaks? Why do you think the TV blew up two days after you bought it? And my laptop, and my phones? And the washing machine, and the refrigerator, and everything else? It's Joanna. When she gets mad, she sends out this surge that messes with the electronics. And she has a pretty bad temper. You have no idea." He let out a long breath. "God, that felt good to say. Finally."

August shook his head, not sure what to think. He hoped the kid just had a vivid imagination. Maybe he remembered Joanna from when she'd been his nanny and had kept her as his secret imaginary friend? A coping mechanism from when his dad left, and then his mom dying elevated it to another level.

Then again, why did the electricity surge every once in a while? He'd had an electrician to the house, and it had gotten a clean bill of health. The electrician had given the recent lightning storm as a possibility, but he'd been clueless as to why the phenomenon continued. A grand later and another credit card maxed, August still had no answers.

No, there had to be another explanation. A reasonable, rational explanation.

"I know exactly what you're thinking, Uncle Auggie. I'm not nuts. You're like my dad now, and it's going to suck if you think badly of me."

August's tension melted. His nephew had been through so much. "I don't think you're nuts, kid. I think you're brave, and I'd be happy to be your dad. We'll get through this, all right?"

"Okay." Nick's shoulders dropped an inch, as if a weight had been lifted. "Joanna said her body was buried in the lot behind the old sugar mill. You know where that is? 'Cause that's where she took Rachel."

"Yep, let's go." Maybe the outing would quell Nick's irrational ideas about ghosts and dead bodies.

~ * ~

Rachel shivered and wrapped her arms around her waist, watching as the sheriff took numerous pictures and two deputies hung police tape around the area. She'd never seen a corpse up close, and she hoped to never see one again.

Joanna had led her to the exact spot—the gravesite—and then disappeared. Rachel understood why she didn't want to hang around to see her decomposed body. Who would?

The grave had been so shallow and apparent, Rachel questioned how no one had noticed it before. She supposed the sugar mill had closed down before Grant had dumped the body here, leaving the area with little to no foot traffic. A perfect dumpsite.

She shuddered, remembering what little effort she'd put into digging—how she'd yanked up a thicket of grass, sifted the dirt, and came across a bone. It was enough proof for her to call 911. Five minutes later, a deputy was uncovering more of the remains. Fifteen minutes after that, here she was, leaning against a squad car and trying not to pass out.

The sheriff handed over the camera to one of the deputies, his expression grim as he stared down at the corpse.

Poor Joanna. She'd been so young, her life barely beginning. And her family… They'd never known the truth.

As if on cue, Rachel's cell phone rang, and she picked it out of her pocket to see that her mother was calling. She pressed ignore, not wanting to worry her mother anymore than she already would. Her shaky voice would undoubtedly give her away. Her mother was perceptive. And caring. Judgmental as she may have been, she did care.

Rachel sent her a quick text saying she was busy and would call her back as soon as possible.

She stuffed the phone back into her pocket just as August's truck veered around the sugar mill and headed this way. Nick sat in the passenger seat.

Nick had told him. Now what would August think of her? She'd happened upon the body of the girl everyone in town was talking about, twelve years after the girl had died.

Should've thought this through more. She'd been in such a hurry to help Joanna and prove Grant murdered her, she'd overlooked something important: The police were going to question if she'd had something to do with the murder. Or if she had ties to Grant Golding.

Dumb. She sucked a deep breath into her diaphragm

and released it, which did nothing to help her queasiness.

Come up with a solution? Yep. She was going to have to come up with a good story, and fast. And preferably one that didn't include a ghost.

Chapter Twenty-Two

"What the hell's going on?" August parked his car behind several police cars and cut the engine.

He spotted Rachel immediately, her face pale, her cheeks pink, her lips frowning. She leaned against the hood of one of the cars. Her chest rose and fell with long, deep breaths.

Without a second thought, August launched from the truck, leaving Nick, and jogged over to Rachel. As he drew close, he noticed her red-rimmed, guarded eyes.

"Honey, are you all right?" He pulled her into an embrace, consumed with the need to protect her from whatever was going on.

Her stiff, trembling frame slowly relaxed, and she molded into his arms. A sigh escaped her lips followed by a sniff. "Yes, fine."

He rubbed her back as a sob shuddered her body. Then another. Jesus, he wished he understood what was going on inside her head. He'd do anything to help her, to make her happy.

It wouldn't hurt if he could figure out why the area was covered in crime scene tape. One of the deputies took pictures of a dirt pile while another leaned down staring, shaking his head, pointing, and talking. Seemed like a lot of excitement for these small-town cops.

The sheriff, headed their way, looked wary.

"Rache, the sheriff's coming. What happened? Can you tell me?"

She leaned back and swiped the stray tears rolling down her cheeks. "Um." She sniffed, and August could tell she was trying to gain her composure. "I found the body of the missing Amish girl." Her voice broke, but she continued. "The teenager who worked for Ella twelve years ago. She was in a shallow grave just over there."

Oh, man. So Nick had been telling the truth about Joanna's remains. August shot a glance at Nick, who hadn't left the truck. He looked out the window, averting his gaze to the sugar mill. Odd, considering the police activity seemed a lot more interesting than a deserted building.

Nothing made sense today.

August gave his attention back to the woman in his arms. "That's incredible. How did you find her?"

She pressed her lips together as fresh tears flooded her eyes. She blinked and glanced toward the sheriff.

Hell. "It's okay. We'll talk about it later. It's been a long day." Already.

Rachel and Nick were doing a good job of making him question his sanity. It seemed the ghost story was sticking, or at least until one of them owned up to the real story.

Sheriff Moody stopped in front of them and raked a hand over his balding head. "My hunch says the body is the missing girl. Joanna Schwartz. There've been no other local missing females. Just in case, I'm bringing in the state police. They have more resources. We'll have to get a DNA match, and the coroner'll examine the remains. God willing, we'll discover the cause of death." His gaze steadied on Rachel. "And who buried her here."

"Probably a good hunch." August didn't know what else to say, and Rachel wasn't talking.

Sheriff cleared his throat. "Rachel, I'm going to need you to come into the station and give a statement about the events leading up to you finding the body. Any further help you can give us will be appreciated."

Like how she came upon the body. She was going to have to tell the truth, but a ghost story wouldn't do. He hoped she hadn't already let the "g" word slip around the sheriff or the deputies. Who knew what they would do?

Rachel nodded, her lips still clamped shut.

"Right now?" August tightened his grip on Rachel's waist.

"In about an hour. Can you give Rachel a lift to the jailhouse?" Moody's expression read more like, "Can you keep an eye on her?"

Either way, the answer was, "Yes. Absolutely." Rachel wasn't leaving his sight. Not any time soon.

~ * ~

Rachel needed to pull it together. Only problem was she kept seeing Joanna's skeleton. The dead body of a sixteen-year old girl. She understood why Nick stayed in the truck. Joanna's spirit seemed alive and well, but her remains were a kick in the gut with the harsh reality. Grant Golding had killed her and buried her body.

Rachel followed August to his truck, mentally setting aside her grief in exchange for anger. Grant was going to pay for this atrocity. She momentarily thought about calling her father, the defense attorney, and asking for advice. But then she'd have to explain why *she* might need a defense attorney in the very near future. In an hour, she was supposed to give a statement as to how she'd known where to find Joanna's body. She just might have to plead the fifth. They couldn't arrest her if they didn't have probable cause. And her only connection to this town, up until she'd stepped into it, was Ella.

Ella. Where was she? Rachel had so many questions

for her. Did she know Grant had murdered Joanna before disappearing? Did she ever question why Joanna never returned? Did she have any suspicions?

Rachel opened the truck door, and Nick moved over for her to have the window seat. He swallowed hard, obviously holding back tears, and doing a better job of it than she was.

"It was her, right?" Nick asked Rachel as August slid into the driver's seat.

"Good probability," August said. "They'll have to run DNA tests to be sure."

Nick swallowed again and crossed his arms, slumping into his seat. "It's her. I know it."

August started up the truck. Rachel studied his handsome-yet-somber profile, wondering what he thought about all this. She'd barely believed in ghosts when they'd terrorized her apartment. How could she expect to win August over with a simple story? Maybe he just needed time. Or maybe he'd never believe her.

Nick must've been on the same mental wavelength. His narrowed gaze fastened on August. "So now you know we're not making it up, Uncle Auggie. Joanna led Rachel to the grave. There's no other way she'd have known where to find her."

"Let's just take a few moments to think about this." August drove away from the crime scene, stopping at the Main Street four-way stop.

"I don't need a few minutes," Nick said. "You should just believe me. My mom would've believed me."

"Hell." August exhaled and pulled into an empty parking lot that paralleled the hardware store and the covered stalls where the Amish parked their horse-driven buggies. He shut the engine down and turned toward them. "Okay, let's talk it out now, because you both have me really confused."

"Tell him, Rachel. Tell him we both see Joanna's spirit."

August pinned her with a warning look. "Be careful what you put into this kid's head. He's been through a lot."

Rachel's mouth gaped as her heart sank. "I understand what he's been through, August. That's why I think it's important for you to listen to him. And to me. I would never do anything to harm this family. I love you guys. All of you."

"We love you too." Nick's gaze shot toward August, as if daring him to argue. "Don't we?"

August's guarded expression slowly melted into the tender look she'd grown to adore—tilted head, the hint of a half-grin, warm blue eyes that promised forever whether he realized it or not. His broad shoulders dropped as he centered his gaze on her. "We do. We love you more than you know."

A whisper of breath escaped as Rachel absorbed his words. She tried not to analyze the depth of them when he'd been put on the spot. But the "more than you know" gave her hope. Yeah, at his office he'd said he'd fallen in love with her, but it had been during the heat of an argument, and he'd seemed regretful, as if falling for her had been a mistake.

Nick's face lit up with a wide grin. "Awesome. Let's go home. Auggie, I'll introduce you to Joanna."

"Wait just a second." August's guard slammed back down, eradicating his warm expression. "We can't go around pretending we see ghosts. Not with a murder investigation underfoot."

"I understand your worry, August." She really did. "We can't freely admit our ability to communicate with spirits. But Nick's not pretending. And neither am I."

"I don't know what to say anymore. I'm at a loss." He opened the truck door and exited, rubbing a hand down his face.

"I'll talk to him." Rachel gave Nick a reassuring smile before meeting August at the front of the truck.

August stared up at the sky.

"It's a lot to take in." Rachel kept her hands to her sides, stifling the urge to reach for him. "I understand why you're upset."

Flustering seconds passed before he met her gaze, his navy-blue eyes searching her soul. Or at least it felt as if he were trying. He stepped closer, reaching out to run his hands up her arms. Like always, her skin flushed and tingled under his touch. The effect he had on her was both warming and unnerving. How could she go back to her normal life after this? After knowing how intense true love could be?

His hands reached higher, and he gripped her shoulders. "Rache, can you please tell me how you knew where the body was?"

"What explanation would you believe, August?"

"The truth. Tell me the truth."

For the love of... "The truth is I didn't know anyone in this town before Ella came to me, asking me to help you." *Oh, no.* She shouldn't have admitted that. He'd frazzled her, frustrated her.

"What do you mean Ella came to you?" He dropped his hands and stood back, taking his warmth with him.

Might as well tell him. He already thought she was delusional, needing medication, which was exactly what she'd wanted to avoid from the start. But it couldn't be helped, not when Nick shared her same fate. She needed to fight for them both.

"Ella's spirit came to me." Rachel straightened her spine, lifted her chin, and summoned her determination. "She asked me to visit you and the boys to make sure you were all okay. Then she persuaded me to help you." *More like bribed me.*

When August didn't respond—obviously stunned silent—she continued, bent on admitting everything.

"Spirits have visited me for about a year now. They're the reason for my anxiety issues, for my panic attacks.

They can be pretty terrifying—and distracting. One of them spurred a panic attack on the second day of the bar. That's why I failed. Ella promised she'd be able to keep the other spirits away so I could study and retake the exam." Rachel hated how this sounded, but she continued. "In exchange, I did her bidding around your house, cleaning where she wanted me to, cooking for the boys, and reviving her garden."

"Stop."

August's one word was enough warning. She'd said too much.

The horses in the stalls twenty feet away stirred and huffed.

"You're telling me you helped us because you made a deal with my dead sister?"

"Yes, it benefitted us both." Rachel took a breath. "I'm sorry. It was selfish of me to bombard your life. But I was desperate. She promised me a break from the madness of being haunted day and night. I couldn't afford to refuse her offer. But then something unexpected happened, August. I wanted to continue seeing you because I fell in love with you." She clamped her mouth shut, realizing too late what she'd admitted. She didn't just love his family, she loved him. So much.

"In love with me," he mumbled under his breath. His cheeks took on a shade she hadn't seen before as he scuffed his shoe on the ground, kicking a loose rock too hard. He whispered a curse.

"August," she started, but didn't know how to finish. So she waited.

"Let's just keep to the facts, all right? You never knew Ella when she was alive then?"

Ouch. Her heart pumped out of beat. "No, I didn't. I only met her in her afterlife. She's yet to cross over, or move on, or go to the light, or whatever it is that they do. Of course, I haven't seen her in a couple of days, so I wonder if she has moved on."

"If that's true"—he pointed to the truck—"and what Nick's saying is also true, I'm to assume Nick also has communicated with Ella since she passed?" His dark brows furrowed in contemplation. Or was that anger?

"Ella explained that she's tried to avoid him, not wanting to hurt him anymore than he already has. So, no, not intentionally."

"Well, hell. At least she's considerate in her afterlife." He threw up a hand. "Honey, you can't expect me to believe any of this."

"It's a lot to take in. Trust me, I don't want to believe it myself. You have no idea how much I wish I could stop seeing them, how much I wish I was oblivious to their existence. I'd love to be normal again. For your sake and mine."

"Medication can help with—"

"I don't need medication, August." She fisted her hand over her heart, both hurt and frustrated. "I might've agreed with you a few months ago, but so much has happened to prove these spirits aren't just an illusion. Everything Ella told me about you was true—where to find you, your names, your neighbor's names. Today, I wouldn't have been able to find that body without Joanna telling me exactly where she was buried."

August rubbed his chin, scorching her with his brilliant eyes. In the sun, they were even more beautiful. If only he weren't judging her from behind them.

"Say something," she said.

"If what you say is true, you lied to me about knowing Ella when she was alive. You lied about the reason for helping me and the boys. How can I trust you now?"

He was right—she'd lied to him repeatedly. And she couldn't be more sorry. But now all she could do was fight for him—to make him see how much she cared.

"I can't take back the past, and I don't want to. If it weren't for Ella, I never would've met you. And Nick and

Zach. I can't imagine my life without you now. I hope you'll be able to forgive my deceit. As you can see, I've transformed into an open book." She spread her hands. "I want to tell you everything. If you'll only believe me."

"Do you see Hayes's ghost?"

The question caught her off guard. A large knot formed instantly in her chest, blocking the breath she needed to release. Unable to form a word, she shook her head.

"You don't?"

She eased out the breath, and the knot unwound. Hayes was her past. August was her future. Undeniably.

"I used to. He had unfinished business after he died. When it was resolved, he moved on. I haven't seen him since. That episode of my life was short-lived, but it seemed to be the trigger that initiated me into this new dimension. It opened up a Pandora's box. More and more, other ghosts started seeking me out. Finding me. It doesn't help that I live across the street from a hospital." She let out an awkward, nervous laugh. "Freshly dead and all, you know? They're mostly confused and worrying about a certain event that happened before they died. Some of them shake off the worry and simply cross over. Others stay and let it fester. Once they realize I can see them, they want me to help them. Like Ella did."

"Right," August said, not giving away any emotions. "I gotta be honest with you, Rachel. If I hadn't gotten to know you before all this, I'd be hauling you to the state psych ward right now, far away from my family."

"But you do know me." And she knew him. He was a good, decent man who loved his family. And *her*. She felt it to her marrow—to the blood rushing through her. He loved her.

"I need some time. You and Nick seem dead-set on this—on wanting me to believe you. All I can promise is I'll think about it. A lot. In the meantime, you can't let the sheriff hear you talking like this. You're going to need to come up with a better story for finding that body."

"I know. And I will." She wanted to hug him. He was coming around. Or at least she hoped. He could be simply telling her what she wanted to hear for now.

His gaze drifted to her mouth, and for a moment she thought he might lean in to kiss her. Then he swallowed and glanced toward the truck.

"We should go home. The bus will drop Zach off in a few minutes, and I don't want him to be alone. Not with Grant still on the loose."

"Good idea."

"And I don't want him finding out about this otherworldly business. It'll only confuse him."

"I won't tell him. I'll leave that up to you and Nick."

August scratched his head, his expression weary. It was only three p.m., and the day had already tired them both.

"We should try to relax before you take me in. It'll help me think of what to say to the sheriff."

He lifted his nose and sniffed. "Do you smell that?"

Rachel glanced around and spotted smoke rising from a couple blocks away. A fire in the direction of August's house.

An anxious twinge hit her body. "Let's go home." She headed back to the truck and slid inside. August seemed just as anxious to leave. He started up the engine, and they sped down Main Street, turning right on Peony Street.

The rising smoke grew larger and closer.

Chapter Twenty-Three

Our home is on fire.

Rachel couldn't take her eyes off the tragic sight. She and Nick jounced as August slammed on the brakes too hard, abruptly stopping the truck along the street.

August's stunned stare took in the blazing inferno. "My goddamned house's on fire. I gotta stop this."

"No, it's too dangerous," Rachel said. And hopeless.

Flames licked up the entire first story of the house. The front porch was engulfed in angry swirls of orange and red, black smoke rising from the top.

Rachel called 911 as August and Nick jumped out of the truck and strode toward the front lawn. She quickly gave the operator the address and pertinent details. After disconnecting, she rushed to stand beside a fidgeting August.

The acrid smell in the air was almost too much to bear. She held her shirt over her nose while her heart plummeted. Everything they owned was in that house. She couldn't imagine how helpless and desperate August must be feeling. And poor Nick. His life was being yanked upside down once again.

"Joanna," Nick said, looking to Rachel. "Joanna

might be in there."

He had to understand she couldn't be hurt—she was already dead. But the anguished look on his face said he still worried about her.

"She'll be okay." For a ghost. "Everything will be okay." Rachel rubbed his tense back, wishing she could do something to help. What could've started the fire anyway? She'd never seen one in real life, but this one seemed to be moving fast.

"She's over there." Nick pointed to the side of the house.

Rachel spotted Joanna hovering over the garden. A pale three-dimensional hologram with a long brown dress and black bonnet. Rachel would never get used to seeing a ghost, much less one dressed in Amish attire.

Sirens called out in the near distance. The firehouse was only a couple miles away. At least there was that.

"Who is?" August glanced around, obviously not seeing Joanna.

"Look!" Nick waved furiously in another direction. "It's him, isn't it?"

Grant Golding. He rounded the corner of the house, a red gas can tightly clenched in his fist and a crazed look in his eyes as he stared up toward the second-story window. He yelled unintelligible words while shaking his other fist violently in the air.

"Son of a bitch." August hunched forward, as if ready to attack. "He did this."

Rachel grabbed his hand, hoping the gesture would calm him. Getting any closer to the fire would be dangerous. They watched on as Joanna crept up behind Grant, smiling and mocking him. She laughed when he swung around, eyes wide with horror.

If only August could see.

This was Joanna's revenge, Rachel thought. Joanna was driving the man insane, taunting him, forcing him to reveal the horrible person he was. What a shame it had come to this.

"Burn, damn it!" Grant threw the gas can at the charred siding, causing a crackling explosion, forcing him back several feet.

"He's going down." August launched forward, taking off across the yard toward Grant.

"Wait." Rachel grabbed for him but missed. "August, stop!"

He didn't listen. He ran full-force, shoving Grant to the ground, straddling him, and getting in a hard shot to the man's jaw.

Two fire trucks pulled up along the street, and several firefighters hurried to their positions, dragging out supplies and rolling out the water hose.

Rachel's attention vacillated between the firefighters and the struggle ensuing on the lawn. Though it wasn't much of a fight. August threw a few punches while Grant held his arms in front of his face.

"The house is haunted," Grant screamed. Or at least that's what it sounded like he said. Then, "It needs to burn. She needs to die."

August stopped hitting Grant and sat wide-eyed.

A forty-something fireman ran up beside Rachel. "What are they doing? They need to get away from there."

A second later, Dana, hair wet and wearing a bathrobe, rushed across the street, her horrified gaze pinned on the burning house.

"Grant!" She broke into a jog, but a young, brawny fireman easily held her back, telling her to go back home and stay out of the way.

The firefighter beside Rachel nodded toward the house, his frown deepening. "Damn it. What is that kid doing?"

Kid? *Nick.* Amongst all the commotion, Rachel had lost track of him. She scanned the area and saw him kneeling at the garden, digging furiously at the loose dirt. Joanna suspended beside Nick, speaking to him about something.

"Nick!" Rachel started toward him, but the fireman took hold of her arm.

"We'll get them. Stay here."

August jumped off Grant, shoving him one last time, before heading toward Nick. He gripped Nick by the shoulder just as the boy lifted a box with both hands. August helped him to stand, and they both sprinted toward Rachel. Joanna followed behind.

Two police cars zoomed up and slid to a stop behind the fire trucks. The sheriff jogged over, his gaze centered on Grant, who was picking himself off the ground—firemen worked around him.

"What happened here?" The sheriff kept a brisk pace past Rachel.

"Grant was holding a gas can. He threw it at the house." Rachel said. "I can only assume he started the fire."

The sheriff continued on, his hand settling his gun holster.

Nick and August reached Rachel, as two policemen and the sheriff took a disgruntled Grant into custody. He'd surely do prison time for arson, if not murder. Is that what Joanna had planned? She seemed pleased with the results of the day, judging from the sheepish grin creeping across her ghostly lips.

"It's okay, Uncle Auggie." Nick handed August the mysterious box. What was inside? "My mom left us this. We can build a new house."

"Build a new house?" August seemed dazed. He clenched and unclenched his swollen fists, already bruising from the punches he'd thrown. "What are you talking about?"

"She left us fifty thousand dollars."

Money? Ella left money behind?

"She hid it under the floor in my room. Joanna showed me where it was. Then we thought it was a good idea to bury it in the garden. You know, in case something like this happened." He glanced at the house. Firemen continued to spray their hoses at the inferno. It seemed pointless. What hadn't burned would be soaked. Destroyed.

Everything the family owned, including all of August's treasured instruments. Rachel's heart squeezed as she gulped down her sadness. She hoped they had good insurance that protected them from arson. Fifty grand would only go so far in building a new life. But at least they had that. *Ella, wow, where did you get the money?*

"They'll be fine," Joanna said, as if trying to soothe Rachel's thoughts. "They have a new father, and that evil man will never bother them again." Her ghostly form faded in and out in the afternoon sun.

Rachel wondered if the glitching was normal or if Joanna was in the process of moving on—her earthly business complete after all these years. She'd protected them from the man who'd murdered her. The man who was now sitting in the back of the sheriff's sedan.

"How brave you've been," Rachel said to her, realizing the burning house before them was only a small part of the journey—the ending of Joanna's. "You did this for Nick?"

"Yah. For my boys." Joanna turned to Nick. "I have to leave you now. I'm going to heaven." Her smile spread, brightening her face.

"Is she here?" August asked, looking in the direction that captured Nick and Rachel's attention. "Joanna?" His face paled.

"Not for long." Rachel explained, surprised at August's question. Did he believe?

Her heart warmed as Nick attempted to hug Joanna's dimming spirit.

"Goodbye, Nicholas. I know you'll grow to be a good man."

"I will." Nick's voice broke with a sob. "I promise I'll

do my best. I'll miss you, Jo."

"I'll miss you too. And remember, I'll always love you." Her words faded as her body vanished. A light brighter than the sun shone down and disappeared just as quickly.

"I love you too." Nick gushed out the words—too late.

"She's gone," Rachel told August. "She just needed to know that Nick and Zach were safe for good." She gestured toward the sheriff's car. Grant's head was down, a look of shame marring his profile. At least the man appeared to have somewhat of a conscience. Too little, too late.

August hugged Nick, taking the boy's attention away from Grant. "It's going to be okay, buddy. We got each other. No matter what, you're stuck with me, got it?"

"I know." Nick gulped back a sob. "I know."

Rachel sniffed as new tears broke free. There was still hope for a happy ending for this family. She had no doubt August would give them a new place to call home and be the best dad possible.

The only question was whether she'd be welcomed back in to share the love.

~ * ~

August sat in the lobby outside the sheriff's office, waiting impatiently for Rachel to be released from questioning. The one-story building wasn't large, but it held a couple offices for the deputies, the sheriff's office, this lobby, and down the hall were two small detaining cells. August had toured it once and remembered thinking it was more than adequate for a town this size. Though, at the moment, he preferred to have more space between him and the woman sitting on the other side of the lobby.

Dana was unusually quiet as she chewed on her acrylic fingernails and tapped her bejeweled flip-flop in an annoying offbeat pattern. August clamped his lips shut to keep from shouting for her to hold still. It took enough self-control to not barge down the hall to where Grant was being held, just so he could ask the man what the hell he'd been thinking. He was a dangerous man. There was no doubt.

Thankfully, after all the day's events, Nick and Zach were safe, unharmed, and eating dinner at Loretta's house. Loretta had kindly opened up her home to them until they could find a new place to live. Sometimes the woman wasn't so terrible. It was one less thing to worry about.

August had already given his statement and hoped his answers cleared any doubt that Grant was responsible for both the house fire and Joanna's murder, though the latter was sketchier.

He went over the answers he'd given.

Yes, Grant was walking in front of my house, carrying a gas can. Yes, he threw said gas can at my goddamn house. Yes, I do think the motherfucker lit my house on fire.

Okay, so he could've been a little more succinct and a lot less angry. August shifted in his seat. The next set of questioning was more difficult. But he had no reason to lie. Rachel was innocent of any wrongdoing. His gut told him so.

No, I don't believe Rachel had ever met or had any communication with Grant Golding. No, she'd never mentioned Joanna Schwartz before hearing about her disappearance at Dolly's this morning. Yes, I do believe Rachel knew my sister Ella.

One way or another, Ella was the reason Rachel had entered August's life.

August glanced down at his bruised fist, remembering how bittersweet those punches had felt. He was lucky he hadn't been questioned about attacking Grant. Maybe Sheriff Moody was giving him a break and looking the other way. Or maybe Grant felt enough shame not to press charges. The man had been out of his mind, looking crazed as he screamed about the house being haunted. He'd believed there was a ghost, just as Rachel and Nick had sworn. It seemed like too much of a coincidence. Did his nephew and his girlfriend really see ghosts? What were those people called?

Mediums? Psychics? Someone with a sixth sense?

He'd never been one to believe in what couldn't be proven, but he also had to admit not all *could* be proven. Not scientifically, anyway. Seeing Nick talk to the ghost had given him chills. Rachel translating what was going on with the spirit seemed all too real. For a moment, he'd believed. Whole-heartedly. And now?

"Dana?" August needed answers—ones that he could dig his teeth into.

She looked up, scrambling to hide her chewed nails between her thighs. "What?" Her expression was a rare frown with taut features and raised eyebrows.

"What happened with Grant? He was staying at your house?"

"It wasn't a big deal. I thought he'd wanted to see the boys, but then he started acting strangely." She sighed. "I'm sorry. I should've told you he was in town."

"No kidding." August stuffed down his anger. It wouldn't get him anywhere with Dana. "How was he acting strange?"

"Well." She sighed again, this time with her whole body. "He mentioned that Ella had left behind some money." Her hand slapped to her heart. "Of course, I didn't want to have anything to do with that. But you know how bad of a temper he has. I was afraid to argue with him."

"Argue with him about what?"

"About searching your house for the money. He was determined to find it. Apparently he owes money to some bookies. He'd mentioned that, so there's his motivation." She shook her head, disbelievingly. "I told all this to the sheriff. I refuse to responsible for what happened."

"You mean you don't want to be charged for anything, so you outed Grant. That's noble of you. Probably a little too late though. Aiding and abetting a criminal? And you have to wonder how much time a person can get for harboring a murderer."

Dana gasped, and August wondered if she'd been rehearsing her expressions in front of the bathroom mirror, because this one was a doozy. Mouth gaped, eyes wide.

"August Kline, what are you insinuating? I would never intentionally aid a criminal. Grant has never been charged for anything until today, and there's no proof he killed that girl."

"Other than her corpse being found buried behind the old sugar mill he used to work at and the fact that he left town right after her death. Who knows what the forensics people will discover? It'll be interesting to see." August was enjoying goading his neighbor—probably more than he should. But she deserved it.

"If he committed murder, I didn't know anything about it. I'm completely innocent. Maybe even a victim."

"Right." August sat back and crossed his arms. "Did you know he was going to burn down my house?"

"No." To her credit, her eyes misted up. So she did have some amount of empathy. "I'm going to have to live next to an eyesore for God-knows-how-long. And then the construction noises when you rebuild? I would never have let Grant burn down the house had I known his intentions."

Never mind about the empathy. This woman had narcissism down to a T.

"You're not the only one hurt here. He destroyed my garage—tore everything apart."

"Oh, yeah. Is that where he got the gas can?"

"How should I know? I don't take inventory." She rolled her eyes. "I just want this nightmare to be over."

"We all do, Dana." August was done talking to the nutcase. Rebuild his home across the street from her? Maybe he'd just sell the land and move into a different neighborhood. The homes across the street from the high school had always been appealing. And the boys wouldn't have to take the bus.

Only problem was finding the means to move. He had homeowner's insurance. He'd call them tomorrow to get an investigation going. No doubt it would be a long process. It might help if Grant was convicted of arson.

August blew out a breath, trying to clear his mind. If he didn't relax, he'd give himself a headache. Things would work out. They always did. And he was lucky no one had gotten hurt in the fire.

Yeah. That's what he needed to do—think positive.

Now to wait and see how Rachel explained how she found Joanna's body.

Chapter Twenty-Four

Rachel glanced at her cell phone sticking out of her purse but stifled the urge to call her father. She'd make it through this without his help. Sure, the smarter choice would be to call in for legal backup. But this was just another step she needed to take to break away from her parents' hold.

She had all the tools she needed, she reminded herself, so she remained resolute, waiting for the hard questions. At this point, exercising her Fifth Amendment rights seemed the logical choice. She had no tangible reason to give, no story to tell that would make the sheriff understand how she'd found Joanna's remains. On the other hand, the police had no solid reason to hold her.

Sheriff Moody scribbled on a notepad. The man took a lot of notes. The outdated PC sitting to his right seemed to be a dust collector at most. When he found a pen that worked, he looked up and blessed her with a warm grin.

Rachel returned the smile and tried not to stir in her seat. She'd already answered his questions regarding what she'd seen outside August's house. She'd been open and honest, wanting to help August and the boys.

Sheriff leaned in closer, studying her.

267

Here it comes.

"Now, Miss Spencer, I admit I'm a bit mystified by how you came upon the body this morning. You knew right where she was, almost as if someone had pointed you to her."

Rachel stared at him, not offering a word and attempting her best lawyer face—the one she'd practiced in front of her bathroom mirror, hoping to mimic her father's cool facade that had worked well for him when defending the dirt of the earth.

The sheriff's focus didn't falter. "I'm on your side, Rachel. Everyone in this town has talked about how much you've helped the doctor and his boys. We all think highly of you."

Rachel blinked, urging herself not to roll her eyes. The Curlville townsfolk had been anything but complimentary. Suspicious was more like it... Though they did have a right to be. She *had* been deceitful about knowing Ella once-upon-a-time. But they didn't know that.

"You can save us a lot of time and resources if you tell us everything you know." He tapped his pen on his notebook, waiting. "I'm sure the victim's family will be grateful for any information, as well."

Rachel's throat began to itch, and her eyes began to water. *Crap.* She'd forgotten one important detail—she was nothing like her father. She couldn't lie to save her life. She couldn't stand by and let a criminal walk—*help* a criminal walk. And her lawyer face sucked.

She cleared the itch from her throat. "I'm sorry, Sheriff. I don't believe I can tell you anything helpful."

He opened his mouth but was interrupted by a knock on the door. He sighed, weariness apparent on his face. "Come in."

One of the deputies peeked in. "He's talking," the man said, and Rachel assumed he was referring to Grant.

She didn't know whether to feel relieved or

concerned. Who knew what the man would admit or deny?

"Excuse me for a moment, Miss Spencer." Sheriff Moody rose from his seat. "I promise we won't hold you for longer than necessary."

Rachel nodded, and the sheriff left the room. Her mind instantly wandered to August. She'd been separated from him right after the police arrived at his home before she'd had a chance to hug him—to help ease at least some of his tension. She wanted nothing more than to wrap her arms around him and tell him she loved him. And that she'd do anything to help him and the boys through this.

Even go so far as to ask her parents for enough money to help August get them back on their feet?

Probably not that far. But she'd do everything else. She had some jewelry she could sell, some bonds she could cash in.

"What about the money?" Ella's voice startled Rachel out of her seat.

Rachel glanced around until Ella's body appeared behind the sheriff's desk. The spirit, clad in her knit top and capris, plopped down in the sheriff's leather chair.

"Where have you been?" Rachel said too loudly, before lowering her voice to a whisper. "I didn't know if you were gone for good."

"I wouldn't do that without saying goodbye." She rubbed her temples. "I've been watching from afar. Grant gives me a headache. I can't deal with him, and I knew you'd figure things out."

"Um, I didn't figure anything out, if you haven't noticed. Your home is destroyed, and I'm sitting in the sheriff's office."

Ella ran her hand over the desktop, her gaze landing on the picture of the sheriff and his wife. Her frown deepened, and she stopped her movement to tip the photograph. The silver frame hit the solid wood with a *thud*.

Odd. Did Rachel's favorite translucent visitor have a

history with the Moodys?

Ella sighed and gave Rachel her attention. "Sheriff Moody will do the right thing. He's a stand-up guy—annoyingly so. And he's very good at his job. Very perceptive."

Rachel set the picture upright. "I'm a little perceptive myself. What's the story with you and Moody?"

"Long. But I'll shorten it, because it just might help you in this little situation you've gotten yourself into."

"Spill. Please."

"Louis is a married man," she said, using the sheriff's first name with familiarity. "When I met him, I was married to Grant. But whenever Louis and I bumped into each other, there was instant undeniable chemistry. We both felt it but hid it—until one evening. I'd run out of gas just outside of town on my way home from work. I started walking toward the gas station. Louis saw me and picked me up, helped me fill the gas can, and escorted me back to my car. He stayed to talk. When I laughed at one of his jokes, he leaned in and kissed me. I kissed him back." The dreamy look in Ella's eyes explained just how she'd felt about that moment.

"Oh, wow. I had no idea."

"No one did, and no one will. Except you. Louis stopped the kiss before it got out of hand and apologized profusely, saying he'd never cheated on his wife and couldn't believe what he'd just done. He hurried off, and we never spoke of it again. It was like it never happened."

"But it did." The rejection must've stung. Rachel reached for Ella's hand across the desk.

Ella snatched it back. "I'm fine. It was a long time ago. And he was right. We were both married, and we would've ended up making a mess of our lives and our families, not to mention the community. Dolly had always been a good friend, and I felt guilty for betraying her…even if it was just for a moment."

"Did you tell Grant?" It was hard to believe Ella had

been married to such a depraved man. A psychopath. Who knew what further harm he could've done if he hadn't been caught today?

"No, and I didn't feel guilty as far as he was concerned. He'd been screwing around with Dana since we'd moved into town. Our marriage was hanging by a thread. It didn't surprise me when he disappeared, but I always wondered what had happened to Joanna." Ella covered her heart as anguish blanketed her face. "I should've put two-and-two together. I should've investigated, found Grant, and made sure he was prosecuted. But something in my subconscious stopped me. Maybe it was the boys. I hated that they'd had a father like Grant. I was ashamed. I was glad when he left and didn't return. I wanted—*want*—so much more for my sons."

"They have August now. And Grant'll be prosecuted to the fullest. I'll make sure he never interferes with Nick and Zach's life again." Geez, wouldn't putting Grant away for life be satisfying? Maybe prosecution was in her future.

Ella shook her head as if trying to erase the memories. "Here're my thoughts." She cozied into the leather chair and tapped her chin. "You should tell Louis the truth."

"Excuse me?" Rachel sat back down, hoping Ella's advice would get better.

"Tell him you're a medium, and you knew where to find Joanna's body because Joanna's spirit led you there. The truth," she reiterated with a confidence Rachel didn't feel. "If I'm right about Moody—and I'm certain I am— he might take a while to digest the news, but he'll believe you."

"How could you possibly be certain about that?"

"He's open-minded, not as black-and-white as August has been about the situation. Which surprises me a little. I guess August is more like me than I realized." She grinned half-heartedly. "Louis's belief system is more flexible, like

Dolly's. You've been in Dolly's salon. See all the *unusual* paraphernalia? She fancies herself a tarot card reader, thinks she can help guide people with their problems. And Louis eats it up. They've both gone to a psychic to have their fortunes told. In fact, Louis once hired a psychic to solve a serial burglary case. The town newspaper made a big deal about it, and everyone was all aflutter. But they'd shushed up when he found and arrested the perpetrator with enough evidence to send him away."

Rachel leaned forward, hopeful and intrigued. "No kidding?"

"I wouldn't joke about this. Not when so much is at stake. Besides, we have extra ammunition. You'll tell him you can communicate with me too. If he doesn't believe you, feel free to mention our long-forgotten rendezvous. That should bring him around. Like I said, we promised never to tell another soul. I might even want to say goodbye to him, if you'll translate for me, that is."

"Huh. That's actually not a bad idea. If he believes me, I can tell him everything. About you. About Joanna and how I found her body. And about Grant."

"Exactly." Her grin turned somber briefly before spiriting up. "You know, once this is all cleared up, you and August can get married. You'll make a happy couple. A parenting team to be reckoned with."

"Married? I'll be lucky if he talks to me when this is over."

"And you tell me not to underestimate him." Ella folded her hands in front of her. "Maybe we should both give him the benefit of the doubt."

Rachel smiled. "What'll I do without you, Ella? I never thought I'd say this to a spirit, but I don't want you to cross over."

"Oh, I have a feeling I'll be here for a while."

~ * ~

August jumped to his feet when Rachel walked out of the sheriff's office. As the time drug on, he'd grown more and more worried about her, wishing there was something he could do. Now, seeing her smiling and laughing at something Moody had said made his worrying seem needless.

The sheriff nodded at August. "You two are free to go. Sorry for detaining your lovely lady for so long." His gaze veered to Dana, his expression hardening. "You can leave too, but don't go far. I'm sure I'm going to have more questions for you."

Dana didn't speak as she quickly made her way out the door, her frowning face looking down. Was that a hint of shame?

August didn't have the energy to care. With an overwhelming need, he pulled Rachel into his arms and hugged her tight, kissing her temple, feeling her slight frame against him, safe and secure. He'd missed her in just the small amount of time she'd been out of his sight.

Moody cleared his throat a couple times before August finally released Rachel. She smiled up at August with her pretty pink lips, and his heart thumped hard against his ribs. Damn, the woman did crazy things to his body.

"Sorry to interrupt." The sheriff stepped closer, forcing August to take his attention away from Rachel. "I thought you should know Golding confessed to everything from pushing Joanna Schwartz down his stairs twelve years ago, to burying her body in the shallow grave, to breaking into your house, and then setting it afire. The only thing he didn't do was implicate Dana in any of his crimes. We'll keep an eye on her though, since she seemed to know more than she should, given the circumstances."

"Good news for the most part." August drew in a long breath, filling himself with bittersweet relief. He hadn't realized until that moment how exhausted he was. The day had taken a toll on him.

"We're lucky." Moody winked at Rachel. "The man was spooked. Something sure scared him straight, and he'll be locked up for a long time after all is said and done."

August looked at Rachel with curiosity. What had she told the sheriff?

"I'll explain later." Her grin brightened her beautiful face.

"Yes, do that," the sheriff said. "Rachel, do you mind if I hold onto your phone number? Just in case I need your services?"

"Sure. If I can help with anything, I'll be glad to."

"What services?" August asked, but was wary to be let in on the secret.

"She's a keeper there, Doc," the sheriff said. "A special woman. You take care of her." Moody didn't wait for a reply as he practically skipped out of the room, heading down the hall.

"What is going on?" August couldn't help but return her grin. "Did you put him under a spell?"

He wouldn't be surprised, considering the spell she had him under. Even after the bizarre day full of irrational reasoning and revelations, he still couldn't get enough of her. If only he could take her home and make love to her— If only he had a home to take her home to.

"Let's just say Sheriff Moody is a believer. A *huge* believer."

"Believer of…?" August didn't finish his question. It was obvious what she meant. Sheriff Moody believed her ghost story. "You told him Joanna guided you to the gravesite?"

Rachel nodded, swallowing. "Apparently he's tried to contact psychics and mediums before to ask them about Joanna but got nowhere. He was excited to hear my story. Are you upset?"

Was he? No. August shook his head. He was happy as long as his loved ones were safe.

"I'm glad," she said, but her smile withered.

He wanted to say something to bring back her joy but worried he'd only mix up his words. For whatever reason, he still couldn't get behind the idea of Rachel being a medium—and being able to talk to Ella. There was something very troubling about that. Something too painful. Too raw.

"The boys are spending the night at Loretta's house." He changed the subject. "She was happy to take them in for as long they need a place to stay."

"That's nice of her."

"She spoiled them with ice cream and video game rentals. They're doing okay, considering. Mostly, Zach was worried about his clothes and shoes—all replaceable. Nick seemed in high spirits, amazingly."

"Like a weight had been lifted?"

"Exactly like that," August said. "How did you know?"

"I assumed. He'd been Joanna's only confidante for years, and he had no way of helping her. Today all that was resolved when Grant was arrested and she was able to cross over."

"Interesting." August didn't know what to say. But he was glad Nick no longer had a burden on his shoulders—whether it was real or not.

He changed the subject again, too fatigued to further that particular conversation. "I promised them we'd look at new houses closer to their school. That cheered Nick up. A lot of his friends live in that neighborhood."

"That's a great idea. I hope—" Rachel paused, looking away. "I hope I can help in some way."

August grabbed her hand, wanting to ease whatever ailed her. He ran his fingertips along her wrist and watched as her cheeks flushed, thankful he still had that effect on her.

He caressed her cheek with his other hand. "Loretta's house only has two bedrooms, so—"

"You can come home with me." Her words spilled out fast, and she met his gaze, scrunching her brows nervously. "I didn't break the lease on my apartment yet."

"You didn't?" Because she wasn't sure about him, he could only assume. Hard to believe just that morning she'd moved her things into his house. But apparently not *all* of her things.

"I had a huge secret, August," she said as an explanation. "I wasn't sure how you'd react once you figured it out. Turns out you've discovered the secret sooner than later."

"I get it." August stared at her, not sure he cared about the details. Or rather too tired to care. So she was eccentric? He'd known a lot of unconventional types when he'd lived in New York. To each his own, he'd always thought. But he'd never been in love with any of them. Never wanted a future with any of them.

But now he couldn't imagine his future without Rachel.

He glanced at the wall clock. A quarter after ten. The longest day of his life. He'd lost everything he owned. He couldn't imagine the musical instruments he and his mother had collected over the years had withstood the fire, smoke, and water damage. He'd miss them the most. Everything else could be replaced—like he'd told the boys.

His mind spun at how he'd be able to afford the avenue to where his life was leading him.

"You must be exhausted." Rachel squeezed his hand. "I suppose my apartment is a bit far. Do you want me to drive you to somewhere close?"

"Close would be good. Mrs. Taylor, the inn keeper, texted me and said she'd leave a key for one of the rooms, if we needed it."

"That was kind of her."

"But I want you to stay with me, Rache. I need you." His eyes stung as he said the words. Hell, when had he become so emotional? But it was true. He did need her. "Will you stay?"

"I—of course. I need you too." Her gaze took on a sheen of unspent tears. She'd been through her own hefty amount of turmoil today.

"I'm sorry about whatever you lost in the fire. Just let me know what you brought over, and I'll compensate you."

"Oh, August, I don't care about material things. I just want you."

The sweetness of her words hit him profoundly, and his worries dissipated. If only for tonight. Everything else could wait until morning.

Chapter Twenty-Five

Rachel followed August into the quaint room filled with a king-sized quilt-covered bed, a grandma rocking chair, white-lace curtains, and sturdy oak furniture— probably handmade. Fresh-cut daisies added a homey touch. The floral bouquet was arranged in a glass vase on a two-seater dining table in the corner of the room. Rachel took a second glance and noticed a plate of cookies next to the flowers. Lavender-scented candles flickered along the window sill and atop the dresser. Someone had gone to some trouble to make August feel welcome. Either Mrs. Taylor had a crush, or August was well-loved. Maybe both. Who could blame her?

August found the key where Mrs. Taylor had left it, under a rock outside the door. Such a small-town mentality. Rachel found it endearing and comforting. She hadn't just fallen in love with August over the past couple months, she'd fallen in love with Curlville. With Nick and Zach. The quiet streets and nosy neighbors. The clip-clop of the horses' hooves as they pulled the Amish families on their carts. The historic homes and architecture. The country farmland that surrounded the small town. The protective attitude from the townsfolk. The smiles and waves of them calling out to each other. She loved it all.

And she wondered what it would be like to have that love returned. To be accepted as she was. With the positive way the sheriff had responded to her claims of being a medium, she kindled a flame of hope. She certainly hadn't expected him to be receptive to the idea and was glad Ella had been there to guide the conversation.

August lifted a note card off the dresser and furrowed his brows. "Mrs. Taylor wants us to know there's pasta salad, a couple of sandwiches, and half a strawberry-rhubarb pie in the mini-fridge. Not to mention the cookies." He motioned toward the table. "You hungry?"

"We can't be rude and *not* eat it." She tried for humor and was awarded with a brief grin.

"I don't know about you, but I can't stop smelling smoke." He kicked off his shoes and scrubbed his hands over his head. "I should shower."

She sniffed her shirt, noticing the lingering odor for the first time since leaving the station. The smoke had clung to their clothing and hair. Definitely time to get rid of that reminder. Yawning, she slipped off her tennis shoes and stretched her arms in the air, stretching her neck back and forth to get out the kinks.

August's penetrating gaze didn't go unnoticed. Her skin warmed under his attention as he visibly skimmed her body. She wasn't sure how she could feel sexy after a long day consisting of breaking up with the love of her life, finding a dead body, watching a house burn down, and being interrogated by the town sheriff, but she did. August had a way of changing her mood for the better.

He started toward her, and her entire body buzzed, tingled, and fluttered. Kinks be damned.

"Join me in the shower, honey." His hands inched around her waist, grabbing the hem of her T-shirt and lifting.

She raised her arms, helping him slip the cotton shirt over her head. Their break-up argument from earlier today seemed to be forgotten or forgiven. She was glad. She'd hated hurting him. But now that everything was out in the open, she still felt vulnerable.

"Or a bath." His voice was soft against her ear as he unzipped her jeans. His fingers skimmed under the denim waist, massaging her lower back.

Need pulsed low in her belly. His hands were magic, kneading her muscles in just the right spots.

"Both sound wonderful." She worked on his belt, unclasping it before unbuttoning the rest of his shirt. She wanted him like never before. Only that vulnerable niggling in the front of her mind, tickling her throat, stopped her from continuing.

Make a stand. Be strong. Say something.

"August." She said his name with more force than she'd intended.

The kisses he whispered along her neck halted, and he lifted his gaze to watch her. She missed his touch immediately. Shoot. How should she begin so they could—with any luck—get back to the good stuff?

The worry wrinkles between his brows formed a V when she waited too long to speak.

Oh, to hell with it.

"I love you," she said, confident of her feelings. "I love everything about you—all of your quirks, your expressions, your mistakes, your triumphs. All of it makes you who you are, and I very much want to be with you. And I need to know if you feel the same way about me— as I am, after everything you've learned. Because I'm not—no, I *can't* give you more of my heart if you can't accept me, ghosts and all."

There. God, that felt good. Her shoulders lifted, weightless.

He inched back and stood straighter, tenser. He seemed taller, gigantic. Or maybe that was because she couldn't bring herself to meet his eyes.

"Rachel." His hands bracketed her jaw as he tilted her

head up. "Look at me," he said, when she closed her eyes.

She gulped and opened one eye at a time. The dim lighting in the room cast somber shadows under his weary blue gaze, and she suddenly felt guilty for bringing this up tonight, after all he'd been through.

"Thank you." His words surprised her and held her hostage.

Thank you? Not exactly what a girl wanted to hear after declaring her love…again. But she waited as patiently as possible, hopeful.

"I needed to hear that from you." His lips angled into his sigh-worthy half-grin. "It makes so much sense."

The knot in her throat swelled. "What does?"

"Why I'm so damn in love with you."

"What?" She wanted a rewind button so she could hear it again.

"Honey, I'm crazy in love with you. So crazy, I might be the one who needs medication."

"Oh." She wanted to say more but her vocabulary was suddenly insufficient. She held her breath, waiting for the conditions. The "but" or the "if only."

"Breathe, Rache. You need to breathe."

"Right." She released a long breath.

"Better? I want to explain, but you need to be conscious."

She nodded, laughing nervously. "Wide awake."

"Good." He kissed her cheek and met her stare again. "When everything seems so complicated, you tell me how you feel, and it all seems so clear." His thumb grazed her cheek, and a warm smile lit up his face, soothing her.

"What's clear?"

"You love me for who I am. I can count on you to stay and not want to change me. You have no idea how happy that makes me, and I want you to feel the same way."

"I do," she dared to whisper.

"Rache, when it comes down to it, I wouldn't care if

you were best friends with Elvis... Well, I might be a little jealous of that. But you know what I mean."

Rachel laughed again as a jolt of relief hit her. "Really?"

"Yes. Unconditional love isn't something I've ever truly felt—not since my parents passed away." His smile dimmed briefly, and Rachel wondered if he thought of Ella. "I want that with you."

"You have it, August. Like I said, I love you for who you are." *So much.* She wrapped her arms around him, feeling a warming calm, as if a light switch had been flicked on inside her chest.

His expression brightened, eyes resplendent. "I won't ever ask you to change either. I might not understand it at first—how you do what you do, but I'll try. Do you believe me?"

"Yes."

"I'm sorry for being an ass and making you think otherwise. This day got the best of me."

"Understandable. I hit you with a lot." To put it mildly. She'd never dreamed he'd understand her little otherworldly gift. Not that he was a hundred percent on board, but this was a good start. She smiled, glad she'd gathered the courage to tell him how she felt. She deserved love—his love—just the way she was.

"We can start the day over. What do you say?"

Rachel held his hand and gestured to the bathroom. "I say we have all night. How big is the tub in there?"

~ * ~

Rachel braided her damp hair, watching August slumber peacefully next to her. He'd collapsed on the bed a couple hours earlier, after their shower, and had immediately fallen asleep—but not before satisfying her completely with his hands and his mouth. She'd reciprocated, giving more of herself than she'd ever thought she could allow. He'd sparked a part of her she hadn't known existed.

After, she'd tried to fall asleep alongside him, but her body was restless and her mind was on overload. She checked the digital clock on the bedside table. Twenty after three glowed back at her. It was the day after the most difficult day of her life. She should feel a sense of relief it was over and that she hadn't experienced a panic attack…or lost everyone she held dearly to her heart, but a niggling, unnamed anxiety still kept her awake.

Her gaze roamed over August. She envied his deep sleep, his even breaths.

In the light of the moon filtering through the lace curtains, his presence—partially covered by a white cotton sheet—was the anchor she needed to keep her mind from drifting too far. She examined his half-naked body further. His arm was tucked under his head, propping up his gorgeous face—lips just full enough, a masculine jaw line. Dark thick eye lashes shadowed his cheeks. His hair was ruffled from going uncombed after their shower romp. Her gaze slid down over his broad chest, fit abdomen, long athletic legs. The sheet covered his, uh, more manly parts, but her eyes fixated there…at the rounded curve where the sheet fitted against him. God, he was beautiful.

Oh, geez. She'd turned into a pervert. This was all his fault, though, with the wickedness he'd aroused inside of her.

Needing closeness, she stripped off her bathrobe and scooted up against him, brushing her naked curves against his side. As if instinctively, he opened his arm and made a cozy space for her, and she nestled up against him. His breathing hastened just so, and she wondered if she woke him. The selfish side of her wouldn't mind.

She slipped her arm over his chest, running her fingers over the soft sparse hairs there.

"You want me." His sleep-heavy sexy voice pulsated low in her abdomen.

She smiled, way too happy to have roused him. "You shouldn't be so addictive."

"Mmm… I promise to be a healthy addiction." He shifted quickly, surprising her by rising and coming back down on her.

Rachel welcomed him and wound her legs around his thighs. His apparent erection pressed teasingly against her belly.

He propped up on his hands, staring down at her. His sleepy-sensual expression was breathtaking, particularly with the shadows dancing around his handsome features.

"Healthy, how?" she managed to say, lack of oxygen and all.

"A thriving sex life can help reduce stress and anxiety. I'm glad to offer you my services."

Rachel laughed at his impish expression. "You're adorable."

"Yeah? And sexy? Impossible to resist?"

"Definitely. I've been eating you up with my eyes for the past hour while you've been helplessly asleep."

"Really?" He lifted a brow. "You should've woken me sooner."

Rachel caressed his cheek, and he dropped down for a kiss. His lips were firm but tender, purposeful and determined. Intuitively, she returned the kiss, their every move in sync. Like a couple who'd been married for years, they were in tune with each other. The thought drifted to their lovemaking, reminding Rachel how incredible sex with him had been. She wanted that again. Now.

"Make love to me." The words rolled off her tongue.

Without a second wasted, August reached over to the bedside table and retrieved a condom. He quickly ripped it open and slid it on. His hand curved over her breast, his thumb teasing her budded nipple. Rachel arched up as a spasm of need zigzagged from her breast to where his erection pressed against her center. His beautiful lips covered her nipple, and he sucked, inspiring more nerves to alight. Warmth smoldered low and deep where his finger found her ready and needful. He pressed his finger inside of her, and she thought she might orgasm on the spot.

"Please." She skimmed the back of her hand down his chest.

"Rachel"—his moan rumbled against her ear—"I want to see"—he licked her lobe—"hear"—his lips skimmed along her jaw—"and feel your orgasm, honey." He kissed her lips.

"Oh, God." Her thighs tightened around him. "I need—" She gasped when he entered her in one long drive.

Her body jolted up, meeting his. Her hot core contracted around him.

"Yes, baby." August shifted inside her, his length filling her, pressing higher. His movements quickened and slowed and then quickened again.

Rachel moved with him, lifted her hips, meeting his thrusts. She savored the sweet pressure, the way he moved. His off-and-on-again kisses were hot and needy. He had lips she wanted to bite into, a tongue she wanted to suck.

A wicked sensation built, consuming her thoughts, her mind, her body. "I'm coming," she heard herself say.

"Good God." His voice was thick, heated, as he continued his sensual maneuvering.

Just when Rachel thought she'd explode with pleasure, another deeper smoldering heat convulsed inside her. Higher and higher he drove her. And she heard herself moan loud and out of control. So unlike her, but she didn't care who heard. The pleasure erased all thoughts. Mindless. She was mindless.

August dropped onto his elbows, slowing his movements. Rachel's breaths began to even out as her body tingled and slackened onto the mattress, spent. But hearing him grunt and give into his own orgasm jolted one last shockwave through her. His body rested heavily on hers as he settled in, hot breaths in her ear. She lazily ran her fingers over his back, loving him and enjoying how completely relaxed her body was.

She smiled, thinking August was, without a doubt, the best stress-reliever medication ever prescribed. She'd gladly take him up on his services offered.

"I love you, honey." He pressed his lips to her cheek and lifted off, pulling her in front of him in a warm embrace.

"I love you too." *So much*, she thought, cuddling against him as she started to drift off.

Her mind at ease.

Though not for long. August's phone buzzed and lit up on the nightstand, a call coming in.

"Nooo—" He held her closer.

"What if it's the boys?" She skimmed her fingers along his arm, snuggling in. "Or a patient in need?"

"That's what I'm afraid of." He heaved a sigh and reached for the phone. "It's Loretta," he said and answered it, putting it on speaker phone.

Rachel listened, trying to keep her eyes open, as he spoke to his nursing assistant, who requested that he come in to the office. A child had fallen off a couch hours earlier, cutting open his forehead on a coffee table. The parents hadn't wanted to bother August after all he'd been through, but the wound looked bad and probably needed stitches.

"Of course they should call me." August kissed Rachel's temple and rose from the bed. "I'll be right in. Hopefully it's not a concussion."

Moments later, Rachel felt his lips on her again. "I'll be back soon, Rache. Get some sleep. Love you."

~ * ~

What seemed like hours later—though the sun had yet to rise and shine into the room—Rachel stirred awake. An eerie tension in the air had her sitting up straight, her heart racing in a distressing pattern. She hugged the sheet to her body, blinking rapidly to wake her sleepy eyes.

"August?" She saw him first, her foggy brain taking

him in. He sat at the table, his back rigid, his lips taut and frowning. Something was very wrong. "Is your patient all right?"

"He'll be fine," he said in a dull, strange voice.

"What's wrong?" Rachel followed his gaze to the other side of the room, where Ella sat on the rocking chair. *Rocking* the rocking chair. In full sight of August.

Oh, boy. Here it goes. Rachel quickly pulled her bathrobe on and tied it shut.

"She's here, isn't she?" August knew. How could he not with a chair moving on its own?

What was Ella up to? Rachel's eyes adjusted to the dimness in the room to see Ella's somber expression. Were those tears running down her cheeks?

August stood and walked toward the bed. He grabbed Rachel's hand and sat beside her.

"Tell me." He looked sad and curious at the same time.

Rachel squeezed his hand, seeing no reason to lie. "Ella's here. Yes."

His gaze jerked to the rocker again, as if he might see his deceased sister somehow. He shook his head, frustration apparent. "Is she saying anything?"

"Not yet." Rachel looked to Ella, searching for some type of guidance. This could end very badly. Fingers crossed, Ella's intentions were pure.

"Of course they're pure." Ella shot her an annoyed look and shot up from the rocker, making it bounce back and sway. "This is my baby brother. I practically raised him." She straightened her cardigan and tapped her healed shoe on the wood floor.

"What would you like to tell him then, Ella?" Rachel returned her own stern look, a warning to be nice. She scooted closer to August, and he guided her to sit on his lap. A protective barrier she was glad to provide.

His arms wrapped around her as he stared at the swaying rocker coming to a slow stop. Rachel shifted to get a better look at him. This close, she could tell his face had paled, and his body trembled. Understandably, the visit was shaking him up. Might as well light a torch to any doubt August had remaining about the spirit world.

Ella paced a ghostly path, her feet barely touching the floor. "I never wanted to leave my sons," she said, staring down as if thinking her words through before speaking. "I thought I was the only one who could raise them properly. I wanted to protect them from all that was bad in the world. So when it was my time to go, I couldn't. I just couldn't."

Rachel relayed the words to August. His lips pressed tight.

Ella moved to the bed and stood before them. "You two love birds are so sweet together." She smiled and wiped her tears. "I'll get to the point so I can leave you alone."

"You should say whatever you need to say," Rachel said. "I'm sure August wouldn't mind hearing it. You both need closure."

"Yes, please say your peace, Ella." August's voice croaked with emotion, causing Rachel's eyes to burn. "I miss you and love you. And I want to do right by you. I always have. Just let me know what you want me to do, and I'll do my best."

Ella placed her hand over August's. "August, look at me."

His eyes widened and seemed to center on the ghost. "Ella?"

"Yes, it's me."

August jolted off the bed, taking Rachel with him. He set her down and turned to where Ella stood. "I can see you." He glanced at Rachel. "I can see her. She's very faint, but I can tell she's there." He sounded excited yet cautious. "Shit, this is insane."

Rachel covered her mouth, hiding her smile. Was it wrong that she felt deliriously happy to have this in common with August? No. This was a good thing.

She hoped. "Did you do this, Ella? Did you make August see you?"

Ella nodded, clasping her hands. "August had to believe. His emotions showed him the rest of the way." Her gaze didn't stray from August as she spoke. "I'm so sorry for all the hurt Grant has caused you." Her eyes teared up. "And all the hurt I've caused you. You deserved my respect. You deserved my unconditional love, and I let you down."

"No you didn't, Ella." August took a cautious step forward. "You became my guardian before you were ready. You did what you could. Hell, you helped put me through medical school."

"That was mostly our parents. They had enough vision to have life insurance, unlike me." She sighed. "And it was you, Auggie. You worked hard, and I never told you how proud I was. But I am proud. No matter what path you've taken, you've always risen to the occasion. Always so smart. Whatever you do, you excel, whether it's medicine or music"—she sniffed—"or raising Nicholas and Zachary."

August grinned. "Now you're just playin' with me."

"I'm not." Ella smiled too. "Rachel's showed me how wrong I've been. It's true I didn't want to leave my boys, but I'm so grateful they have you. They love you and can depend on you." She clasped her hand to her chest. "Our house was destroyed today. My house that I once thought brought good luck and happy memories was burned to the ground. I used to commute three hours a day, so that I could live in that damn house. Why? Because I thought I could somehow control my destiny. Isn't that funny? Ironic how that long drive was my demise."

"And now that the house is gone"—she shrugged—"I couldn't care less. The house doesn't matter. It never did. What mattered was the people in it and how you've all come together as a family."

Rachel sniffed back tears as she watched August attempt to embrace Ella. Her transparent form reached out, doing what it could to return the sentiment.

"I promise to raise the boys right," August murmured. "You can rest easy with no fears or worries."

"I know that now." Ella patted his shoulder and stepped back. "You'll be a wonderful father to them."

"A father," August repeated. "You don't mind if I adopt them as my own?"

"You have my blessing. I'm happy you want to." Ella's shoulders shook with emotion. The digital clock on the nightstand blared and then fizzed out, smoke rising from the top. "Shoot. I should go before I ruin any more of Mrs. Taylor's electronics."

"I'll replace them." August coughed and rubbed at his eye. "I'm glad to be able to see you again. I never thought I'd get the chance."

"Thank Rachel." Ella's image began to fade. "I love you."

"I love you too," August said as she completely disappeared. "She's gone. Holy shit."

"Are you okay?" Rachel grasped his hand and brought it to her heart.

"Yes," he said, yet his eyes were glossy with suppressed tears.

One escaped and Rachel wiped it with her thumb.

"You're pretty amazing, Auggie."

His sexy smile returned. "I'd be lost without you. Thank you for coming into my life and giving me that time with Ella. I'm truly sorry I doubted you."

Rachel released a contented sigh and leaned into him, his body warm and secure. *Hers.* "Make it up to me," she whispered.

And he lifted her into his arms and carried her to bed.

Epilogue

Rachel sniffed the vibrant pink rose bouquet. The soft scent of roses filled her nose and soothed her excited nerves. Behind her, her mother fussed with the ribbon on the back of her dress—an elegant number Rachel had found secondhand. With some minor tailoring, the wedding dress turned out to be a stunner. And under budget. Even though her parents had insisted on paying for the wedding.

Rachel had wanted a simple ceremony in the garden at Curlville City Park—across the street from their new home.

The reception afterward would take up most of the budget as most of the town had been invited, thanks to the women at Dolly's salon. Even Dana would be there—somewhat reformed. She'd gone above and beyond trying to seek forgiveness, going so far as to bake the wedding cake and gift her photographer's services. Even Loretta was impressed with the effort.

Rachel smiled to herself. She'd grown fond of the nosy woman with the biting sense of humor, especially since August was no longer considered *Don Juan* but rather *Dr. Kline*. Loretta had formed a new respect for August

291

after he'd purchased the space next to the office to expand his practice. He'd hired an RN and given Loretta a raise. Ella's fifty grand had helped with the renovation, and August proudly called the new space Ella's Wing. On weekends, he used the extra space to teach music lessons. It was his way of giving back to the community and a way to fulfill a long-life passion. As payment, he accepted second-hand instruments in honor of his mother.

"Your new home is lovely," Rachel's mother said with a surprising sincerity, interrupting her thoughts.

"Thanks, Mom." Rachel and August were lucky to finagle a good deal—and even more lucky August's homeowner's insurance settlement was enough to get them into the gorgeous four-bedroom Victorian home. Truly a dream home. And there was an office downstairs that Rachel could use for the launch of her practice.

Estate planning. She wanted to help people so they had *zero* unfinished business after they passed.

"Hopefully, the old home is ghost-free," her mother said so low, Rachel almost didn't hear the surprising words.

"Excuse me?"

"Honestly, Rachel, I don't know why you never told me about the spirits."

A chill rounded down Rachel's spine. She turned to face her mother. "Mom? How did you know?"

"At the rehearsal dinner." She sneered the words, obviously still not approving of the modest dinner held in the back room at the local restaurant. "Your officiant-to-be, Sheriff Moody is his name? He mentioned you're a medium and that you'll be helping him with cases in the future, if need be. How convenient for him."

Rachel studied her face, astonished her mom was taking the news so well. Unless... "Did you believe him?"

"Do I have a reason not to?"

"No." Rachel hesitated. Today was a huge day, and she didn't want anything to ruin it. But something about her mother's expression made her think there was no better time than now. What was she hiding? "It's true. I can communicate with spirits."

Dora sighed. "I never wanted this to get passed on to you. I'd hoped to leave this nonsense all behind when I left home."

"Mom, what are you talking about?"

"My grandmother was a medium for a time, and my mother was clairvoyant on occasions, or so they'd claimed. I didn't want anything to do with the craziness."

Rachel stepped back, shocked. Well, that explained why she'd only visited her grandmother a few times before she passed away several years ago. She'd always assumed the reasoning was because of a dysfunctional upbringing. Or maybe that was the case.

"You didn't believe them, but you believe me?"

"I didn't want to, but after all I'd witnessed as a child, I have to admit it's difficult to argue with." She gestured to Rachel. "And now you."

"And now me," Rachel repeated, staring at her mother in a new light. Her curiosity piqued. "What about you? If it runs in the family, have you ever had a supernatural experience?"

"No. My mother and grandmother explained that the universe had a way of giving certain people 'gifts'"—she air-quoted—"needed to deal with life issues. Apparently, I've never had a life issue big enough to materialize a so-called gift. Which is fine by me." It didn't sound fine. Sounded like her mother was a little hurt.

"That's really interesting. So you're saying this ability I have might be temporary?"

"You don't want to keep it?" Her mother sounded surprised—and pleased.

"Not really. It's why I didn't pass the bar the first time around. An enraged ghost harassed me." Ella had come through for Rachel the second time, as promised, staying beside her through it all. Her spirit moved on shortly after that—after she'd given Nick and Zach their closure with a heartfelt goodbye. After everything Rachel had been through with Ella, it was difficult to watch her go. But it was for the best. Spirits weren't meant to be stuck in limbo, unhappy with their life choices.

"No wonder." Her mother swept a loose hair from Rachel's face. "I told your father your failure had to be a fluke. I should have known then."

"You should've told me." Rachel glanced at the door. Her sister/maid-of-honor was running late. "Do you think Becca has a gift?"

Dora sighed. "You know as well as I do Rebecca can't hold in a secret."

"I suppose that's true." But still. She'd have to keep an eye on her younger sister.

"My grandmother used to burn sage to keep the spirits away. You could try that."

Rachel smiled and kissed her mom on the cheek. "That may just be the best wedding gift I'll receive. Thank you for sharing."

"Of course."

The door to the bedroom flung open and Becca rushed inside, looking windswept and frenzied. Her bride's maid dress was twisted, as if she'd dressed in a hurry. But she looked beautiful.

"You made it." Rachel hugged her sister.

"I wouldn't miss your wedding for the world. So sorry I'm late." Becca held the embrace a moment longer, holding tight. "Late night, hot date. You know how it goes."

"You're fine." Rachel stepped back as dizziness overcame her. She tripped over her hem and collided into Becca again.

"Whoa, there." Becca helped her gain her balance. "Has Mom been plying you with her favorite gin?"

"No. No drinking for me." Oh, cripes. She shouldn't have said that. As soon as the words left her mouth,

Becca's eyes brightened. Of course her sister would catch on to Rachel's secret—the one she'd been hiding from everyone, including August. At least until she confirmed it with her ob-gyn.

"No way!" Becca clapped her hands. "Rachel, you're pregnant." Her voice echoed in the room and, no doubt, through the walls and down the hallway.

A clanking crash sounded in the next room over—the room where August was getting dressed for the wedding. Thumping footsteps quickly pounded the hardwood, followed by the door swinging open and August appearing, mouth agape, looking gorgeous…and half-dressed. From the waist up, he had on his shirt, navy blue cummerbund, and tuxedo jacket. Waist down, he wore black boxer briefs and black socks.

Rachel clasped her hand to her mouth to keep from laughing, but Becca didn't hold back.

Her mother started toward him. "August, you cannot be in here."

He didn't take his gaze off of Rachel, jetting past her mother. "You're pregnant?" He held Rachel's face as a cute grin cut across his.

"I think so. I didn't want to make any assumptions before the wedding—with all that was going on."

He kissed her cheek and whispered in her ear, "the time after I proposed?"

She nodded. "Probably." August had proposed under a starry Curlville night, after a romantic midnight picnic. She'd said yes and things had quickly got out of control—without protection. She couldn't help it—he was irresistible.

"That is—"

"August." Her mother used her stern tone. "You need to leave. It's bad luck to see the bride before the wedding."

"Oh, Mom," Becca said, "that's just a superstition. Look at them. They're adorable and so in love. Let them have a moment." Her sister, bless her, successfully maneuvered their mother out the bedroom door, leaving Rachel alone with her soon-to-be husband.

Her stomach fluttered at the thought. "Do you believe in superstitions?" she asked him.

He cocked his head. "Should I?"

"No. We'll make our own destiny."

"Definitely. We're ahead of schedule already." His hand planted on her belly as he pressed a kiss to her lips. "I love it."

"Me too."

He cleared his throat. "Do you think our baby will have your gift?"

Rachel considered the revelation her mother just sprang on her. "Only if she needs it."

"Yeah?"

"I'll explain later." She drew in a breath and cupped his handsome cheek, still unable to believe how lucky she was to have found him.

He scrunched his forehead into worry wrinkles. "How are you feeling? Any nausea?"

"I'm fine, Doctor. Now let me finish getting ready. I have vows to rehearse and a hot man to marry. And you"—she pointed at how his package filled his boxer briefs nicely—"should probably put some pants on."

"Oh." He glanced down and grimaced. "Right. Pants. Sorry."

Rachel laughed. "I'm glad I'm not the only one who's excited. Or is it nerves?"

"Honey." He pulled her close. "I've never been more excited about the life ahead of me. Ahead of *us*. And I never thought I'd say this, but I'm happy you communicate with spirits. Otherwise we would never have met."

"That's the sweetest thing you've ever said." Tears burned her eyes. Geez. Pregnancy was already making her emotional. "You're right. Without Ella, I never would have met you and fallen in love." She smiled and sniffed. "Want to get married?"

"More than ever."

Miss out on Book One in the *Bewitching Women Series?*

Meet Sofia and Gray

BEWITCHING YOU

A love spell gone wrong. An interfering ghost. A nosy mind-reading grandmother. And a psychic man-hating mother. To say Sofia Good's life is a mess might be the understatement of the century. But when her visions forecast a love worth fighting for, she's willing to do just about anything to meet the man of her dreams.

Grayson Phillips lost his twin brother in a senseless accident, and now he's trying to gain back control by maintaining a safe and uneventful "life plan." But after sexy, quirky Sofia crash lands into his world he's forced to rethink his strategy.

Available now from a variety of online retailers!

ABOUT THE AUTHOR

Viola Estrella loves a story with humor, flawed characters, paranormal elements, and romance. She tries to include these aspects in all that she writes and loves every minute of it. When she's not reading, writing, or designing book cover art , she's spending quality time with her husband and sons in their Colorado home.

Viola is a 2010 RITA® finalist. Also in 2010, she was honored by her local RWA® chapter, Colorado Romance Writers, with the Writer of the Year award.

Find out more about Viola Estrella's writing at www.ViolaEstrella.com.